I0598833

Star Spangled Banner

Triple Star Ranch series, Book 3

Siobhan Muir

Copyright © 2020 Siobhan Muir

All rights reserved.

ISBN-13: 978-1-947221-14-7

DEDICATION

Dedicated to Terry Kemmitz, reader, fan, and lover of
Wyoming cowboys. Thank you for your encouragement
and patience while waiting for this story. I hope you love
Enrique and Suzie.

ACKNOWLEDGMENTS

Writing a book is never really a one-person job, and writing a series is especially difficult alone. Keeping track of details is so much easier when you have help. Not only does it take a great deal of hard work, editing, and research on the part of the author to get things correct, but without my compatriots, there'd be a lot more mistakes.

Great thanks to Paige Prince for checking my military references, particularly pertaining to the Navy, and for editing this story that seemed to be in a bunch of random flash fiction pieces. Huge thanks to Mary Decker and Terry Kemmitz for encouraging me on this story even when in the midst of my move! And great thanks to Kris Norris for designing the cover with the perfect barrel racing image. You rock.

As always, great thanks to my readers for cheering me on. Y'all make my writing worth the detailed effort.

SIOBHAN MUIR

CHAPTER ONE

Suzie put her head back, closed her eyes, and inhaled the scents of heat, horse, and sweat. This was exactly where she wanted to be. Painted Dog Tired, her bay paint Quarter Horse, stood beside her, nose down, hind foot cocked, apparently asleep. But she knew better. He'd gotten his name from his sleepy look, but it was just for show. The moment he got into the arena starting gates for their barrel race, his head came up, ears flickering, and his body vibrated with suppressed excitement.

"You're not fooling me, Painted Dog." She thumped his shoulder and one brown eye opened to give her a mild look of reproach.

Maybe he's meditating before the run.

Maybe she should think about doing the same. But the energy of the track behind the area buzzed with excitement and anxiety. Women of all ages had come to compete in the Cheyenne Frontier Days barrel-racing championship and this was it, the day everyone both hoped for and dreaded. Suzie had trained and worked with Painted Dog relentlessly on the Triple Star Ranch when her doctoring skills weren't needed and this was her year. After this, she wouldn't have the time to devote to training. The Triple Star Therapy

Ranch had become too popular and successful for her to take time away for barrel-racing at a championship level.

She slapped Painted Dog again. "That's okay. It's our year, isn't it, buddy?"

The horse gave a long-suffering sigh as he switched to resting the other back foot.

She chuckled and shot a look at the stands. It was Cheyenne Day, where residents of Cheyenne and Laramie County all got into the Daddy of 'Em All rodeo for a hefty discount. The stands sat fuller than previous days and she let the excitement and pleasure of the crowd seep into her. Earlier, the Thunderbirds had flown their aerial display over the south end of town, and the Leap Frogs, a group of Navy SEALs who leapt out of perfectly good airplanes, would descend upon the Frontier Park arena as a special treat. They didn't usually do it on Cheyenne Day, but the schedule worked out that way.

Suzie didn't mind.

She laughed at herself. While she enjoyed watching hot men fall out of the sky as much as the next heterosexual woman, she never let it go beyond that. T-type personalities, always seeking the next thrill, and egotistical men infuriated her too much to find any pleasure in their company. The few she'd met while doing her PTSD training had tested her considerable patience, but she'd written it off to their affliction.

Despite that, she still scanned the sky for the C-130 "Herky Bird" as the start time for the rodeo approached. The arrogant SEALs might not be fun to talk to, but they sure were pretty to watch when they did aerial acrobatics with their colorful chutes. The few times she'd seen them before, they made her nervous, swooping and twirling in the air like one of the helicopter seeds from her grandparents' maple tree. But they always came down safely, as sure and confident as the professionals they were.

The rumble of propeller engines made her breath catch

and she focused on the sky. From her position at the north end of the arena, she could see the big, gray airship roaring across the sky with the cargo door open at the back. *Soon, now, real soon.*

The rest of the crowd cheered as the announcers shouted out to "our Navy SEALs, the Leap Frogs" and Suzie strained her eyes to catch the little black dots of the men tumbling out of the back of the C-130. She bit her lip as they fell without chutes for a few moments, but the blue and yellow sails opened and the men stopped short. She let her breath out and shot a guilty grin around to her fellow contestants, but no one noticed her unease.

Two of the men fell in tandem, their feet locked together, and the other two fell separately, one twirling and swirling like his chute was caught in a wind vortex. Her heart crawled up to her throat until he leveled out. *Glory be, I hate it when they do that.* Not that they weren't consummate professionals, but the appearance of being out of control scared the daylights out of her.

The tandem pair broke apart and one dropped an American flag while the other dropped smoke to leave trails in the sky. The whole team performed flawlessly, though the few "out of control" swirls still made Suzie hold her breath. The announcers commented on the performance the whole way down and it was a sight to behold these powerful men falling precisely into the center of the arena.

The first guy touched down amid cheers from the audience, waving before he gathered up his chute. The first member of the tandem team hit the ground, his NAVY chute fluttering to the ground along with the smoke.

But when the second member of the tandem team hung no more than fifty feet up, the SEAL's chute folded like a burst balloon. He immediately looked up and tried to maneuver into the portion of his chute still inflated, but his speed increased.

Oh dear glory!

Somehow, the SEAL twisted in midair and gathered up the American flag before he hit the ground in a jarring thud that sprayed the sand of the arena out in all directions. The announcers shouted in panicked surprise as the landed members of the team turned toward the downed man.

Suzie squeaked and took two steps forward to the rail, looping the reins to Painted Dog onto it before she vaulted over the side into the arena. She was running before her mind even caught up to what was happening. Fortunately, he'd fallen close to her end of the arena and she was the first to reach him.

She skidded to a halt on her knees beside him and scanned his body to determine where he was most hurt. He didn't even moan, but his face blanched white under his tan and his lips were drawn into a tight line though his eyes remained closed.

"Sir, my name is Dr. Suzie Appleton, can you hear me?"

The man moaned but didn't open his eyes.

Sweet glory, let's hope he didn't break his neck.

"I'm going to check you over for injuries, sir."

She thanked all the watching deities he'd uncurled onto his back, but she worried he might have broken something internally. One arm lay curled protectively around the bundled American flag. *Always ready to protect the flag.* The other lay across his body at an odd angle and she suspected he'd used that arm to slow him down when he landed. His ragged breathing made her listen closely. His wheezing suggested a compression she couldn't see.

She checked his pulse just as the other members of his Leap Frogs team gathered around him.

"Miss, you need to get away from him." A gruff man reached for her, but she shook her head and dipped out of the way.

"That's Doctor to you, Sailor, and I'm checking him for injuries. He's broken his right arm and I suspect he's broken a rib or two, given the sounds his breath is making. He needs to get to a hospital ASAP to check for internal hemorrhaging and injuries."

"The SEALs take care of their own, *doctor*." The gruff man growled and tried to grab her again.

"Then have your corpsman get his ass here fast, *sailor*, so you can save your teammate. You're gonna need to stabilize his chest if you want him to live."

She didn't know for sure if that was the case, given she couldn't see inside his body armor, but she wouldn't give an inch when her expertise was questioned. No one knew they were SEALs when they wore street clothes. The same pertained to her when she competed in the barrel-racing events. She couldn't exactly wear a white lab coat.

"Damn, Suzie, you get here fast." Helena Lindstrom, the head medical organizer for CFD. "You think we can let the others take him now?"

Suzie nodded. "Helps that I was gonna ride in the championship barrel race." She pointed to the different portions of the broken man's body. "He's got a broken arm, and from what it sounds like, he's got somethin' going on in his chest. If I had to guess, I'd say broken ribs that might have punctured a lung. Make sure you're gentle when movin' him, and make damn sure the corpsman sees him before they tell me I'm right."

Helena laughed as they moved back out of the CFD medical personnel's way. "Will do."

Suzie nodded, but tugged Helena closer. "And have them check his parachute for holes."

Helena's gaze sharpened. "Holes? What kind of holes?"

"The bullet kind." Suzie swallowed hard. "I think someone took a shot at him while he was in the air."

"Are you serious?" Helena shook her head. "There's no way anyone could get a rifle into the stands. We check every bag."

"I'm sure you do, but his chute shouldn't have folded like it did unless someone shot it. Just have them check, okay? He could've died, and still might." Suzie squeezed her arm.

"Okay, okay. I'll tell them." Helena nodded to where Painted Dog stood at the rail. "You still gonna compete?"

Suzie blew out a breath and shook her head. "I'm gonna try, but my concentration is shot. Maybe Painted Dog can get us through if they let us. I suspect this is gonna throw a wrench in the schedule."

Helena snorted. "Don't be so sure. Those boys like their money. They can't postpone for just one injured sailor. Once we're clear, they'll make a relieved announcement and it's back to business."

Suzie scowled. "Well hell, why would we care that someone got injured performing for their little shindig?" She shook her head as the med staff hustled the wounded man off the arena floor. "I'm gonna compete, but I can't say I'll do well. Thanks for backin' me up with the growling sea-ape."

Helena laughed. "You're welcome. And I'll check on the bullet hole theory. Good luck on your ride."

"Thanks."

Suzie hoped they'd find out who made the holes in the SEAL's parachute because she had no doubt they'd be there. Memories of her own bout with a deflating chute crowded her mind before she shook her head harder to dislodge them. She wouldn't go to that dark place again. Instead she focused on making it to Painted Dog's side and hoped he'd pull out the best run of his life.

CHAPTER TWO

"Petty Officer Sanchez, can you hear me?"

That was the wrong voice. What happened to the sultry feminine voice Enrique had heard when he first hit the ground? He remembered the gentle western twang, not heavy like Texas, but definitely country. Damn, but he loved that cowboy accent. He loved it even more when it sharpened and she gave one of his teammates the edge of it when he questioned her expertise. *Doctor, she said.* So where was that doctor now?

"Petty Officer?"

"Yes, sir. I can hear you." He dragged his voice out of the depths of his chest, down deep where it hurt to breathe.

"Good. I'm Dr. Lyttle and you're in the Cheyenne VA Hospital. We managed to reset your humerus and add pins to stabilize it. It should heal just fine given enough time and rest."

Enrique nodded, glad to hear it. He didn't really want his Leap Frog career to be over so soon.

"We also were able to extract your broken rib from your right lung and repair the puncture. That, too, should heal up just fine given enough time and rest. I've spoken to your CO and he understands that you'll need at least six weeks to recover."

Enrique must have grimaced because Dr. Lyttle sighed. "I know that look, Petty Officer Sanchez. You're planning to push for early release from sick leave, but here's the thing—his isn't a muscle you can retrain by flexing or going to the gym. This is your *lung*. You have to give it the proper time to heal or you won't be able to breathe right ever again. Copy?"

Enrique swallowed hard and nodded. "Copy that, doc."

"Good. We're going to keep you a few days to make sure that puncture in your lung heals correctly, but if there are no complications, you should be released in about ninety-six hours." The doc made some more notes on his tablet before he narrowed his eyes. "How is your pain level? On a scale of one to ten, where are you sittin'?"

"I'm at about a five, sir." There was no way on God's green earth he'd admit more than that. He might be wise enough to take pain meds, but he was still a SEAL. Superhuman came with the job description.

"Uh-huh. Okay, sounds good. Ninety-six hours. You'll let us know if that rises, right?"

Oh sure, right after I win the Miss America pageant. "Yes, sir. Thank you, sir."

"Heh, I know that isn't what you wanted to hear, but I have faith in us and our ability to get you back on your feet quickly if you listen to your body, and my recommendations." The doc's face crinkled with his smirk.

"Yes, sir. I know, sir."

Dr. Lyttle sighed. "And you don't believe me." He shook his head.

"I didn't say that, sir."

"You didn't have to, Petty Officer. I was a Marine-trained Navy Corpsman. Been there, done that, saw it all. Just try to rest. That will get you better far faster." He gathered up his papers and headed for the door.

"Yes, sir." Enrique was done negotiating. "Can I ask a

question, sir?"

"Sure." The doctor waited.

"Who was the doctor who treated me at the arena? Does she work here at the VA?"

Dr. Lyttle frowned a moment. "I wasn't aware there was a doctor at the arena. Are you sure?"

"Yes, sir. She identified herself." Enrique frowned a moment. "Dr. Suzie something. Do you know her, sir?"

Dr. Lyttle's eyebrows went up. "Dr. Suzie Appleton?"

"Yes, sir. I think so."

The doc nodded. "Yes, I know her. I didn't know she was scheduled for Cheyenne Frontier Days."

Relief cascaded through Enrique. *Thank all that's holy I didn't imagine her.* "Would it be possible to thank her? I didn't get a chance."

"Oh, yes, of course. I'll have one of the nurses see if she can be contacted. She doesn't work at the VA very often."

"Thanks, Doc."

"You're welcome." The doc slipped out of the room.

Enrique sighed. He hated hospitals. *Where people go to die.* He'd be out as soon as he could and back to work. But the few days here might give him a chance to see the lady doc if she came into the VA.

In the meantime, he closed his eyes and focused his mind on envisioning his injuries healed and gone. His brother SEALs had laughed at him for his belief, rolling their eyes and giving him shit. But his injuries healed faster than usual, even as he aged, if he took the time to focus on moving healing energy into those spots.

"Are you doing your Nicaraguan mumbo-jumbo thing again, Sanchez?"

The gruff voice made him open his eyes. Chief Petty Officer Andrew "Bruiser" Kent stood beside the bed, his arms crossed over his massive chest. The reference to his paternal grandmother made him narrow his eyes and smirk.

"Wouldn't you like to know? But it's only for true believers and you ain't one o' them."

"Yeah, yeah, whatever." Kent shook his head. "How are you doin' for real? The docs treating you okay?"

"Yeah." Enrique scowled. "They say I have to lay low for a few days and rest, but I need to get back to it."

Kent nodded. "Yeah, I feel you. But for once, I gotta agree with them. You impacted hard and punctured a lung. Ain't nothing you can do but heal. What the hell happened out there?"

Enrique shook his head and resettled himself in the bed. "I dunno. One minute the drop was going fine, and the next, the chute folded and I hit the dirt. Did you look at the chute?"

"Not yet, but it's on the docket this afternoon and the rest of our jumps are canceled." Kent frowned. "Did you hear anything, like shots or ripping to tell you it was collapsing?"

"Nope. Not a damn thing. Between the wind and the crowd, I didn't hear anything." He tilted his head. "Why?"

"Because the CFD med lady said the doc at the arena, who looked like a fuckin' cowgirl, said to check the chute for bullet holes."

Enrique scowled. "Bullet holes? Was someone shooting at me?"

"I'll have more intel this afternoon. But we'll be checking security cameras to see if we can get a fix on anything like a shooter." Kent rubbed the back of his neck. "Still can't believe she was a doc when she looked like a damn buckle bunny."

Enrique snorted. "You don't really look like a SEAL in civvies, either, Bruiser. More like a badass biker thug ready to throw down. No one would expect you at High Tea with lace doilies."

Kent grunted. "Yeah, well, I wasn't gonna let just anyone take a look at you. But she didn't back down."

Enrique nodded. "Good to hear. I wanna meet her and thank her in person. Think you could get that done, Chief?"

"Yeah, I see nothing wrong with that. You can congratulate her on her win."

"What?"

"Yeah, she won the championship in barrel-racing right after she rescued your ass. The woman's nuckin' futs, but damn, she can ride."

Enrique would've liked to have seen that. Damn, just her voice alone had soothed so many hurts. But to watch a woman handle a horse like the *caballeros* he'd see at his grand uncle's place in Nicaragua would've hardened his cock. A woman who could ride was sexy indeed.

"I'll definitely congratulate her when I see her."

Kent grinned. "Yeah, you do that. Give me ten mikes."

Enrique nodded. "Roger that."

He settled back into the bed, ignoring the jump in heart rate as Kent ducked out the door. How could he be this excited to meet a woman he knew for a matter of seconds, and only by voice? The answer wasn't there, but the excitement remained.

****

Suzie stood on the porch of her bungalow on the Triple Star Ranch, grinning to herself. The sky was the perfect shade of Wyoming blue stretching over the green rolling hills beyond Logan Creek. Though she couldn't see or hear the water, the cottonwoods and cattails in the foreground of her view gave the stream away.

But that isn't what's making you smile.

Nope. She grinned because she'd roped the 2018 barrel-racing championship on Painted Dog. She wasn't sure she'd be on her best game after helping the Navy SEAL who'd been shot down in the arena, but she and Painted Dog had been in the zone. They'd ridden their hearts out and left the competition in the dust behind his flying hooves.

Not bad for a Ranch doc. She lifted her coffee mug in salute. *Never give up, never surrender.*

She laughed just as her land line rang. Frowning, she ducked back inside and picked it up.

"Hello?"

"Dr. Suzie Appleton?"

"Yes. Who's this?"

"My name's Petty Officer Enrique Sanchez. I met you at the Cheyenne Frontier Days arena?"

"Oh! Yes, Petty Officer. I remember. How are you feeling?" She immediately switched into doctor mode.

"I'm good, thanks, Doc. Hey, I have leave because of my injuries and I wondered if I could take you out for coffee or dinner in thanks for working on me right there in the arena."

Suzie's jaw dropped. He was asking her out? She scrambled to get out of doctor mode.

"Uh, well, I'm on call today."

"How 'bout tomorrow? You can meet me here at the VA hospital."

The hint of accent in his voice warmed her in ways she hadn't expected. "I don't know, Petty Officer. I don't normally fraternize with patients."

"But I'm not really your patient. You were the triage doc, so I got myself a whole new doctor now. You're not my doc, but I'd like to thank you in person anyway."

"I'm not sure it's a good idea."

"Why, do you have a boyfriend or are you lesbian?"

She laughed. "No to either of those."

"Then I can't see any more reasons not to get together for coffee. Whad'ya say, Doc?"

She shrugged. "All right, Petty Officer. You got yourself a date."

"Hooyah, ma'am!"

She laughed at the delight in his voice. "I'm glad you're looking forward to it."

"Yes, ma'am. What time should I expect you?"

"Hmm, why don't I meet you at the hospital at ten hundred?"

"Oooh, a woman who knows military time. That's sexy." He must have realized what he said because he paused as if evaluating his words. "Sorry, Doc. That just slipped out."

"Don't be sorry. I learned it from the time when my dad was in the Army. Being a military brat gave me an appreciation for twenty-four hour clocks." And uniforms. Damn, now she'd be imagining Petty Officer Enrique Sanchez in his dress blues. Talk about sexy.

"Hooyah, ma'am. Ten hundred it is. I'll be the guy walking slow with a broken arm."

"How are your ribs and lung? Are you breathing all right?" She pictured him pale under his tan as he lay in the dirt of the arena. "What is the prognosis?"

He snorted, conveying disgust. "Rest and recuperation. No heavy lifting or working out until the puncture heals." He snorted again. "I've had worse."

"You do know you're talking to a doctor, right?" She shook her head. "Who's your Primary Care Physician?"

A short silence filled the phone. "Dr. Lyttle. He didn't contact you to convey my thanks for saving me in the arena?"

"No. I haven't heard anything from Dr. Lyttle." She waved her hand. "I'm sure it got lost in the shuffle." She frowned. "How did you get this number if Dr. Lyttle didn't offer it to you?"

"Uh, well, I have a lot of time on my hands and there aren't too many Dr. Suzie Appletons in Cheyenne, Wyoming." She could hear the shrug in his voice. "It wasn't that hard to find out you worked at the Triple Star Ranch. You're listed on their website."

"Ah yes, I'm definitely listed there." She nodded, some of her unease fading.

"I guess we can talk more tomorrow, but did I read the description right? It's a therapy ranch specializing in PTSD recovery?"

"Yes, that's exactly right."

"You get a lot of vets coming through there?"

"Yes. Our owner, Trip Colton, is an Army veteran himself, and he wanted to do more for those in traumatic situations." Suzie let her pleasure come through. She'd been honored to take this job which kept her in Cheyenne so she could compete in Cheyenne Frontier Days. "But we also help others who've had trauma at home. Domestic violence survivors, car accident victims, emergency personnel with trauma. Everyone and anyone who needs help with PTSD."

"Damn, Doc, you sound like an advertising brochure."

She laughed. "Can you tell I like what I do? I'm the medical side of it, but watching how Trip and the other therapists help people is incredibly inspiring."

"That sounds amazing. Maybe I'll have to come out to see it. But I'm definitely looking forward to tomorrow."

"I'm glad you called, Petty Officer."

"Enrique, please. I'm just glad you decided to answer me. Damn it!" The phone made some weird noises, as if it had been jostled and dropped, before Enrique's voice returned. "Sorry. Dropped the stupid handset. I'm usually not this fumble-handed. But I'm still in recovery."

"Tell you what. I have to get to my morning appointments, so you take care of yourself and I'll see you for our date tomorrow. Deal?"

"Yeah, deal, Doc. See you tomorrow."

"Roger that."

"Oh, damn, that's so sexy. Talk to you tomorrow."

"Tomorrow." Suzie hung up the phone and allowed a grin to curl her lips. Who ever thought she'd accept a date from a Navy SEAL way out in the middle of landlocked Wyoming? She snorted and shook her head. *Something straight out of a romance novel.* Yup, and she'd take it.

CHAPTER THREE

Enrique practically vibrated as he waited at the front doors of the Cheyenne Veterans Administration Hospital, his gaze taking in all the people visiting. He couldn't quite remember Dr. Suzie Appleton, but he'd know her voice. He'd been so excited to go out with the doc that he'd overexerted his arm with the physical therapist and now it ached like a sonuvaprick. *Yeah, I think we pushed too far in the workout.* He rubbed it and grimaced.

All his pain was forgotten when a woman with dark brown hair pulled back in thick ponytail and the kind of curves to make a man drool stepped inside the doors. Enrique clenched his jaw to keep his tongue firmly in his mouth.

Sweet glory in heaven. He swallowed hard as she sauntered toward him, her hips swaying with each step. He loved how her legs fit her denim capris and the V-necked t-shirt showed hints of firm cleavage. *Damn, it's been a long time since I've had a woman.*

"Good to see you, Petty Officer Sanchez. I'm Dr. Suzie Appleton." The goddess in denim offered her hand to shake and grasped his with a firm grip. "I hope you weren't waiting long."

"No, ma'am, not long." *Just all my life to meet someone like you.* Jeez, when had he started waxing poetic? The guys would give him hell just for the thought. "How was the drive into town?"

"Eventful, which is why I'm a bit late."

"Now that sounds like a good story."

She smiled. "Let me take you to my favorite coffee shop and I might tell you."

"Yes, ma'am." He hurried in front of her to hold the doors open. "After you, ma'am."

She nodded and walked through but stopped other side as he joined her. "I appreciate the gesture, Petty Officer, but there's no need to stand on ceremony when you're injured."

He nodded. "I understand that, but it's hard to go against the training my *abuelo* and my father taught me. And I want to make a good impression."

"Again, I appreciate it." She nodded again, her expression pensive. "How about we compromise? You let me open the doors for you while you're injured, thus saving time and the possibility of further injury, and I'll acknowledge your efforts to be a gentleman due to your upbringing."

Though he didn't like going against everything he'd learned about interacting with women, he recognized her point. "And I take it you like everything efficient?"

She shrugged. "I'm a doctor. Wasted motions and time can lead to the death of a patient."

He laughed. "Yeah, we wouldn't want that. All right, ma'am. It's a deal until I heal." He winked at his rhyme. "And you can call me Enrique."

"Right, Enrique. It suits you." Her smile filled her face and damn near stopped his breath. "My name's Suzie."

"Not Doctor?" He grinned to show he teased as they headed to her car.

"Not today. Do I need to explain why?"

"You are here and that's good enough for me. Plus as I recall, we agreed this would be a date, right?"

"Yes, right." She unlocked the doors and opened the passenger side for him. "My favorite coffee shop is downtown. It's not far from here, but too far to walk. I hope you don't mind letting a woman pick you up and drive."

"No, ma'am. You know the town better than I do." This was only his first year doing the Cheyenne Frontier Days rodeo.

"That makes sense." She closed the door behind him and walked around the car before getting in. "It's not that big a town, though it is one of the "metropolises" of Wyoming."

She started the car and they headed into downtown. She was right. It didn't take them more than ten minutes to get to the coffee shop and most of that was looking for a place to park. *Hell, it would've taken longer than that to get out of the hospital parking lot in Coronado.*

Suzie turned off the car and got out, but he managed to push the car door open and get out on his own. She gave him an appraising look as he stood up and he couldn't help but preen a little.

"So where's this place?"

"It's about two blocks down." She tilted her head and bit her lip, hesitant for the first time. "May I take your uninjured arm? I don't want to be too forward since we've just met."

"Hell no, Suzie. I'd love for you to take my arm." He'd like nothing better.

He held it up and she wrapped her hand around his forearm. He resisted the urge to shiver with pleasure as her body brushed his. Damn, it was gonna be hard to keep from getting hard with her that close. She smelled of leather and the sweet scent of alfalfa hay, and it reminded him of his grandparents' horse farm and lazy summer days.

"So do I remember right? You're a championship barrel-racer?"

Her smile widened. "I am now. My horse Painted Dog Tired and I came out on top this year."

"Congratulations. How's it feel to be the best of the best?"

To his surprise she smiled and frowned at the same time. "I don't really know. I've definitely worked for this and wanted to succeed, but now that I've done it, I'm sort of over it." She grimaced. "It doesn't make sense, I know. Lots of women strive for this honor and it's hard to reach. But though I love barrel-racing, I like being a doctor more."

"You can't do both?"

She shook her head. "Not at professional level. It takes a lot of hours of practice to get that good and I just can't spare the time away from my medical practice." She shrugged. "But I'm starting to think I don't want to, anyway. Maybe next year, I'll volunteer to be one of the on-call arena docs just in case more men fall out of the sky."

He laughed, but unease slid through him. He still didn't know why his chute had collapsed on him, dropping him to the ground to destroy his arm. He hadn't heard back from the rest of the team as to what happened, but he'd find out. In the meantime, he'd enjoy being with Suzie.

"Yeah, well, that's the last time I'm gonna drop. Fall with style, but not drop."

She nodded. "You definitely fall with style. Speaking of that, how did you get involved with the Leap Frogs?"

"I spent some time in various places around the world jumping out of airplanes and getting to be the best in my squad at it. My CO at the time put my name up to join the Leap Frogs when an opening came up."

He'd been in Columbia trying to recover a downed intelligence satellite and his team had taken heavy fire before they could hump the thing out. They'd only lost one man, but Enrique had made it out with a commendation and a new tour.

"The CO thought I was the best at HALO jumps, and he recommended me to the Leap Frogs team. When an opening in the Leap Frogs came around, I thought I'd give it a shot, so I jumped at it." He grinned as she snorted. "Pun intended."

"How long have you been with this outfit?" She released his arm as she reached for the door to The Tilted Teacup coffee shop.

"This is my first year, and my first Cheyenne Frontier Days."

Suzie scowled. "I'm very sorry, Enrique. That's the worst luck."

He shrugged. "Yeah, it sucks, but so far no one has told me I can't get back to work after I heal and I count that as a good thing. As my CO says, when life hands you lemons, find a way to rig an explosive and blow the hell out of everyone's expectations."

She laughed again as they stepped up to the counter and his dick saluted to the joyous sound. He noticed the other people sitting around the coffee shop looked up and smiled as well. *That's right, this gorgeous woman is hangin' with me.* He stood a little straighter despite the sling around his shoulder.

They ordered some unusually named coffee drinks and took them outside onto the sidewalk where a couple of tables stood in the shade of their umbrellas. She allowed him to pull out her chair and settled into it with a graceful sway of her hips. His dick saluted to that, too.

"So what did you do before you joined the Navy?" She sipped her coffee as he settled into his seat. He fumbled with the lid to his coffee and she deftly opened it for him. "Thanks. Actually, I helped my family raise championship dressage horses. *Mis abuelos*, my grandparents, have been raising horses for dressage for generations and my father has carried on the tradition. I helped as much as I could, but I was always sneaking off to play in the ocean when I was done with my chores. But I can ride, gentle horses, and clean stalls, mend fences, and pick out good horseflesh if the need arises."

"Sounds like you'd be at home on a ranch as much as in the ocean."

"Yeah, I could pretty much be anywhere. But then, that's what SEAL stands for, isn't it?" He grinned as she nodded. "I love flying and jumping out of the planes. I love swimming and riding the currents in the ocean, and I can ride just about anything that moves, though I'll leave the bulls for the real crazy *vaqueros*."

"Not into bull riding? I'm shocked." Sarcasm filled her voice, but her smile mellowed it. "Considering you jump out of perfectly good airplanes to fall with style, I think you have the crazy covered."

"You mean like asking my triage doctor out?"

She grinned and shrugged. "It's definitely unorthodox."

"We SEALs have a saying. Take the opportunities when they present themselves because they probably won't come back around again." He sipped his coffee. "I wasn't gonna miss the opportunity to get to know you better if I could. Not with a voice like sultry country singer."

"You think my voice sounds like a country singer's?" She shook her head. "I can't carry a tune with both hands and a bucket."

"That's okay, maybe I'll sing to you." Where the hell was this sappy guy coming from? He'd never sung to a woman in his life. That gift was only for his family and to entertain himself, never someone else.

"You can sing?"

He shot a look around the coffee shop, but there were too many people around to show her.

"Yeah. When I was a kid, my brothers and sisters used

to joke that we should all be in a mariachi band. My youngest sister is now a concert violinist, my oldest sister can play any kind of keyboard, and my youngest brother is a *guitarista*. I wasn't much of a musician, but I could sing."

"If you come out to the Triple Star, maybe you can sing for me." Suzie blushed when she realized what she'd said and sipped her coffee, her gaze sliding away. "I'm sorry. I don't know why I said that. I'm sure you're headed back out of town as soon as you heal up. You probably won't have time to visit the ranch."

Her impromptu invitation delighted him and he wondered if he could convince Bruiser to let him recuperate on the ranch. Once he'd healed enough, he could drive and renting a car to travel back and forth to the hotel if need be wouldn't be a problem. Hell, technically, he was on leave to recover.

"Actually, I might be able to visit if I get permission from my CO. Technically, I'm on medical leave and I can pretty much go anywhere I want as long as I don't injure myself too much."

She frowned. "Wouldn't you want to go home for that? I mean, wouldn't you be more comfortable there?"

He thought of going home to his parents' house and all the hubbub that went on there. "Actually, I think it would be more peaceful here. My family is big, loud, and close, and I wouldn't get much rest."

"As a doctor, I wouldn't counsel such an environment. But as a person who knows the value of family to healing, I'd say that's probably the best place for you. Love has an amazing effect on bodies and injuries."

Enrique agreed with her, but his romantic soul didn't want his family's love to heal him. *How is this still a thing in me?* He'd sworn the Navy and the SpecOps community had killed anything as tender as romance in him. He'd seen the worst the world offered in the killing zones on four continents, and yet the idea of spending more time with this beautiful cowgirl doctor made his heart pound with yearning. Bruiser would say he'd gone soft in the head.

Despite the razzing he'd get from his teammates, he resolved to ask to spend his leave here in Cheyenne, and see if he could get the doc to spend time with him.

****

Now why the hell would I say that?

Suzie buried her face in her coffee and burned her tongue, but it was better than meeting Enrique's gaze. There was truth in her words—love made people heal a lot faster and completely, but though she'd spoken of his family's love, she'd been thinking something quite different. Something a lot more mature with the possibility of midnight rides and rolling around in the sheets. *He's injured. He doesn't need sheet rolling. Or riding.*

Even if that was something she'd be willing to do for him.

Rein in those lusty wild horses.

"Yeah, well, don't you work for a therapy ranch? That's a good place to heal, isn't it?"

She laughed. "Yes, it is. But that's for patients seeking therapy for PTSD and other traumas."

He tilted his head. "I bet if we checked with the VA here in Cheyenne, I could get special permission to do my PT there. Do you work with the VA?"

She blinked. Why hadn't she thought of that? *Because I don't want him to be my patient.* No, she wanted to go out with him and she didn't date patients.

"Yes, I often work with the VA for some of the veterans who need special care for PTSD." She nodded slowly. "But I don't want you there as my patient."

He raised an eyebrow. "No?"

"No. I don't go out with patients and I'd very much like to go out with you."

Where the hell had that come from? She wasn't this bold with men, at least not in her personal life, and she'd never been so forthright. *Fortune favors the bold.* She just hoped it didn't turn him off.

A sultry smile curled his lips. "Roger that, ma'am." Intense heat flared in his chocolate brown eyes before he banked it a little and sat back. "I'll need to keep up my PT despite my injuries and working on a ranch would help with that. If I get my CO to request a transfer to the Triple Star Ranch for recuperative PT, would you back him up so the request can go through?"

Suzie bit her lip. Did she really want the handsome Navy SEAL out on the ranch so close?

Hell yeah.

She nodded. "Yes, I think that could be doable. I'm sure Trip and Tom Colton could come up with a physical therapy regimen that would allow you to heal while you keep your strength up."

"Hooyah, ma'am." He grinned and pulled out his cell phone. "I'm gonna text my CO right now."

She laughed. "Right this moment?"

"Yes, ma'am. I don't want to waste a single minute. The sooner I can get started rebuilding my strength, the better." He sat up a little straighter. "Getting out of the VA hospital and doing something useful would make me happy. Studies have shown that the happier a patient is, the faster he'll heal."

She laughed. "That's very true. All right, Enrique, have your CO give my name as the coordinating doctor at the Triple Star, but make it clear that Trip or Tom Colton will be overseeing your PT. I'm just there for the medical side of things. You know, cuts, scrapes, and broken bones."

"Yes, ma'am."

His fingers flew over the touch screen of his phone and she settled back to enjoy her coffee and the warmth of the late summer day. She liked the idea of Enrique Sanchez being out on the ranch. Not only could he help with some of the day-to-day chores, but she'd get to see him more often. And she definitely wanted to see more of him.

Yeah, naked, sweaty, and totally satisfied.

Okay, yeah, that too.

Enrique set down his phone and smiled as he picked up his coffee. "Done."

"That fast?"

He shrugged. "Maybe not quite that fast, but it won't take long. Bruiser doesn't mess around when it comes to his team."

"Oh, I remember that. He wasn't too keen on me taking a look at you in the arena. Took him a while to realize us country folk can be doctors, too." She hammed up her Wyoming accent and winked.

Enrique laughed. "You mean you don't barrel race in your white doctor's coat? That's where your problem lies."

She grinned. "I'll make a note to add that to the official barrel-racing uniform."

"Good plan."

She pointed to his coffee. "Are you done with that?"

"Yeah, why?"

"I want to show you something."

"Oh yeah?" His lips curled into a sexy smile as he rose to throw out his cup. "I'm up for that." He extended his arm to her again. "Shall we?"

Suzie grinned and took his arm as they stepped out the door. She wasn't usually so tactile but she loved feeling his hard body next to hers and the strength in his good arm. She also liked his scent, a wicked combination of male musk and cinnamon. *He's definitely got masculine fire.* And she liked having him beside her as they walked down toward the Depot.

"So where are you taking me, doc?"

"I want to show you one of my favorite, hidden secrets in Cheyenne."

Enrique raised an eyebrow. "Hidden secret, eh? Will I have to file this away under Top Secret?"

A smile curled her lips as she leaned close. "No, but don't blab it about. Can't give away all our unique details."

"Yes, ma'am. Mum's the word." He whispered it in her ear and she shivered with his closeness.

Heat slid down her body, pooling between her legs and making her nipples tighten into peaks. What was it about this man that set her off? She hadn't felt like this about anyone for years. Not since before her medical residency.

What would it be like to have a fling with a Leap Frog? She'd known military guys, but she'd never encountered one from the SpecOps community. At least, not that she'd been aware of. Did those skills make them more accomplished lovers? Or were they just so quick and quiet they left no trace or memory?

Why the hell am I even thinking like this? She didn't often give into frivolous fantasies about men of any kind, and her thoughts about Enrique were silly.

"A penny for your thoughts, Doc."

"Hey, today I'm on a date. I don't have to be your doc."

He grinned and squeezed her arm to his side as they crossed Lincoln Way. "Yes, ma'am. Sorry, ma'am. It's Suzie, right?"

"Yes, it is."

"So, a penny for your thoughts, Suzie."

Damn. She'd hoped he would forget his question, but apparently not. How was she going to explain she'd been thinking of what he was like in bed? She'd have to come up with something that had nothing to do with sex. She didn't want to give away just how celibate she'd been lately.

She shot him a look to gauge his expression and found him watching with intense interest. *Oh, glory. Now what do I say?*

"Random thoughts." That sounded plausible. "Like did

he like the coffee shop? Will he really come to the ranch to recover? Did that guy just cross over two lanes to take the right without signaling? And why is that woman stopped at a green light?"

Enrique nodded as they headed for the Cheyenne Train Depot. "Yes, I liked the coffee shop and I'm really gonna go to the ranch for rehab. And yeah, that guy did cross over from the left hand lane to take the right, but the woman is moving now once she put her damn phone down."

She laughed. "You were paying attention."

"Always. It becomes habit after all the training Uncle Sam has put me through."

"I guess so." She pulled him into the Depot under a tall arched doorway. "Through there is the museum and gift shop. If you're into trains or have nieces and nephews who are, it's pretty cool. But what I wanted to show you is through here."

The doors to the left opened into the main room of the depot. At one time it had been where travelers waited for their trains to take them to destinations both new and familiar. But now it sat empty except for weekend events the community planned.

Perfect.

On the floor against the north wall, a map stretched the length of the room between the exit doors. Different stones had been used to depict the Wyoming Territory and the railroad that connected the different towns along the route. It started in Omaha, Nebraska and stretched all the way to Promontory Summit, Utah in the west. She loved the old map for the history it represented and the geology used for each marker.

"This is what I wanted you to see. It's a map of the original railroad across the territory back in the day."

"Yeah, I can see that." He strode along the floor, his feet making very little sound on the stone as he moved. But he never let go of her hand with his good one. "Did they

27

put this map in when they built the building?"

"Yes, spared no expense to make this place beautiful if not as grand as New York or Chicago." She smiled at the swirling designs in the stone. "I like it because the map shows the craftsmanship of the designers."

"It's definitely beautiful." He stood gazing down at the stone cartograph with his hand warming hers. "More so because you're here showing it to me."

Heat bloomed across her cheeks and she gave a one-shouldered shrug. "Did you know they tried to entice women to come here from back east by saying they'd have the vote? It worked which is why we have that statue of the women with her bags out front. It's called "A New Beginning" and it was meant to represent the chance to start a new life."

Damn, she was babbling. But his nearness and his compliments unsettled her.

"I can imagine your *abuelas* coming out here to start a new life and tackling it head-on."

It took her a moment to translate the word *abuelas* into grandmothers and she could almost picture them stepping off the train and striding into this depot on their way to a new life. Some had been mail-order brides. Others had simply been women with skills and determination to live as much on their own as they could.

Enrique turned to face her, releasing her hand to rest his at her waist. "Strong, determined, fierce women who wanted something new." He gazed at her. "And beautiful, like you."

She snorted. "Some were mail-order brides. Beauty had nothing to do with it."

"Not to your *abuelos*. I bet they were here in this depot, anxiously waiting for the ladies who'd change their lives forever." He stopped and his gaze slid down to her lips. "Like you've changed mine."

"How have I changed your life?" Was that her voice

all breathless and excited?

"*Querida*, you saved me from losing everything." He brought his good hand up to cup her face as he gazed into her eyes. "Without you, I could have died."

"I couldn't let that happen."

"I know." He dropped his gaze to her lips and she swallowed at the blatant interest she read on his face. "*Muchas gracias, señorita.*"

He leaned forward and brushed his lips across hers, and desire flared in her chest. His kiss was gentle at first, teasing her with soft touches. She tilted her head to get closer and opened her lips, wanting him to deepen the kiss more than she'd wanted anything in a long time. She wrapped her arms around him and moaned when his tongue stroked hers.

A deep answering growl rumbled from his chest as his hand slid into her hair and tightened on the strands. His tongue danced around hers, stroking and stoking her fires while the fingers of his injured hand rested against her hip to hold her close. She loved his heat and his hard muscles pressed against her body. She wanted more, preferably without clothing between them, and she kissed him back, hoping she could convey her need as much as she felt his.

They would've kept going except a family with young kids came into the room, the mother herding her brood toward the bathrooms at the other end. Suzie stepped back and Enrique released her as the herd passed them. They stared at each other, out of breath, but didn't say anything until the group disappeared through the door.

"Oh, my glory." She licked her lips and straightened her shirt. "I, uh, I should get you back to the VA."

"Are you sure you don't want another kiss, *querida*?" The smirk mixed with his dark eyes promising pleasures straight out of her fantasies and she swallowed hard.

"No, I'm not sure at all, which is why I should get you back to the VA."

He laughed and adjusted the crotch of his jeans before offering his hand again. "Yes, ma'am. A good, solid plan."

"Yeah. Good plan." She took his hand but forced herself to keep her inner Saloon Girl locked up tight.

CHAPTER FOUR

Enrique still hadn't completely caught his breath by the time Suzie dropped him off at the VA. Oh, he'd managed to make some sort of conversation with her on the drive from downtown, but his dick was still hard and his heart continued to race after that kiss in the depot. He'd kissed lots of women during his time as an active duty SEAL, but none of them had left him breathless. Not for this long.

He watched her car drive out toward the gate before he turned and entered the VA hospital. Bruiser sat with Petty Officer First Class Mike "Skywalker" Ingalls and Petty Officer Second Class Lloyd "Scout" Gutenburg. Enrique swallowed a groan. If they were all in the waiting room of the VA, it meant Bruiser had informed the team that he'd been changing venues for his medical leave. Hopefully, he hadn't mentioned that's where Suzie worked.

"Kickin' that relationship up to full throttle, aren't you, Sanchez?" Skywalker smirked while Scout winked.

So much for keeping it a secret.

Enrique shrugged. "Just movin' to the best place to get my arm rehabilitated. The doc at the Triple Star Ranch was the one who got to me first in the arena. I can't help it if she's had the most experience in rehab around here."

He had no idea if that was true, but he'd stick with it. He wanted the chance to stick around Wyoming a little longer.

"You could go home to Coronado to the med center there." Scout raised his eyebrows. "What's keeping you here?"

"Dude, if I go back to Cali, *mi familia* will be all over me like flies on shit and I'll never get any rest. Plus I'll get fat from my mama's enchiladas." That was only partially true, but he was staying in Cheyenne. *Suzie's worth it.*

Bruiser snorted and shook his head. "I might just stop by your parents' place to get some of those enchiladas. They might put some meat on Skywalker's skinny bones." He lifted a manila folder and waved them at Enrique. "Here are your papers for the transfer of rehab venue. Be sure to look 'em over and sign 'em at the bottom. You can head on over to the ranch tomorrow once your doc okays them."

Enrique nodded, reading over the documents. "Is the Navy gonna cover a rental car while I'm here?"

"Yup. I made sure to get that requisitioned, but don't think you're gonna get a Beemer."

Enrique snorted. "I was thinking of driving a Jeep just in case I have to take any dirt roads. This is Wyoming, bro."

Bruiser snorted. "Believe me, I know. I'm ready to get out of here. Just take those to your doc and have him sign off on the change. Shouldn't be a problem."

"Right." Enrique grabbed a pen and signed the papers. "What are you gonna do while I'm kickin' back?"

"We got the jumps up in Sturges for Bike Week. It's the 78th anniversary so they're doin' it up big." Skywalker practically salivated. He'd always loved the different kinds of Harleys on display. Word was he'd once been in a biker club in Colorado, but he'd left it to join the Navy and the Leap Frogs.

"Right, but first we're headed to Seattle for Seafair and then to Sturges, and then to Chicago for the Air and Water show." Scout ticked the shows off on his fingers.

"We'll keep tabs on how you're doin' while we're off actually doing work." Bruiser gave Enrique one of his rare smirks.

"Yeah, yeah, if it was work, you wouldn't be doin' it, bro." Enrique thumped his CO's shoulder with his fist.

Bruiser snorted. "Just get the paperwork signed and heal up completely because I'm not gonna go easy on you when you're back to one hundred percent."

"Yeah, I've heard that before." Enrique smirked but nodded. "Thanks for this, Chief." He waved the papers.

"Yeah, you're welcome. Just get better. I don't like being a man short."

Petty Officer Second Class Avery Hightower barked a laugh as he joined them, looking down on their CO from his height of 6'5". "Sir, you're always a man short. Or maybe just a short man."

"Shut up, Hightower. You find anything out or you still got your head in the clouds?" Bruiser scowled, but amusement sparkled in his gray eyes.

Hightower lost his grin and he nodded. "Let's take Sanchez back to his room so he can gather up his shit and I'll tell you what I know."

Enrique's gut clenched with unease as they all trooped down the halls to his assigned room. Hightower was the chute specialist, though each man in the Leap Frog team inspected his own equipment. But Enrique's chute failure was unusual and they weren't taking any chances.

They filed into his room and Bruiser shut the door, leaning against it. "What did you find?"

Hightower scowled and with his dark skin, he looked sinister. "The doc was right. Someone shot the chute. I found two bullet holes in the upper canopy. We're just lucky Sanchez was close enough to the ground and had some mad skills to keep from dyin'. Someone definitely aimed for him."

"Are you shitting me? 'Cause I'm not finding this funny." Enrique widened his eyes.

"Not bullshittin' you, bro." Hightower shook his head. "Someone smuggled a weapon into the arena and shot at us."

"Fuck." Bruiser scrubbed his face with his hands. "Who else knows about this?"

"No one, yet. I checked with CFD security and they don't have cameras up in the grandstands. But they do have cameras at the gates. Tae is down there reviewing them right now. He said he'd text when he got something."

Petty Officer Third Class Aaron "Tae Kwan Do" Chin had been an electronics and communications specialist when in the SEALs.

"How does he know what to look for?" Skywalker frowned.

"I dunno." Hightower shrugged. "But he says he's done this before and I figured I needed to get this news back to you ASAP."

"Shit, this show went FUBAR in a damn hurry." Scout shook his head. "What does this mean for the rest of our shows? Do you think someone was aiming for Sanchez specifically or were they going after any one of us?"

"That's a good question." Bruiser frowned. "I don't think we should rule anything out until we have more information on the shooter. But none of us have any identifying marks on us when we jump, so it might have been a crime of opportunity."

"Except to bring a weapon into a rodeo when they check shit at the gate takes planning and intention." Skywalker ran his hand over the back of his head. "The shooter might not have had a specific target in mind, but they were definitely aiming for one of us."

"And I got lucky." Enrique scowled at his broken arm.

"I didn't hear any shots or see anything when my chute collapsed. I was more worried about making a good landing."

Bruiser nodded. "Don't worry about it. We'll get this figured out. Just work on your rehabilitation while we coordinate with local LEOs and the rodeo staff. But keep an eye out and your phone charged. We'll keep you up-to-date as the investigation goes."

"Yeah, go romance that lady doc while you're at it, Sanchez." Hightower flashed a dazzling smile. "She did save you after all. She's a hero."

"You don't have to tell me twice." Enrique nodded and couldn't help the smile curling his lips.

Dr. Suzie Appleton was more than a hero. She made his heart beat faster than a salsa number and yet she was smooth as silk over skin. He'd really like to see her in nothing but silk and lace lingerie, but he thought it might be too early to bring her something like that. Nevertheless his cock thought the idea of Suzie in his bed was worth the salute.

"I'm gonna go get the doctor to sign these papers and arrange for a car." He shifted his body to downplay the tenting of his shorts.

Bruiser grinned. "Yeah, you do that. What time you think you're gonna take off?"

Enrique shrugged. "If the doc is fast, I'll see if I can get up to the ranch tonight and get started on the physical therapy first thing *mañana*."

"Roger that. Our flight's first thing tomorrow too, so we're gonna hang at the hotel bar."

Enrique winked. "Sounds like a wild night. Don't play too hard, bro."

"Shut up. It's gonna be better than cow-tipping on that ranch out there." Skywalker rolled his eyes. "At least they have TVs with the game on at the bar."

"I bet I'll have that in my room and no sweaty drunks

to go with it." Enrique laughed as Skywalker thumped him on the shoulder, but he sobered quickly. "Good luck on the rest of the jumps. Try not to get shot at, okay?"

"Copy that." Skywalker bumped knuckles with Enrique. "Watch your six."

"Roger that."

Enrique waved to his team as they headed out to their rental and couldn't help the disappointment and yearning to go with them. Jumping as part of the elite Leap Frog team of SEALs was his passion. He loved the rush of falling only to be brought up short with a silken canopy over his head. He loved the flow of the air past his body and the pure joy of a precise landing, even when the wind tried to fuck with him.

But even if Bruiser would let him go, his body wouldn't handle a jump. He hated to admit it, but the only way to get back into peak condition was to heal. *Dammit.* At least he'd be able to see Suzie. That would definitely make up for missing a few shows.

It took him a few minutes, but Enrique found Dr. Lyttle finishing his notes after seeing a patient.

"Hey, Doc. You got a moment?"

"Ah, Petty Officer Sanchez. Yes, a moment, but not much more than that." He gave Enrique a tired smile. "What can I do for you?"

"I need you to sign these papers about a change in location for my therapy." He handed the doctor the papers and Lyttle frowned.

"A change in location?" He scanned the papers and his eyebrows went up. "You're moving to the Triple Star Ranch Therapy facility?"

"Yes, sir." Enrique shrugged, for some reason wanting to downplay the real reason for his move. "I've heard it's the best therapy location near Cheyenne, and my CO needs me to recover fast. Can't argue with that and if Uncle Sam is footing the bill, might as well go with the best."

"Who will be overseeing your therapy?" Lyttle's frown deepened.

"Uh, Tom Colton, I think." Enrique craned his head to look at the papers, though he'd memorized the pertinent details. "Yeah. Dr. Suzie Appleton is the medical doc out there coordinating with the VA, but Tom Colton will be overseeing my recuperative PT, sir."

Lyttle said nothing as he read over the documents with more care than Enrique expected of a busy doc. *What the hell has his cajones in a bunch?* When Lyttle raised his gaze, distance and disdain flashed across his face.

"I'll okay this transfer, but keep in mind if you're doing this to get closer to Dr. Appleton, you're wasting your time." Lyttle signed the papers with more flourish than necessary.

Enrique's gut clenched in unease but he kept a mild and amused expression on his face.

"Why do you say that, Doc?"

"Because Appleton is a hard-ass with no time for love-struck patients." Lyttle's voice was flatter than a tortilla. "She doesn't date patients. Hell, she doesn't date at all. So if you're hoping to get close to her by being at the ranch, you're in for disappointment."

Enrique offered a faded smile and shrugged. "I'm just going there for the PT, Doc. I'm glad Dr. Appleton is the medical professional on site, but it's the PT I'm after."

Lyttle narrowed his eyes, trying to read Enrique's face, but whatever he saw there must have reassured him because he nodded and handed Enrique the papers.

"Then you're good to go, Petty Officer. Make sure you schedule a checkup with me in the next few weeks so we can check your progress."

"Yes, sir. Thank you, sir."

The doc nodded and turned away to finish his rounds. Enrique pulled an about-face and headed toward his room, turning the conversation over in his head. What the hell was up with Dr. Lyttle? He'd essentially been warning Enrique off Suzie Appleton. But Suzie had made it clear that she didn't want Enrique to be her patient specifically so she could go out with him. Why would the other doc warn him off?

Enrique shook his head as he let himself into his room. *Maybe other patients had tried to get into Suzie's pants and it ended badly.* Enrique shrugged. He'd take it as it went. Now all he had to do was pack his gear and go rent a car. One-handed.

He sighed.

The only easy day was yesterday.

****

Suzie dropped her keys on the kitchenette counter and headed to the bathroom. While it wasn't a long drive from Cheyenne, it was long enough that she had to pee the minute she walked in the door. She finished using the toilet and returned to the living room just as her phone rang.

"Dr. Appleton."

"Hey, doctor lady, how was your date?"

Suzie laughed at her best friend's question. "Man, you don't miss anything, do you?"

"Hell no. My best friend in all the world finally goes on a date with a guy and you think I'm not gonna pay attention?" Seychelles *tsked* on the other end of the phone. "Honey, I'd be lettin' you down by doin' that. So tell me how it went."

Suzie laughed. "It went...very well."

"Oooh, I like the sound of that. How well is very well? Will you see him again?"

"I'm definitely going to see him again. He'll be coming here to the Triple Star Ranch for rehabilitation therapy."

"How the hell did you swing that?" Seychelles

sounded impressed. "Wait, he's not gonna be your patient, is he? 'Cause that would suck for ethical reasons."

"No, he's not my patient. He'll be either Tom or Trip's patient and I just oversee the medical issues if they arise." Suzie couldn't keep the giddy grin off her face. "You know I don't date patients."

"Just checkin'. I didn't want you to sabotage yourself out of this opportunity."

"What do you mean by that? When have I sabotaged a relationship?"

"Seriously? What about Deacon Malloy back during your residency?"

Suzie rolled her eyes. "It was during my residency. I didn't have time to wipe my ass, much less take on a relationship with a needy bar owner. Besides, he had body odor from the Bog of Eternal Stench. That wasn't going to work with my nose."

"Okay. Well, what about Isaac Easton?"

"The trucker? That should say enough right there."

"Hey, I know a lot of truckers who are great guys, plus worldly and funny."

"There's nothing wrong with truckers, per se. But Easton had a foot fetish and he was never here. I need someone who's gonna be around a lot more."

"Oh, like you're the epitome of 'never busy.'" Seychelles's sarcasm oozed through the phone. "And you're not getting out of telling me how it went with the sailor boy. Who could be deployed at any time and not around, either."

"First off, he's not a boy by any stretch of the imagination." No, he wasn't. He was hot, masculine, sexy, and adult. Suzie wanted him so badly her panties were soaked just thinking about him. "Second, we had a really nice time. I took him to The Tilted Teacup and then we went to the Depot to check out the map on the floor."

Seychelles groaned. "Oh my glory, Suzie. What the

hell were you thinking? Why would you show him that stupid map? It's the dorkiest thing ever."

"Hey, I love that map and he liked it, too. But he said he would sing to me."

"Sing to you? Why would he do that?"

Suzie shrugged as she settled into a chair on her tiny covered porch. "He said I had a sultry country singer's voice but since I couldn't carry a tune with both hands and a bucket, he'd sing to me."

"Be still my beating heart." Seychelles moaned in delight. "Who knew a Navy SEAL could be such a hardcore romantic?"

Suzie frowned. "How is singing particularly romantic? I think it would be kinda embarrassing in public."

"Oh, come on. Between the country boys like Henry Bright singing ballads or Mariachis playing dancing tunes, you gotta admit a man singing is sexy as hell."

Suzie shook her head. "He was already sexy as hell. Have you seen a Navy SEAL's physique? Sweet glory." She fanned her face even if Seychelles couldn't see it. "So hot. And hotter still, he kissed me in the Depot."

"What?" Seychelles squealed into the phone. "Oh my glory! Was it awesome? And he's still coming to the ranch for rehabilitation? Yeehaw, darlin'. Well done with snaggin' him!"

Suzie held the phone away from her head as Seychelles carried on for a few moments. She thought her friend was overreacting. It was a kiss and a date. He'd be leaving as soon as his body healed enough for him to get back to work jumping out of airplanes. Granted, she didn't date anyone she didn't think she'd have a chance at something more than a quick fling with, but Enrique was going places other than a small town doc in Cheyenne, Wyoming.

"Calm down, Sey. It was one kiss."

"Yeah, but he's gonna be at the ranch and you'll be able to hang with him after work each day. This is gonna be so awesome." She squealed again. "You know, he could be the One, the guy you finally find who will do the whole husband, kids, and white picket fence thing you always talked about."

Suzie rubbed her face with her hands. Sey wasn't wrong. She'd always dreamed of being a doctor and finding the right man who pushed all her hot buttons, made her happy, gave her children, and made a home with her. It was her dream, and she'd held out a long time to find the right man to fill that role.

"Maybe, but I'm pretty sure it's just a quick fling, something we both can enjoy while he's recuperating." Hope sang in the back of her mind, but she shoved it away. "Why are *you* so excited about this? It's not like you're going out with him, Sey."

"No, but I gotta live vicariously through you. There's no one on my love life radar for miles, so you're it."

"What about Derek?"

Seychelles snorted. "Derek decided that he needed to find himself in the bright lights of LA with women who are size zero."

"Aw, I'm so sorry."

"Eh." Suzie could hear Sey wave her hand dismissively. "It's okay. He wasn't doing it for me sexually anyway. Kinda a "sixty second man" sort of problem. By the time he was done, I was just starting my run to the finish line, and he'd roll over while I used my rabbit. I might as well not put up with the man invading my space when I get more satisfaction from a toy."

She definitely had a point.

"So, I'm getting all the good points with none of the drawbacks through you. Did the Petty Officer smell good?"

"Okay, enough. I'm only willing to share details so far. But now I need a shower and I gotta prep for the morning." Suzie laughed. "I'll talk to you tomorrow, Sey."

"Yeah, well, I'll want a full report then, too." But

Seychelles was laughing.

"We'll see. I'll talk to you later. Love you."

"Love you, too, doctor lady."

Suzie ended the call and headed for the bathroom. She wanted a long leisurely shower to relax. She adjusted the water and thought about Enrique. She liked his smile and his athletic physique, and she wanted his hands on her body. She loved men's hands. There was something about the strength and elegance of them, and she closed her eyes as she ducked her head under the spray.

Oh glory, I want his all over me.

It had been a long time since anyone she liked had touched her and she used her hands as surrogates, imagining Enrique in the shower with her. His smile would turn sultry and determined, a trait she'd seen in other military men, as he'd slide his palms down her sides and over her ass.

In her imagination he trailed one hand around her hip and cupped her mound, his fingers stroking between her pussy lips. She moaned as she leaned into his touches and he growled as his cock flexed between his thighs. She wanted to grasp his hard length, but he swiveled his hips out of reach and chuckled deep in his chest.

"Not tonight, *querida*. You will have your chance later. Tonight is for you."

He wrapped one hand around her breast and tweaked the nipple as he thrust his fingers into her dripping pussy. Suzie gasped as his mouth latched onto her nipple and he rubbed his balls against her thigh. That wasn't nearly close enough, but she'd take it as long as he didn't stop stroking her clit.

Instead of stroking, he gently pinched her hard nub between his fingers and she whimpered, letting her head drop back against the shower wall. Hot water splashed against her skin as he went to work, thrusting and stroking her sensitive flesh with his fingers. Her orgasm built with relentless power and she whimpered with each thrust of the fingers in her pussy. She watched his expression, unable to look away from his intense gaze.

"Come for me, *querida.* Come on my hand."

The words, said in his sweetly accented voice, pushed her over the edge of pleasure and her orgasm burst through her. She keened her pleasure into the shower's spray, glad her bungalow wasn't anywhere close to the others. The last thing she needed was members of the staff knowing when she got off.

Suzie shuddered a few times, resting her head against the tile wall before she straightened and turned off the water. Enrique had long since faded from her imagination but the memory of his words and his hands on her, even if just a fantasy, stuck with her as she dried, dressed, and made a small meal before crawling into bed.

Enrique would be coming the next day to the Triple Star Ranch and she thanked her lucky stars he wasn't her patient. She shouldn't be fantasizing about patients, and Petty Officer Enrique Sanchez would definitely occupy her fantasies and dreams from now on. A smile curled her lips as she settled in to sleep.

CHAPTER FIVE

Enrique was up and packed well before dawn, but he couldn't head to the Triple Star Ranch until he secured his vehicle. He'd tried to go the day before, but the local rental car company didn't have anything available until this morning. He'd joined his team at the bar last night, but hadn't drunk more than a single beer before they dropped him at the VA. It sucked to bid them goodbye.

They're probably already in the air headed to Missouri.

To keep himself occupied, he used the VA's track to go for a four mile jog, just something to keep him from losing his stamina. His arm twinged with each impact on the ground and his ribs reminded him that they'd only recently knitted, but it felt good to run. He took it slow, per doctor's orders, and he didn't ache too badly when he finished.

By the time he'd showered and dressed, the sun had risen and the VA was stirring. He made sure he hadn't left anything in his room and headed to the lobby to wait for his taxi. A few of the nurses nodded to him on their rounds, but mostly folks left him alone until the taxi drove up.

Once he'd gotten his rental car, he stopped at The

Tilted Teacup for a cup of joe and a bagel. He took them to-go and headed for the freeway. The sun painted the rolling hills a golden green as he sped north on I-25. As much as he missed jumping with the team, his heart thundered at the prospect of seeing Suzie again.

Because he didn't leave for the ranch the previous night, the guys had razzed him for switching therapy venues. Skywalker and Hightower had a bet as to how quickly he'd get the doc into bed, while Bruiser and Scout maintained the doc would play hard to get like Dr. Lyttle suggested. Enrique had rolled his eyes at their shenanigans, but kept his mouth shut. Suzie was his and he wasn't ready to share. How their relationship worked out wasn't anyone else's business.

It didn't take him long to reach the ranch and he drove under the arch with a sense of anticipation. He parked his car in front of the lodge and stepped out into the sunny morning. The day was beautiful but he could smell water in the wind and suspected they'd have rain later in the day. His brothers and sisters always teased him about his weather sense, but it had helped him in the Navy and in the Leap Frogs. He'd always been able to call when they'd be grounded.

He headed into the lodge, removed his cover, and stopped at the desk where a young redheaded man tapped away at the computer keyboard.

"Be right with you." His name tag read "Andrew" and he finished what he was doing before he looked up with a smile. "What can I do for you?"

Enrique extended the paperwork from the VA. "My name's Petty Officer Enrique Sanchez. I'm scheduled for physical therapy here at the Triple Star Ranch."

Andrew took the paperwork and looked it over. "Oh, right. You'll be working with Tom Colton. I'll just page him and he should be right over. In the meantime, could you fill out these forms so I can get your room all situated?" He handed Enrique a clipboard with papers and a pen with a little cowboy hat on the end.

"Cute pen."

Andrew grinned. "Yeah, that was Doc Bright's suggestion for low-key promotion. They always make folks smile."

By the time the paperwork was done and he got his key, a tall man strode into the lobby area with a rolling gait. He looked like the stereotypical cowboy with a chambray shirt, faded jeans, low-heeled boots, and a weathered straw hat. His eyes looked like they'd seen a lot, but his smile brightened his whole face as his gaze lit on Enrique.

"Petty Officer Sanchez, right?" The cowboy held out his hand. "Tom Colton. Welcome to the Triple Star Therapy Ranch."

"Thank you, sir."

"Aw, you don't have to call me sir. Tom'll do." He shook firmly but without the tightness of a man establishing dominance. "I understand you're here for some physical therapy to get you back into peak condition. That right?"

"Yes, sir. Er, sorry. Old habit in the military." Enrique grimaced.

"'Sokay. Let's go talk to Doctor Appleton. I understand she was the first one on the scene of your accident." Tom turned and gestured toward a hallway into the lodge.

"That's right." Enrique's heart revved up but he kept his expression mild. "Dr. Appleton was in the arena when I landed. I don't remember much, but she was there and got me stabilized before I was taken to the VA."

Tom whistled. "You're damn lucky she was there. Best rural doc around. Hell, in some ways she's better than the docs they have at the Cheyenne Medical Center."

"Then I'm doubly glad she was there that day."

"Hell yeah." He paused by the door to a small clinic. "I

don't think she has any patients yet this morning so she should be able to explain your doctor's orders and we can set up a recovery regimen that'll benefit everyone." He pushed the door open and waved to the receptionist. "Hey, Casey. Is Doc Suzie in?"

"She sure is. Her first patient comes in at nine. Want me to buzz her?"

"Please."

Casey nodded and picked up the phone. "Dr. Appleton, Tom Colton is here and wants to see you. Do you have time?" The receptionist listened a moment before nodded. "Yes, ma'am. I'll tell him." Casey looked up after hanging up the phone. "Go right in, Mr. Colton. She's waiting on you."

"Thanks." Tom nodded and headed through the door to the few patient rooms.

Enrique's hear rate ramped up with his anticipation. *I get to see her. She's here.* Excitement roared through his body but he kept a tight leash on his expression. No need to alert Tom to his feelings for the doctor.

"Hey Doc, I brought in Petty Officer Sanchez. You remember, the Leap Frog who fell out of the sky?"

"Yes, Tom, I remember."

Suzie rose from behind the desk at the far end of the room. Cupboards and drawers lined both sides of the long room with two large windows bringing in natural light. A few personal items sat on the shelves behind the desk, but most of the space was filled with books. She looked at home in the office/exam room, and he imagined the patients she saw found the space relaxing and welcoming. *Or maybe that's just how I feel about Suzie.*

"Good to see you, Petty Officer. How are you feeling?"

"Better, ma'am." He nodded and lifted his arm in its cast. "Not much pain in my arm now that it's stabilized, but the ribs give me a twinge every now and again."

"Yes, ribs take a long time to heal." She grimaced. "I'm sure in your service you know that, but I wanted to reiterate so you don't overdo things here at the Triple Star."

"Which is why we've stopped by, Doc." Tom handed her the paperwork Enrique had brought with him. "I'm plannin' on puttin' him to work, but I don't want to do anything that'll aggravate his injuries. What sorts of things do you think would help him work on strength training?"

Suzie frowned as she scanned the orders from Dr. Lyttle. "Shoveling, tossing hay, and lunging horses are out. Those jobs will pull too much on his arms and torso." She shot Enrique an apologetic smile. "But grooming, with the exception of using a hoof pick, grain distribution, and helping Doc Bright hold the animals would be fine."

"Damn, Doc, that's a lot of standing around. Can I at least go running?"

She shook her head. "Not for another week or so. I know you Navy SpecOps types. You don't just jog, you push your bodies until they break, which isn't conducive to healing a punctured lung. Given how healthy you were before the fall, I suspect your body will heal faster than most ordinary folks, but you have to give it a chance."

Enrique couldn't help the scowl pulling at his lips.

"I know it's not what you wanted to hear, but I won't undo all the healing your body has already done. You didn't think I'd just let you run around here, did you?"

"Leave anything for me to do that's real heavy." Tom clapped a hand on Enrique's shoulder. "Trust me, draggin' around a grain wagon one-handed will get you winded, especially after restin' for a few weeks. I won't let you get soft, Sanchez."

Enrique tightened his jaw and nodded sharply, hating his injured status all over again. *Guess Lyttle was right and Suzie's a hardass at work.* He didn't like being proved wrong but there wasn't much he could do about it.

"If you can write up what you're planning to use for a

regimen that would be very helpful. I can look it over and sign off on it, and y'all will be good to go." She signed the bottom of the paperwork Lyttle had sent with Enrique and handed them back to Tom. "Follow Tom's regimen, Petty Officer, and you'll see faster results than if you ignore it."

"Yeah, yeah, Doc."

Her lips tightened as she gave him a dry look. "Your choice, and your time." She turned from him, her back straight, and returned to her desk. "Now, if you'll excuse me, I have a patient coming in a few minutes. Good to see you, Petty Officer, and good luck." She gave him a polite smile as she settled into her chair.

"Thanks, Doc. We'll see you later." Tom waved before he ushered Enrique out of the room.

Enrique followed silently, his thoughts churning with frustration and recrimination. Why the hell had he thought he'd have it easy even if Suzie wasn't his doc? She'd still do her job to the utmost of her ability. She'd be a doctor first and his...what second? Date? Girlfriend? Lover? None of those terms fit their relationship.

"Hey, don't worry about it, Sanchez." Tom gave him an easy smile. "I'll work you hard enough without pushing your injuries, and you'll be fit as a fiddle soon enough." He grinned and it coaxed a smile out of Enrique.

"You ever had a punctured lung and a broken arm at the same time?"

Tom snorted. "Hell yeah. Well, not the lung, but I did have broken ribs, collarbone and arm at the same time. Made breathing a bitch, and ridin' even worse."

"Riding?" Enrique raised his eyebrows.

"Bronc ridin', yeah."

"Shhhhhiiitt. You rode broncos?"

"Hell yeah. Won the championship three times before quittin'." Tom chuckled at Enrique's impressed look as he led him out the back door to the yard behind the lodge. "Ah hell, it ain't nearly as tough as what y'all have to do as a

SEAL, and no one was givin' me hazard pay. Let's get you settled in your place before I show you what all you'll be doin'."

Enrique followed Tom outside where a paved path led around a large duck pond edged with cattail reeds. The barn and covered arena sat off to the left and another building stood ahead of them. It resembled a two story western motel sporting covered balconies with wrought iron railings. A few people sat on benches around the pond, relaxing, while others followed an instructor in a yoga class.

"Wow, this place is nice."

"Thanks." Tom beamed. "We've worked pretty hard to make this one of the best places to come for therapy in Wyoming. My dad recognized the need for it after his time in the Army and as a bull fighter."

"Bull fighter?" Enrique raised his eyebrows. "He challenged bulls?"

"Oh, no, not the way you're thinkin'." Tom shook his head as he opened a door into an interior hallway of the motel building. "Folks used to call them 'rodeo clowns' back in the day. Now they're called bull fighters because they distract the bulls from the cowboys who are dumped off them."

"*Dios mio*, that's a helluva job to have." Enrique pulled out the keycard to his door. It had three stars in a triangle on black background. "I think the guy at the front said I was in room 225."

"Alrighty. That's up on the second floor about half way down on the left."

Tom showed him to the room and when he opened the door, a sense of warmth and comfort flowed over Enrique. The interior had been decorated like a western cabin with oak walls and dark colors for the carpets, drapes, and bedding.

"Wow." He hadn't meant to sound so impressed but

the quality of the accommodations blew all the other hotels he'd stayed in with the military out of the water. "This place is amazing."

He strode to the sliding glass door of the balcony and stepped outside. His view encompassed the duck pond, the barn, and some bungalows out beyond them. A stand of cottonwood trees marked the edge of a river while horses grazed in the pastures disappearing around the edge of the building. He might actually get a chance to relax in a place like this.

It would be more relaxing if Suzie was here with me.

And she was. Kinda. She was the ranch doctor. *But not mine. Not directly.*

That was the only saving grace to the news she'd delivered this morning. Technically, he didn't have to listen to her, but she did have to sign off on the plan and ignoring her would be tantamount to disobeying a direct order. It would also piss her off and get him shipped back to the VA. He respected her too much to blow off her advice.

"You good?" Tom leaned against the entryway wall, a pleased smile on his face.

"Yeah, good." Enrique closed the sliding door and dropped his paperwork on the small desk. "Is there a place I can park my car closer to my room?"

"Nope. The only parking we have is near the lodge or at the barn. Most folks get brought here from Cheyenne as part of the rehabilitation service. It saves on space and pollutants in the ground." Tom stepped out of the room and waited for Enrique. "But since you drove here, you can park in the staff parking lot behind the barn."

Enrique nodded, already calculating how he'd get his gear to his room one-handed. Maybe the staff had a luggage cart of some kind. He said nothing as he followed Tom back out into the sunshine and down the path toward the barn.

"Let's get you started on the few jobs that'll give you

somethin' to build up your strength and stamina while you're healin'. And I'll introduce you to my dad and the two vets who care for our animals." Tom held the door to the barn open.

Enrique nodded and stepped through, inhaling the scents of horse, leather, and hay. He loved the sea and everything that went with the surf, but horses and a barn full of hay felt like home. *I need to call Mama and Papá when I get a moment.* They'd be pleased to hear from him, but not thrilled to learn he'd been shot at. He frowned. Maybe he wouldn't mention the last.

"What branches are the vets from?"

Tom shot him a confused look as they walked down the center aisle between stall doors. "Branches?"

"Yeah, of the military." Enrique touched his dog tags.

"Oh, no, veterinarians." Tom laughed as he led Enrique into a very clean and modern animal clinic. "Though my dad is an Army vet, but Byron and Henry are animal vets."

A long-haired man about Tom's age stood at the counter looking at something through a microscope. He wore jeans, boots, and a flannel shirt rolled up to the elbows as he peered through the scope, and he reminded Enrique of someone he'd seen before.

"Hey, Henry. You got a moment?" Tom gestured Enrique forward. "I want you to meet Petty Officer Sanchez. He's gonna be here to get some physical therapy before he heads back out with his team."

Henry looked up and gave them a friendly smile. "Hey, Tom. Nice to meet you, Petty Officer. Why are you bringin' him down here?"

"He's got broken ribs and a broken arm, but we need to find stuff he can do for strength trainin'. I figured he'd be able to help hold animals for you and Byron to check 'em over, and he could groom those for the therapy classes."

Henry nodded slowly as he looked Enrique over with an assessing eye. "Yeah, that might work. How long you been in that cast, Petty Officer?"

"Just under four weeks, sir." Enrique stood a parade rest with his arms in front of him. He wanted to present the best image of health. The last thing he wanted was to be put on bed rest or light exercise. He'd never get back to his team in time to finish the event season if that were the case.

Henry nodded and Enrique couldn't help but think he'd seen the guy before.

"All right. Do you have any experience with horses?"

Enrique nodded. "Yes, sir. I helped my family raise championship dressage horses. When I'm at one hundred percent I can ride, gentle horses, clean stalls, and mend fences." He raised his splinted arm with a grimace. "But not for a while."

"Great. Then I won't have to go over the basics with you." Henry nodded. "Work out a schedule with Tom here. He'll get you squared away with the feedin' times of the horses and goats, and I'll come collect you for the vet's rounds for some of the gentler horses."

"Gentler, sir?" Enrique raised an eyebrow.

"In light of your ribs and arm, I don't need any of the more rambunctious critters makin' your life a livin' hell. We'll reassess in about a week and see if you can use it a bit more. I just don't want to undo all the work you're body's doin'."

Enrique grimaced. "You sound like Doc Appleton."

Henry laughed. "Yeah, well, we're all about healin', even if she has the more ornery critters."

"Hey now." Tom scowled but his eyes twinkled with mirth. "Old Mags was damn ornery."

"Yeah, but Old Mags turned downright sweet once we found the problem and she's been grateful ever since. Humans can be reasoned with and they're still ornery." Henry shook his head. "I'll stick with animals, thanks."

"Yeah, yeah, don't come cryin' to me whenever you can't figure out what's wrong." Tom shook his head.

"Ain't happened yet." Henry smirked.

"Come on, Sanchez. Let's let Doctor Doolittle get back to work." Tom waved toward the doors. "I'll show you where the stuff is for feedin' the critters and we'll work out a schedule."

"Good to meet you, Petty Officer Sanchez." Henry waved.

"Yeah, you too, sir." Enrique followed Tom out, still trying to puzzle out where he'd seen the guy before.

Tom brought him into the tack rooms of the barn, showing Enrique where the grain was kept for the animals. He also offered him a little red Radio Flyer wagon with rubber wheels to drag it around the barn. He only felt a little ridiculous with the grain bucket and scoop sitting in the red wagon, but with thirty horses and twenty-five head of goats, he was glad of the little vehicle.

The only easy day was yesterday. Even if this was hilariously easy in comparison to the HALO jumps, it pushed him to his limits and he looked forward to crashing in his room after his chores were done.

Damn, it's like I'm back on mis abuelos' *farm.* Yeah, but it was good to do mindless physical work again, especially if it got him close to Suzie. He grinned as he dragged the wagon to the next stall. He could definitely get used to that.

CHAPTER SIX

Suzie finished up with her last patient and took a deep cleansing breath. Post-Traumatic Stress Disorder wasn't fun to deal with on the best of days, but on the times it resulted in physical injuries, it was hardest on her. She took a holistic approach to her Hippocratic oath, trying to use what she knew without ignoring the possibilities of other methods of healing, and acting accordingly. But wrapping up someone's arm in a cast after they broke it in a panic attack made her question if she was only a Band-Aid solution.

You can only make them comfortable. You can't defeat their demons.

She had to remind herself of that more often than not. Her job was to repair their bodies so they could continue to fight the demons. But sometimes the physical damage exhausted her and her heart ached for their internal pain.

She had the ability to let it all go when she locked the door of her office. She didn't have to hold onto anything they carried. But it exhausted her all the same.

"Have a good night, Casey." She nodded to the receptionist as she slung her purse over her head.

"You too, Dr. Appleton. Remember we have an early

morning check-out tomorrow. Herman Langley is heading home."

"Aw, Herman." Suzie's lips curled in a bittersweet smile. "He's finally found his way?"

"Yup, back to Oregon. And I understand his daughter is going to put him up until he can afford his own place." Casey sighed and shook her head. "I'm glad for him, you know? He really worked hard at getting both his physical and mental health under control."

"Yes, he did. And now he's getting a chance to live a real life instead of the half-life he had. I'm happy for him." Suzie nodded. "But it's time for me to get my own life for the night. I have a glass of wine and a kiddie pool waiting for me."

"Kiddie pool?" Casey raised her eyebrows. "What's that for?"

"I love sitting out on the back deck of my bungalow and soak my feet in cool water. It doesn't take much and it's easy to maintain." Suzie grinned as Casey laughed. "So I'll see you tomorrow early."

"Yes, ma'am. Goodnight, Doc."

Suzie headed out the back door of the lodge and strode past the duck pond. It never failed to relax her after a long day. With the sun angling toward the horizon and the horses in the field beyond the barn, her worries drifted away with the Wyoming wind. The heat helped relax all her muscles and her walk slowed to a stroll.

"Hey, doc. Dr. Appleton!"

She paused and glanced at the hotel-like building, affectionately known as the Bunkhouse. Someone waved from the second floor and it took her a moment to recognize Enrique in nothing but a pair of low-slung jeans.

Sweet glory, that man's hot.

"Wait for me a moment." He ducked back inside his room and closed the sliding door.

She couldn't stop her heart from fluttering like it had

the morning when he walked in her office. She suspected she'd irritated him when she wouldn't let him run or work hard, but she wasn't about to play favorites. Yes, she was willing to go out with him because he wasn't technically her patient, but that didn't mean she'd ignore her responsibility as a doctor just because she was seeing him.

A few moments later, Enrique emerged from the Bunkhouse dressed in jeans, t-shirt, and running shoes, and she had to swallow to keep from drooling at his physique despite the sling around his arm. He might have been on the injured list, but it didn't slow him down.

"Where are you headed tonight, Doc?" He stopped beside her with a smile.

"I'm going home to my kiddie pool and a glass of wine."

He raised an eyebrow. "Kiddie pool? Doesn't the Triple Star have a spa for that sort of thing?"

She laughed. "I don't want hot water, I want to cool my feet off after being on them all day."

"Ah, okay. Want some company?"

She tilted her head. "Are you offering to join me in my kiddie pool, Petty Officer?"

"Yes, ma'am." He grinned as he fell in beside her. "It's part of the reason I changed therapy venues. Well, maybe not the kiddie pool, but to spend more time with you."

She shook her head in mock disappointment. "Oh, I'm sad you hadn't included the kiddie pool."

"Ma'am, I'm a SEAL. I can recalibrate on the fly to fit the parameters of the mission."

Suzie laughed. "That is an admirable quality."

"Thank you, ma'am. I'm known for achieving my objectives."

She nodded as they continued toward her bungalow. "And what is your objective tonight?"

He met her gaze as a smile curled his lips. "To have dinner and relax with you."

She raised an eyebrow. "Nothing else?"

"No, ma'am."

She shoved the disappointment back behind her eyes. She'd been hoping he wanted something a little more intimate.

"At least not at this moment. Like I said, I'll recalibrate as the mission evolves."

He grinned and she laughed. It was more of an excited giggle, but she chose to ignore the twitterpated quality. Their path took them toward the little bungalows set away from the Bunkhouse where most of the professional staff lived. Tom's wife, Amber, and lived in one with her dog Nimbus before she and Tom connected, and the vet Henry Bright had taken that one when he was hired. But when Tom's dad, Trip Colton had fallen in love with Doc Bright, Henry moved into the lodge with Trip and Andrew had taken over the bungalow. Suzie was his next closest neighbor and they often walked to work together, especially in the summer.

I hope Andrew isn't feeling too neighborly tonight. She didn't really want to share Enrique's presence with anyone. They probably wouldn't be able to do anything given his healing ribs and arm. Not that he wouldn't try if she asked him. But she'd need to rein in her inner Buckle Bunny—or whatever the Navy SEAL groupies were called—and enjoy a mellow evening with him.

"Please come in and if you wouldn't mind, take your shoes off." She removed her own and set them on the rack beside the door.

"Going the way of the Japanese?" He knelt and untied his sneakers.

His t-shirt stretched across his back and shoulders, and she forgot what she was doing to admire the image. She'd seen lots of cowboys well-built from tossing hay bales and roping cattle, but none of them ever captured her attention like Enrique's physique.

When she didn't respond, he stood and raised an eyebrow at her. She cleared her throat and tried to remember what he'd asked. *Something about Japanese shoes...*

"Oh, no, more like I'd prefer to be barefoot everywhere I go, but there are too many needles, nails, and hooves around here to be safe so I stick to it only at home." She hung her keys on the little hooks beside the door and headed for the kitchen, trying to regroup. "Can I get you something to drink? Ice water? Iced tea? Beer or wine?" She found her favorite red and grabbed the corkscrew from the drawer. *I'm definitely gonna need a drink and that kiddie pool.*

"Yeah, a beer would be great."

"You want a glass with it or just from the bottle?" She pulled a beer from the fridge and grabbed a pint glass with a local restaurant's logo on the side.

"The bottle works for me." He took it from her as she picked up the corkscrew. "Here, let me do that for you." He took both the bottle and the tool from her hands. "Is this your favorite wine?"

"Yeah. It's more like grape juice than wine, but I prefer that. Hell, sometimes I just drink regular grape juice from a wine glass and it works." She grinned as he laughed.

"Good to know." He popped the cork and poured some wine into her glass. "This looks a little more red than purple, but in a dark glass you could completely fool anyone."

She took the glass with a smile. "If I ever don't feel like drinking, it keeps people from asking me why."

"Yeah, like if you're pregnant and don't want anyone to know." Enrique winked.

He meant the comment to be flippant, but it rammed through her like a thrown javelin and froze the breath in her chest. *Get a hold of yourself.* He had no idea how much she wanted a child, but between her medical practice and the barrel-racing, there had never been a good time to have a baby. *Or a long-term relationship with anyone.*

When she'd been in college, there'd been a couple guys not far from home who caught her fancy, but they'd all be going places and she'd wanted her medical degree. She couldn't ask them to wait for her.

Still, the loss of motherhood raked across her heart like barbed wire and the reminder hurt more than she expected. Trust her to get maudlin when she had a hot guy in her house for the first time in years.

"Hey, are you okay? Did I say something stupid?"

And trust that hot guy to be very observant.

"No, no. It's fine. Old memories trying to crowd into the present." She forced herself to smile.

"Wanna make better memories to push them out?" He raised his chin with a smile.

She laughed, letting the past remain where it was. "Yes, please. That sounds perfect."

"Good. Then tell me where to find your kiddie pool."

He set his beer down and headed for the sliding glass door to her little patio. She shook her head and followed him outside. "I keep it in that storage space to the side there." She paused and let him open the storage fence barely large enough for some outdoor furniture and a kiddie pool.

The blue plastic pool had various colored fish and sea creatures on it including the Loch Ness Monster, a couple of mermaids, starfish, and one octopus that looked more like a mythical Kraken than a regular cephalopod. She'd found it at a specialty store online and couldn't resist the pattern.

"Wow, I haven't seen one like this." He rolled the pool out and set it in the middle of the patio. "Got a hose?"

"Over there." She pointed to the green coil.

"I can see how you'd make this a tropical paradise with that thing." He grinned as he dropped the hose end into the pool and turned on the spigot. "How full do you want it?"

"No more than three inches of water. I don't need much." She gestured back to the kitchen. "Do you want anything to eat with your tropical paradise and beer?"

"Sure. Whatcha got?" He left the water running and followed her back inside.

"Cheese and crackers, local farmer's market tomatoes, some deli meats, and such. You know, typical carpet picnic." She pulled the items out of the fridge.

"Carpet what?"

"Picnic." She grinned at his raised eyebrow. "You've never done a carpet picnic?"

He narrowed his eyes. "I don't think I'm translating that phrase right. What do *you* mean by carpet picnic?"

"When I was in med school there wasn't much time for outside activities so I figured out a way to have picnics inside, rain or shine, no matter the company." She chopped the cheese and tomatoes. "What do you call carpet picnics?"

He shrugged but a little pink showed on his cheeks. "It's not a subject for polite company or when trying to make a good impression." He flashed a grin. "Let me help with that. Do you have any salsa or corn ships?"

They put together their meal and after five minutes, Enrique disappeared outside to turn off the water. Suzie put everything on a tray and carried it out to the covered patio. Enrique had already positioned her chairs around the kiddie pool with the little glass table between them and sat rolling up his pant legs.

"Wow. You did all this with one arm?"

He gave a one-shouldered shrug. "Mostly."

She tightened her lips but brought the tray and sat down on her chair. She set her feet in the deliciously cool water and picked up her wine, setting aside her doctor self to just enjoy the evening. Black clouds built in the west, like big heavy brows over the setting sun, and she wondered how long they had until the storm dropped rain onto them.

"How fast do your storms roll in?" Enrique sat back and grabbed his beer as he stared out at the sky. Thunder rumbled in the distance but she didn't see any lightning.

"Depends on the winds. Right now it's pretty calm here, but if the winds pick up, so does the storm." She gestured with her wine glass. "I'd guess we have about a half an hour. Forty-five minutes tops."

"I bet it's beautiful to watch this kind of weather."

She gave him a half-smile. "You like thunderstorms?"

"When I'm landlocked, yeah." Enrique smirked. "Out on the open ocean, not so much. That's when the big metal tin can we're floating in is the tallest thing out there. Not nearly as much fun."

As if to underscore his words, lightning flashed in the clouds and thunder rolled across the landscape.

"I revise my estimate to be about ten to fifteen minutes."

He laughed and splashed his feet in the pool. "We might consider taking the party inside."

The wind picked up and blew his words back at him and she bit her lip.

"You might be right." Her gaze slid toward the horizon again and the mountains had disappeared. "I think the storm's coming much faster than I thought. You get the food, I'll get the chairs." She lurched up just as the wall of rain engulfed the fence at the end of the ranch.

"I'll get the chairs, you get the food." He stood up, but she thrust her wineglass into his hands.

"You have one arm and shouldn't strain your ribs. Don't worry, the chairs aren't heavy." The rain had swallowed the back pasture. "Go. I'll be right behind you."

He growled but grasped the plate of food and headed inside. She stacked the chairs and shoved them toward the storage space as the wind whipped her hair into her face. The clacking on the concrete let her know the rain had arrived. *And hail, too. Lovely.*

She hoped her table would survive the onslaught as she dashed back to the door. Rain soaked her back and hail pelted her head as she ducked inside, laughing and squealing. She slammed the sliding glass door shut and turned to find herself damn near nose-to-nose with Enrique. He caught and held her against his chest, his dark eyes boring down into hers.

I want him.

Her reaction to him was immediate and urgent. She wanted to kiss him until she forgot her name. But she held back, waiting for him to make the first move. *Why does it matter?* He was here, it was after hours, and he wasn't her patient. *But I don't take advantage.* Her inner voice snorted. *He's not saying no to any of this.*

But she waited, and she didn't have to wait long.

"*Querida.*" He moaned the word like a prayer and fit his mouth over hers.

He tasted of beer, crackers, and hot man, and she fell in to his kiss. He teased her lips with his tongue, sampling them with utmost gentleness as his one good arm wrapped around her waist. He explored her mouth, growling softly. She moaned against his lips as his tongue tangled with hers and the sensation shot straight to her pussy.

Enrique pulled back and met her gaze, his chest rising and falling against her breasts. She loved being close to his body and wondered what it would be like, skin to skin.

"You take my breath away, *querida.*"

"I could say the same of you." She bit her lip and took a chance. "Would you kiss me again, Enrique?"

A slow smirk curled his sensuous lips. "It would be my pleasure. But let's do this in a bedroom with something soft to lie on. It'll be easier on my ribs."

She narrowed her eyes. "Are you trying to manipulate

me into my bedroom, Petty Officer?"

The smirk widened. "It's possible, but I'm afraid that's need-to-know information and at present I'm more about action than intel."

"Hmm, I do like a man of action." She let him tug her to the bedroom and followed him inside, suddenly glad she'd made the effort to clean up that morning. "And I've always wanted to see a Navy SEAL's physique in person."

He stopped and raised his eyebrows at her. "You've never seen a Navy SEAL undressed, doc?"

She shook her head. "Not that I know of. You're the first I can definitely say is a SEAL."

"Yes, I am. But let me see you undressed, Suzie. I've never seen a doctor naked." He winked then grimaced. "That sounded a lot better in my head before I said it."

She laughed and pulled her shirt over her head. "Yeah, that came out a little on the creepy side. But I understand your meaning." She dropped her shirt over the chair and paused when his heat permeated her back.

"Ah, glory, *querida*, you're so beautiful." His voiced whispered across her ear as his hands slid up her arms. "Your skin is so smooth and your ass is so sexy." He trailed his fingers down her back to her butt still encased in denim. "Let me help you with these."

He followed the waist band of her jean shorts and stopped at the button. With a flick of his wrist, he released it from the hole and pulled the zipper down before he pushed the shorts off her hips. They pooled at her ankles and he steadied her as she stepped out of them in nothing but her black lace-trimmed panties and bra.

"*Dios mio*, you make black lace sinful, *querida*."

Suzie looked over her shoulder at him. "Come sin with me, Enrique."

"*Dios mio*." He swallowed hard and dropped his hands to her hips, sliding his fingers over the lace on her ass. "Give me a moment. I gotta get this sling off."

She turned and grasped the strap. "Let me help you." She eased it over his head, supporting his arm the whole time. "In fact, I recommend you lie on the bed to help your arm stay still."

She set the sling on her chair and led him closer to the bed. "Sit a moment while I take off your t-shirt."

"Aw now, don't go all doctor on me, Suzie." He sat as she asked but the grimace on his face said he wouldn't be pushed much farther. "I've had worse on training missions. I know the score about broken bones."

She snorted as she lifted his shirt. "I'm sure you have. Oh."

Enrique's body showed the evidence of his experience. Bullet wounds, knife scars, and various other marks of battle showed on his coppery skin. They didn't detract from his physique of strength and endurance – they enhanced it. But the bruising around his ribs and the surgery scars showed as new pink additions to his tapestry of endurance.

"I know I'm pretty scarred up."

She nodded. "It's not that. Your ribs are bruised and healing, and while I know you can take it, I don't want to cause more pain." She trailed her fingers over his surgery scar. "How about I kiss it to make it better?"

"I'd take your kiss, *querida*, and anything else you're willing to give me." His smirk returned. "I've never backed down from a challenge, and I'm determined to give you pleasure."

"Oh yeah?" She knelt between his denim-clad knees. "Me first."

She leaned forward and kissed his chest between his pectorals. The left one had a full coating of hair while the right had been shaved for surgery. She tilted her head to brush her lips against his scar and he inhaled sharply, but didn't pull away. She kissed his bruised skin and opened her mouth to lick his nipple, making him moan.

His reactions made her pussy slick with desire and she

hoped she'd given him some pleasure as she sat back.

"Damn, Suzie. We're gonna need a doc like you in every platoon from now on." His eyes watched her with a hooded predatory gleam.

"Oh yeah? Why is that?" She ran her hands down his ribbed abs to the button on his jeans. A hard ridge strained the denim at his crotch and she yearned to let it free.

"'Cause I feel better already."

He bent down and captured her face in his hands, kissing the hell out of her. She closed her eyes and let herself absorb his touches. This was what she wanted and she'd take every moment of it. It had been too long since a man had made her feel good and she wouldn't feel guilty for this one.

"Good. Give me a chance to pleasure you more." She grinned up at him as she pulled the zipper down on his fly. "I have to be sure everything is in working shape."

He chortled, a deep rumbling sound that ramped up her arousal. "Oh, I assure you, doc. My weapon's always in working order."

****

Enrique couldn't believe his luck. The buttoned-up doctor he'd met in town had turned into a confident goddess and she wasn't holding back. His cock flexed as she deftly opened his jeans and pulled down his underwear. He braced his hands on the bed and lifted his hips so she could pull them all the way off.

She laughed. "Your weapon, eh? Excellent. I've always wanted to try military grade."

Then she dipped her head and engulfed his cock with her hot mouth.

Dios mio! He threw his head back as she took him down to the root. He'd no idea she'd be so capable. That would've been enough, but the things she did with her tongue made him see stars. He fisted his hands in her hair – not to control her, but to keep a grip on some form of restraint. The pleasure of her hot, velvet mouth on his flesh destroyed his previously iron will.

"*Ay querida*, what you do to me."

She hummed as she bobbed on his swollen cock, scraping her teeth over the edge of the glans. Stars glimmered behind his closed lids and his arousal surged up from his balls. The sounds of her gleefully enjoying his shaft pushed his endurance to a screaming pitch and he let go of her head to grab her shoulders.

"Enough, *querida*. You must stop."

His cock popped out of her pouting lips as she stared up at him. Hurt filled her expression. "Why? Didn't you like it?"

Oh shit, not the right thing to say.

"No, no, *hermosa*, that's not what I meant. I like it too much and I can't hold back with you." He drew her to her feet in front of him, staring up into her glorious gray-blue eyes. "And a man doesn't leave his lover unsatisfied."

She tilted her head, a mischievous smile curling her lips. "Was I testing your control?"

"Yes, ma'am." He laughed as she grinned. "But now it's my turn to test yours. Come here, *querida*, and let me show you some loving."

He scooted his naked ass up to the head of the bed, his wet cock waving like a banner. She watched it with rapt attention and crawled onto the bed after him. He enjoyed the view of her breasts encased in black lace as he settled back, but his ribs made him wince and she stopped.

"Are you all right?" She paused on all fours, her face creased with concern.

"Yeah, I'm good. Ribs just reminded me why I'm here."

She settled back on her haunches, her arousal slipping farther away. "Do you want to stop?"

"Hell no. I want you to come closer and sit between my legs." He spread his thighs to accommodate her and her gaze dropped to his throbbing cock. "That's right. You'll get to feel all of that, I promise, *hermosa. Ven acá.*"

Her smirk returned as she dropped her knees between his thighs and dipped her head to lick the crest of his cock. He hissed and swore but she didn't stay there. She twisted and settled her amble hips against his legs, wiggling until his cock and balls rested against her ass.

"*Sí, querida.* That's it." He wrapped his arms around her waist and drew her against his chest, careful not to squeeze so hard as to strain his arm. "Let me help you with your lacy lingerie."

He slid his fingers over the sides of her breasts as he laid soft kisses on her shoulder. She whimpered and trembled under his touches, and he slid his hands under the lace of her bra. He rubbed her tight nipples with the balls of his fingers, allowing them to grow harder under the pads. She thrust her chest into his hands and he reveled in their silken softness.

Holy shit, she's sexy.

"Do you like this, Suzie?"

"Oh glory, yes."

His cock flexed with the passion in her voice and she gasped as the hardness pressed against the small of her back. He was going to lose his mind if he didn't get the bra and panties off her. *Focus, dumbass.* He dragged his fingers away from her taut nipples, keeping contact with her skin until he reached the clasp of her bra. He needed both hands to undo the four little hooks but when he succeeded, her full breasts pushed out of the cups with glorious abandon.

Suzie sighed as he slid the straps off her shoulders and down her arms, freeing her silken body from the lace.

"Oh, *querida*, I love your sexy curves." He tossed the bra away and let each mound overfill his hands. "Your body is the kind to give a man distracting thoughts and a hard-on for days."

"*A* man or this man?" She wiggled her hips against his rigid shaft.

"Glory, this man, you saucy minx. I can't think of anyone else."

"Good. I don't want you to think of anyone else." She leaned forward and twisted around so she straddled him again, her large breasts hanging above his chest. "I want you completely focused on me."

"Yes, ma'am."

"Good. Now are you going to let me finish sucking your cock?"

"No, ma'am. I don't think I could hold out to give you the pleasure you deserve."

"What? A Navy SEAL admitting he doesn't have the stamina?" She raised an eyebrow.

"No, ma'am, I'm simply aware of my limits and when it comes to your fuckin' sexy body, I'm completely lost." He grinned at her. "But it's my duty to make sure you receive your pleasure and to ensure that, certain precautions must be taken."

She laughed. "So no cock-sucking this time?"

"Exactly. I'd be happy to indulge in that during our next go-round."

She tilted her head. "You think there's going to be another go-round?"

"Oh, I know there will be." He took her face in his hands and kissed her with all the pleasure and need surging through him. This woman was the perfect combination of curves, sexiness, and intelligence he'd been looking for. She tripped all his triggers and ticked all his boxes.

"Come on, *caballera*, ride me hard. I want to feel this ass in my hands." He dropped his palms to her butt cheeks and squeezed.

She moaned and shifted, the scent of her arousal tantalizing his nose with its sweet muskiness. It reminded him of the flowering bush his mother had planted beside the kitchen window to attract the hummingbirds.

Honeysuckle, she called it. He hoped Suzie tasted as sweet as she smelled.

Rearing up, she pushed her panties off her hips and slid them down her thighs, baring her sweet pussy to his gaze. His mouth watered with the thought of burying his face in her dark curls, licking the plump lips holding her honey. His cock saluted the idea but he lost his focus as she straddled him once more and positioned herself above him.

Oh, yeah, bring your honey pot to me, Suzie.

Shit, a condom! Yeah, he couldn't get her pregnant, but that didn't mean he could just go bareback. As far as he knew he was clean, but he didn't want to take the chance of giving her anything.

"Wait." He croaked the word and she raised her eyebrows. "Condom."

Great, he was down to one word sentences but at least he had some communication skills left.

"Oh." Suzie nodded and reached into the drawer beside her bed. Inside sat lube, condoms, a small vibrator, and a dildo. "Will this do?"

He blinked. "Damn, woman. How many men do you bring back here to your place?"

It was the wrong thing to say at that moment because she swung her leg over him and sat on the bed. Her brows came down as she dropped the condoms.

"I'm a doctor, Enrique. I understand the human body better than most people, and I know what sex does for the health. What, were you expecting me to be a virgin or a nun before you?" She raised an eyebrow. "I suppose I should be unprepared for sex or not interested until some man comes along and clicks my buttons, right? Or maybe you'd prefer me to be inexperienced so you can teach me all the sacred ways of sex that only men know?" She shook her head as the sarcasm smacked him in the face. "I enjoy sex and I take care of myself. Maybe I should ask you how many women you've been with? Do you even remember all their names?"

"Whoa, I'm sorry, Suzie. I didn't think before I spoke." His cock wilted as he frantically tried to salvage the situation. "I've never met a woman like you. I guess I am kinda hung up on the myth that women aren't into sex as much as men, unless they're getting paid for it."

If anything, her expression grew flatter. "So only prostitutes and porn stars like sex, is that it?" She sighed. "Maybe this wasn't such a great idea." She shifted to get off the bed.

Okay, this definitely wasn't going the way he'd expected. And he kept making it worse. *Way to go, cabrón.* He reached for her and closed his hand around her wrist to keep her from leaving.

"Please, Suzie. Don't go. I'm sorry." He sat up and winced, but the pain from his ribs sat second only to his worry that she'd send him back to his room alone tonight. "I admit, it took me by surprise that you'd be so prepared. A man likes to think he's the only one who's been with the woman he likes, even though I know it's not true. It's kinda an ego thing. Please, *querida*, forgive me for being sexist."

There, he said it. His father and grandfather had maintained the myth of women not liking sex, possibly to cover their own shortfalls in that arena, and he and his brothers bought into it. No one dared to ask their mother and he had no idea if she'd shared the truth with his sisters. That was another no-go conversation. He didn't really want to know if his sisters liked sex.

"Are you really sorry or do you just want to get laid?" She lifted her chin, and damn if she didn't look like a regal queen despite her nakedness.

"Would it be bad to say both?" He grinned as she snorted. "I am sorry for being stupid, but I definitely want to make love with you."

"I like your honesty." Her lips curled into a sensual smile. "You keep that up and it'll go a long way with me."

"I promise to be as honest as I can with you, Suzie."

The one thing his father had taught him about women was that honesty worked better than being *macho*, or claiming to protect them. His dad had often warned him women were a helluva lot tougher than anyone gave them credit for, and underestimating their strength would cost him. It had damn near cost him their mother. *Gracías, Papá.* First lesson put into action.

"That's good." She smiled as she leaned forward, her breasts dragging against his hip. "Because I didn't want to kick you out."

His cock responded to both her words and the touch of her taut nipples. "I'm glad to hear it. I would've missed you tonight alone in my room."

"Oh yeah?" She moved to straddle him again, this time dropping her breasts below his balls. His cock flexed with arousal. "What would you have done about it?"

He groaned. "I would've had to jack off imagining your hot pussy and your moans."

"Mmm." She licked her lips then nuzzled his balls and he saw stars. "How do you know what my moans sound like?"

"I know your sultry voice, *querida*, and I have a good imagination."

"Does it sound like this?"

She moaned as she dragged his cock between her full tits. His balls tightened up against the base of his cock and his shaft hardened to granite.

"Fuck, don't do that, *querida*. I won't last for you."

He lifted her enough to bring her large breasts close to his face and wrapped his lips around one taut nipple. She tasted like sweet berries and he wanted more. She moaned as he sucked on it, thrusting her chest forward. His cock tightened and he had to take a breath before he came from the arousal surging through him.

He tore one of the condoms from the strip and rolled it over his aching shaft. Suzie licked her lips as she watched him work between them, and his arousal expanded.

"Are you ready for me, sailor?"

He grinned as she positioned herself over him with one hand on his cock. "Yes, ma'am. Ride me, cowgirl."

She didn't waste any time and impaled herself on his rigid flesh.

Dios mio! She's so fuckin' tight.

They both groaned as she seated him balls-deep. Tight heat seared him through the condom and he had to take a few deep breaths to keep from exploding with the pleasure. Her pussy rippled around him and set off fireworks behind his eyes.

"Oh my glory, you feel so good, Enrique."

He opened his eyes and stared up at her quivering tits as she raised herself off his cock only to slam back down on him. He would've been concerned that she'd cause herself pain if it wasn't for her breath catching with each thrust.

Her pussy fluttered over his shaft and he couldn't decide which was more pleasurable—the pressure of her on his cock or watching her pleasure herself on him. He'd never had less control than he did now, but the magic of her joy in fucking him destroyed his need for it.

"Oh glory, Enrique. I don't think I can hold back. Your cock feels so good." Her voice came out half plea, half demand as she rode him hard.

"Come for me, *querida*. Give me your cream." He thrust up hard as he held her hips and watched Suzie let loose.

She threw her head back and screamed as her pussy clamped down on his cock. Her orgasm set off his and his release shot from his balls. He rode the wave, letting himself go into free fall, shouting her name.

Ecstasy exploded from the base of his spine all the way to the crown of his head, and mimicked the thrill of jumping from a C-130. The rush of adrenaline before the wind caught him and the pure freedom of soaring through the sky.

He'd experienced great sex before. He was no slouch with the ladies. But sharing this moment with Suzie, watching her take pleasure from him, made his other experiences pale in comparison. He cared if she enjoyed herself and it gave him a sense of pride that he'd brought her to the point of breathless, boneless pleasure.

When she collapsed on the bed beside him, he mourned the loss of her intense heat around his shaft. *No, don't go yet.* But he was too wrung out to move and he had to give her points for kicking his ass sexually.

"Oh, sweet glory." Her breathless words made him mentally fist pump. "That was…I'm speechless."

"Then my work here is done."

She laughed and his heart expanded. "Oh no, you're not getting off that easily."

Delight replaced the warmth at the satisfaction and arousal in her voice. "It was pretty easy, but in terms of you getting off, I'm all about working for it, ma'am."

She grinned. "Give me a chance to recover and I'll be ready for round two."

"Hooyah, ma'am."

He'd be ready for anything she gave him.

CHAPTER SEVEN

Consuela scowled at the pews in front of her, despite the Holy Son on the cross above the altar. The *pendejo* sailor she'd shot from the sky had retreated out of town to complete his recovery. *As if I'll let that happen.* He'd pay for Miguel's death. Hell, he'd pay for all the deaths of her husband's men. While she was owed several deaths, she wasn't greedy. That went against God's edicts. One would be enough.

She thought she'd killed the *gringo* when she'd aimed for his parachute and he'd crashed into the floor of the arena at the big rodeo. But that *puta* barrel racer had gotten to him too quickly to let him die in the dirt like he deserved. *Stupid bitch.* She didn't know what she was messing with.

The SEAL had gone to the Veterans Administration hospital in town, but by the time Consuela had figured out a way to get onto the hospital cleaning crew, he'd already transferred to another therapy location. She'd wanted to scream and destroy the VA, but she'd settled for listening in on the doctors and nurses to find out where he'd gone.

The *putas estupidas* wouldn't or couldn't give her the location, but the doctor who oversaw the SEAL's recovery mentioned the Triple Star Therapy Ranch. He seemed obsessed with the doctor who ran the place, even to go as far as saying she was a bitchy hardass to the other doctors. Why he had a hardon for her, Consuela didn't know, but he let slip to his coworker that the SEAL was sniffing around this other doctor's skirt and he didn't like it.

Once she heard that, Consuela found it on the map using her phone and figured out a way to rent a car. She'd need it for her new job at the Triple Star Therapy Ranch. One way or another, she'd kill that *pendejo* for her husband's death.

Satisfied with her course of action, she lit a candle in the Catholic cathedral in downtown Cheyenne, and asked for his blessing as she carried out her vengeance. *I will do right by you, Miguel. They will pay with everything they hold dear. Just like I did.* She nodded to the Holy Son and sailed out the grand doors to her car. She'd make this right and the SEAL would die.

****

Suzie saw her patients that day with an extra bounce to her step. *Hell, not even just today.* It might have something to do with the hot Leap Frog Navy SEAL. Enrique had been spending most of his evenings at her bungalow, and she wasn't regretting any of it.

Turned out her SEAL was very creative when it came to pleasuring her and getting around his injuries. One time he had her kneel over his head as he feasted on her pussy until she came. She'd held onto the headboard to keep from collapsing on him and he'd only licked his face like a cat with a bowl full of cream. She'd been too boneless from pleasure to complain when he shifted her down and inserted his cock, fucking her from below. He'd brought her to another two orgasms before taking his own pleasure.

"You're in a good mood, Doc." Casey smiled as she

handed Suzie the day's patient files. "Something to do with
that hot new stable hand Tom has working here?"

"He's not a stable hand, he's a Leap Frog, and maybe."
She grinned as Casey rolled her eyes.

"I don't know what a Leap Frog is, but Tom has him
doing stuff around the barn."

Suzie raised an eyebrow. "How do you know that?"

"I got eyes." Casey snorted. "And he's hot. I don't
think I've seen that many ripped muscles on the guys
around here." She shivered dramatically. "He's definitely
one to watch when he's working."

Suzie completely agreed though she wanted to keep
her interest low-key. "He needs those muscles to do his job
jumping out of airplanes. He's just here to rehabilitate his
body before he goes back to work."

And she was happy to work his body in other ways,
though she wouldn't share that with Casey. Hell, she
wasn't willing to share it with Seychelles, and her best
friend had been calling for daily updates.

"Couldn't he have done that at the VA hospital in
Cheyenne?" Casey tilted her head with a dry look.

"We are the best therapy facility in southeastern
Wyoming. Why take adequate when you can get the best
on the government's dime? He's a Navy SEAL. They don't
skimp on training or medical care."

That sounded plausible, though his coming to the
Triple Star had been about seeing her more than the quality
of rehabilitation facilities. But she was trying to keep a low
profile to avoid ethics problems.

He's not my patient. I'm consulting only.

That might be true, but they were at the very edge of
technicality and she didn't want anyone asking questions.

"So who's my first patient today?" She didn't really
need to know as she stayed on top of all her appointments,
but it was a good way to get Casey off the scent.

"Amber is coming in for her three month post birth

checkup. And then you have Marine Sergeant Rafferty and Private Dixon back to back." But she frowned.

"Something wrong, Casey?"

"No, well, maybe. Did you come in late last night and go through the medical files on my desk?" She rearranged more of the file folders.

"No, why?"

"Because they were all out of order and Petty Officer Sanchez's file was on top. But you don't have an appointment scheduled with him and I only put out the next day's appointments."

Suzie frowned and shook her head. "No, I wasn't here last night. Maybe one of the night cleaning crew rearranged things and just moved it to the top of the pile. I know I have a checkup with him soon. Maybe it just got shuffled around."

Casey nodded slowly though her brows remained lowered. "Yeah, maybe." She looked up and winked. "Too bad you don't have one with him today."

Suzie picked up the files and shot Casey a dry look. "Mmhm. Send Amber in to exam room one when she gets here."

She headed to her office to get her stethoscope to the sound of Casey's laughter. There wasn't any point to argue with her. She'd just use it as an excuse to tease Suzie more about Enrique. Suzie shook her head as she grabbed her white doctor's jacket and threw it over her shoulders. While she didn't need to wear it, she'd found it made the patients trust her and take her more seriously when she did. Particularly the male military members.

Like in the arena when Enrique hit the ground. His CO would've been a lot more receptive to her advice had she been wearing the coat.

Suzie sighed and grabbed Amber's file as she headed to the exam room. Amber had already settled herself on the exam bed while her service dog Nimbus sat beside the visitor's chair and watched her human. Suzie paused to greet Nimbus when she came in then turned her attention to Amber.

"Good morning, Amber."

"Hey, Doc. How are you?"

"I'm doing pretty well. How are you doing?"

"Good. I'm releasing weight and I'm eating right since the baby was born."

"I'm glad to hear that." She took out her stethoscope and placed it against Amber's chest. "Let me listen to your heart a bit."

While Amber had given birth to a healthy baby girl, the pregnancy had been her first and her body hadn't dealt with it as easily as they'd hoped. Suzie hadn't ruled out a second pregnancy if Amber wanted it, but Amber had mentioned she wasn't ready for another child.

"Everything sounds good. How are you feeling?" Suzie only asked the question to see Amber's reactions. It was an innocuous question, but the way a person reacted to it told her a lot. Their bodies often spoke louder than their mouths.

"I'm good. All the aches from the pregnancy are gone and I finally feel like my body is back to its original shape." She shifted on the bed and pulled out her phone. "I still am a little stiff in the mornings when I wake up and I get sleepy early in the evening, but otherwise I feel pretty good."

A piece of paper fluttered to the floor and Suzie bent over to pick it up. "What's this?" She held it up.

Amber raised her eyebrows. "I don't know. What are you talking about?"

"This. It came out of your pocket when you grabbed your phone." Suzie handed her the scrap of paper.

"Oh, yeah. I found that on the floor on my way here and thought it was yours." She handed it back. "It's not something I recognized."

"My handwriting is a little clearer, despite being a doctor." Suzie snorted as she narrowed her eyes, trying to decipher the note. "I think it says, 'Saturday, 7:30 pm,' but I'm not sure what it's for."

"And you didn't write it?"

"Nope." Suzie tilted her head. "Maybe it's from Tom?"

Amber shook her head. "No, his writing slants to right like cursive." She rubbed her chin. "Flowers…Maybe it's from your new beau. What's his name again? Petty Officer First Class Enrique Sanchez?" She grinned. "Sounds sexy."

Suzie laughed as she tucked the note into her coat pocket. "Hey now, you got yourself a real Wyoming cowboy. I had to find someone different. Like a hot Navy Leap Frog." But a smile curled her lips at the note. "Maybe he's doing something sneaky and bringing me flowers on Saturday."

"Aw, now that's terribly sweet. You've only been together a short time, right?"

"Yes, just a couple of weeks." Suzie waved the thought away. "You, however, are looking good. How's Emerald doing? Feeding well?"

Amber beamed at the mention of her daughter. "Yes, ma'am, and Tom's over the moon about her."

"I bet." She shoved her own baby-need away. She still needed to find the right man for the job because there was no way she had enough time to be a single mom. "How are your nipples? Did the cream I gave you help?"

"Oh glory, yes." Relief colored Amber's voice. "Emerald was wearing them out with all her feeding and the cream reduced the chapping by half in just a day."

"Good. Well your vitals look good and it does seem like the baby weight is coming off." Suzie made some notes in Amber's file. "Keep up your walking regimen and you should be back to your usual. And feel free to take as many naps as you can while Emerald sleeps. Also keep up with the vitamin B12 and glucosamine supplements to help with the sleepiness and stiffness."

"Sounds good. Thanks, Suzie." Amber gathered up her things and reached for Nimbus, but she paused before she moved to the door. "And you and Petty Officer Sanchez should come over for supper one night soon. Are you bringing him to the wedding?"

Wedding? For a moment, Suzie blanked and shot Amber a confused look. "What are you talking about?"

"Trip and Henry, big shindig? You remember, it's happening this coming Saturday here at the ranch?"

"Oh, sheesh, yes, I remember." She frowned as she thought about the note. "What time is it planned for again?"

"Ceremony's scheduled at four, reception starts at five, why?" Amber tilted her head and Nimbus mirrored her motions.

Suzie held up the note. "Maybe this was a handwritten note about a flower delivery for the wedding rather than for me." She shook her head. "But that would be way too late. So strange."

"It's probably nothing." Amber smiled as she headed for the door. "I'll text you some dates to come over for supper and we'll make a plan. It'll probably be after the wedding though. Tom's pretty stressed about making it great for his dad."

"Yeah, I understand. Seychelles said the same about her father. Byron is going to be Trip's best man." Suzie grinned at the thought of the old veterinarian dressed up to stand with Trip. "It's going to be a great day, I think. Nice to see Trip really happy."

Amber nodded. "Yeah, it does. And Henry's a great guy. All right, thanks for the checkup. Do I need to schedule another one?"

"No, I think if you just keep on with what you're doing, you'll be fine. But if you have any troubles, give the office a call and we'll check on you."

Amber gave her a smile. "Will do. And I'll let you know about supper."

"Sounds good."

Amber and Nimbus headed out of the clinic and Suzie made notes in Amber's file, glad the other woman was recovering so well. She was looking good after having a kid and Suzie hoped it would be as easy for her, too. *Still have to find the right guy.* Enrique would definitely fit the bill if attraction and humor had anything to do with being a parent.

But he was a Navy SEAL Leap Frog. While not as crazy as the men on the front lines in extreme parts of the world, they did jump out of airplanes and twirl their chutes in the sky. She'd bitten her lip a few times as they fluttered in dizzying circles before coming in to land. They always touched down like butterflies with sore feet but it still freaked her out a little.

Maybe he's not the right one for long term. No, perhaps not, but he definitely lit her fire now and she saw no reason not to be with him and enjoy his company. Maybe she'd even ask him to come with her to the wedding. *And if he wears a dress uniform?* She shivered with delicious pleasure and forced herself to move on to her next patient. She could fantasize later, but the image stayed with her all day.

CHAPTER EIGHT

"We think we have an idea of who shot at you, Sanchez." Bruiser's voice came through Enrique's earbuds as he raked the clean straw bedding in the stall.

"Who are we looking for?" He couldn't help the growl in his voice, but he kept it down so none of the other stable hands would hear it.

"Someone smaller than average, around five feet in height. Could be a kid or a woman given their build. I'd say no more than a buck fifty in weight." Aaron sounded frustrated. "I went over those videos with a fine toothed comb and then I got serious, and I still didn't get a good look at the face. The unsub knew where all the cameras were and kept their head turned. They were wearing a sweatshirt, which was strange in the heat, but that day a storm came in so it didn't stand out."

"That's not much to go on. We need confirmation before we send anything to the LEOs." Enrique chewed his bottom lip as he thought of ways to catch the bastard. "Did you see anyone with the same look coming out of the gate?"

"Is a frog's ass airtight?" He could hear Aaron roll his eyes. "We got the unsub coming back out while everyone was worried about you in the arena. Again, they avoided the cameras, but I did catch something dangling from their wrist this time. Looked like a rosary and the skin color was darker than Caucasian. It's not much but better than nothing."

"Shit." Frustration filled Bruiser's voice. "Did you get anything from any other cameras at the park?"

"Nothing and it's not like we can be sure what kind of vehicle this person is driving." Aaron's voice had the quiet stoicism that meant he was pissed.

"So we really have nothing." Enrique stepped out of the stall and leaned against the wall, staring down at his boot toes. "Do you think this was a freak, isolated incident or something more personal?"

"To get a weapon like that into the park, it had to be personal. You got any specific enemies, Sanchez?" Skywalker spoke up for the first time.

Enrique shook his head. "Not since I left for the Navy. I mean, there are plenty of people who hate SEALs all over the world, but no one I can think of who's gunning for me specifically."

"He's probably right. They could've hit any one of us that day, Chief." Hightower sounded reasonable though Enrique's blood boiled. "Maybe we need to look at a broader threat."

"That'll narrow it down," Scout remarked drily enough for Enrique to grin. "Should we limit the search to all Catholic supporting countries or just those in the New World?"

"My biggest question is will they strike again?" Bruiser had lost his amusement. "Will this tango find us in Memphis or Sturges? Or has this individual decided Sanchez is the true target?"

Silence reigned on the call as they all digested his concerns. Was the tango just after Enrique? And would they strike again?

"It doesn't matter, Chief." Enrique tried to sound more confident than he felt. "We'll just all have to stay vigilant. Watch your six, guys."

"You, too, Sanchez."

"Roger that."

"We'll inform the LEOs what we have but they might not be able to do anything. Just keep one eye open." Bruiser sounded more dour than usual.

"Copy that, Chief. Talk to you in a few days."

Enrique ended the call and pushed his wagon of straw to the next clean stall, going over his memories of the jump during the rodeo. Nothing about the tango stood out. All he remembered was the jump, his canopy collapsing, and the scent and voice of the women who stabilized him after he hit the ground.

He tried to remember if he'd seen anything in the stands, but nothing came to mind beyond wrestling to slow his fall with a torn chute. *Fuck!* The tango could be anyone and he'd never see them coming. Hell, he didn't even know if they'd be going after him or after the rest of the squad.

I'm probably worrying over nothing. Except his gut said he needed to be worried and it had saved him more times than his logical mind. He'd just keep his eyes open and try to stay ready while he spent time with Suzie.

The thought of the doctor shifted his focus and his body reacted to the memories of touching her. Her soft skin and aroused moans distracted him from the mind numbing job of forking straw into a clean stall and spreading it out. He remembered the taste of her sweet pussy on his lips and how she rode him like the champion barrel-racer she was. Damn, he'd need to take a cold shower before Tom or the vet Henry noticed his wayward thoughts.

"Hey, Sanchez, you almost done there?"

Speak of the devil...

Enrique glanced over his shoulder at Tom where he leaned against the stall door.

"Yes, sir. This is the last stall." He grimaced as Tom lifted an eyebrow. "Sorry. As I said, it's a habit. I'm not sure I can break it."

"Yeah, I guess I can't ask you to try since you aren't gonna be here very long." Tom grinned and shook his head. "But since you're damn near done, I figured I could ask you if you have plans for this weekend."

Enrique took his time setting the pitchfork aside as he considered. As far as he was concerned, he planned to be in Suzie's company, preferably in her bed. But he didn't want to get her in trouble with Tom.

"Nothing special. Just putting my time in to get better. Why?"

"Well..." Tom rubbed the back of his neck, looking nervous for the first time since Enrique arrived. "There's a weddin' this weekend here at the ranch. My dad's marryin' his fiancé on Saturday and we're short a man to be an usher. One of the guys we expected got pneumonia and won't be cleared to be around folks for at least a week. It's not a hard job. Just make sure folks get to their seats for the ceremony and maybe help them find their tables for the reception. You, uh, think you might be willin' to do that?"

"I don't have a tux or anything. Just my service dress blues. Nothing formal enough for a wedding."

Tom nodded. "That should be okay. It's last minute after all, and I'm sure only Navy folks would know the difference. The rest of us wouldn't bat an eye."

Enrique snorted. Probably true. His family certainly hadn't known he wasn't dressed up until he showed them his dress whites. He remembered some of his women cousins being suitably impressed when he came in wearing his service dress uniform. Would Suzie like it on him?

"Will Dr. Appleton be there?"

Tom tilted his head. "Yeah, I do believe she's on the guest list. Why? You sweet on our doc?"

Enrique willed his body to remain still and relaxed.

"Yes, sir. She's the main reason I had my therapy venue transferred here. And why she's the consulting doctor rather than primary care."

Tom nodded slowly, his lips curling into a smirk. "I'd wondered why she's been in such a good mood lately. I chalked it up to her winning the CFD barrel-racing championship, but maybe it's something else. Or rather some*one* else."

Tom seemed to be taking it in stride, but Enrique didn't want to cause trouble for Suzie. "I don't want to cause her grief, sir. We did meet outside before I came here and she's only consulting on my recovery. So far she hasn't treated me any different than her other patients."

"It's not really me you have to worry about, Sanchez." Tom shook his head, his smirk mellowing. "It's her best friend, Seychelles Abernathy. If I've learned anything about women, especially Seychelles, it's they're very protective of their friends. They defend them like their own sisters. If you want to get in good with Doc Suzie, you'd best make sure Seychelles approves."

Enrique sobered and straightened his shoulders. "Duly noted, sir. Where do I find Seychelles?"

"She runs the Twice Tallied Treasures antique store in downtown Cheyenne in the Tivoli building on Lincoln Way." Tom reached for the rake. "Why don't you head into town today and visit the shop? If nothing else it's a good place to find gifts for weddin's, pretty women, shit like that." He winked.

Enrique barked a laugh. "Subtle, real subtle." He shook his head with a grin. "I have to head into town today for an appointment with my regular doctor. I'll make sure to stop by the shop to see what I can find."

Tom lost some of his humor. "But you're okay with bein' an usher?"

"Yeah, as long as you're okay with my less than formal service dress blues."

"Yeah, it's all good. I'm sure the ladies will think you're hot shit." Tom grinned.

As long as one lady does.

"I gotta get a shower. What time to I need to be ready for the wedding festivities?" Enrique stretched his shoulders gingerly, making sure not to pull too much on his ribs. They'd healed pretty well in the five weeks since the fall, but things were still tender.

"Stuff starts happenin' on Friday so we can get the stage floor set up for the reception, but the actual weddin' happens in the arena on Saturday. I'll come knock on your room door on Saturday mornin'. Sound good?"

"Yeah, copy that. I'll be ready." Enrique waved as he headed out of the barn into the sunny afternoon, already formulating a plan of attack for negotiation with Suzie's best friend.

CHAPTER NINE

Enrique parked his car near the front entrance to the VA and sighed. The last doctor he wanted to see today was Lyttle, but as his PCP, it had to be done. There was just something about the guy that rubbed Enrique the wrong way. Oh, he was professional and knowledgeable, and he'd been in the service as a Navy Corpsman, but Enrique's gut kept screaming warnings about him.

The nurse took his weight, blood pressure, oxygen levels, and temperature and made some notes in his file before she said Dr. Lyttle would be right with him. He was left to his own devices in a small room that, while functional and useful, was sterile and cold. It looked like most doctors' offices associated with medical centers around the country. And he'd been in some shabby ones throughout his military career. He immediately missed the clinic rooms of the Triple Star Ranch. They were warm and friendly as well as practical. Lyttle's space made him feel like a number.

Suck it up. This guy is only temporary. Thank glory for that.

After about ten minutes, Lyttle finally made an appearance, and though he smiled, his eyes remained remote. "Ah, Petty Officer Sanchez, good to see you. How are you?"

Enrique doubted the doc really wanted to know so he answered with the standard. "Fine, doc."

"Good. Let's take a look at your arm. If everything looks good we can remove the cast and not replace it. Otherwise, we'll use a nylon brace to remind you not to overuse it."

"Sounds good, doc. I'm really to be free of this weight." Enrique lifted his arm and shrugged out of the sling as the Lyttle readied the saw.

They didn't speak for the short time it took to cut open the cast and peel it off Enrique's arm and that was fine. The man who made his shoulders tighten with unease. Once the cast was off, his skin looked dry, pale, and flaky, but it felt so good to be without the weight.

"It looks good. Let's test how well it's knitted." Dr. Lyttle set the saw aside and gently grasped Enrique's arm, using his fingers to probe the muscles and bones. "Do you have any pain when I manipulate your arm?"

Enrique hissed a little as he ran over the site of the break. "Yeah, it's still tender right there. The rest feels okay, but weak."

Lyttle nodded. "Let's take one more X-ray to verify, but I suspect you're on track to heal correctly. You'll need physical therapy to get it back into working condition. But I think we can go with a nylon brace for the next two weeks. Leave it on as much as possible, though you can remove it to shower."

He pulled open a drawer and removed a blue and black brace that he fit to Enrique's arm. They fiddled with the fit, making sure it didn't rub his elbow or pinch his skin but still held the bones where they needed to be.

After going over the maintenance of the brace and the care for his injury, Dr. Lyttle asked Enrique to remove his shirt to check the surgery site and to listen to his lungs.

Enrique didn't like the doc's hands on his body, but he dutifully held still and breathed deep when asked.

"The lung sounds good and the swelling has definitely gone down. I think you can be cleared for running and mild workouts. You can put your shirt back on." Lyttle turned away and made some notes in the charts and records. "How has it worked out being up at the Triple Star Ranch for therapy?"

Warning bells rang clearly in the back of Enrique's head despite his pleasure at being at the ranch with Suzie. Something about the way the doctor asked made him temper his response.

"Yes, sir. It's a good facility. There's lots of opportunities to keep up my physical endurance while not straining my injuries. I've been lucky to work with Tom Colton." He pulled his shirt on and put his wallet and keys back in his pockets.

"Oh, so you haven't been seeing Dr. Appleton?" Lyttle frowned and shook his head. "I'm sorry. That came out wrong. She hasn't been overseeing your therapy?"

"No, she's just making sure I follow the doctor's orders."

Enrique kept his expression bland and his voice light, but Lyttle's question sounded more of the personal nature rather than professional interest. There was no way in hell he'd tell Lyttle about his relationship with Suzie.

"Good to hear. Anything else that might be bothering you? Everything functioning the way it should?" Again, the question appeared on the surface as an innocuous, but something slithered under it with an intrusive quality.

"Yes, sir. Why?"

Lyttle shrugged. "I see in your file that you've experienced some sterility from actions in the field. Is everything functional? You aren't experiencing any other problems as a result of those previous actions or the recent events?"

Enrique narrowed his eyes. "No, no problems, and yes, everything is functional. What does this have to do with my lung, ribs, and arm, doc?"

"Nothing, just making sure you have nothing else bothering you." Lyttle's professional mask slid into place, but not before Enrique caught the quirk of his lips in a satisfied smirk. "Good to hear you're not experiencing any ill aftereffects. As I said, I've marked down that you're cleared for mild workouts and running, and you should be able to get the brace off in about two weeks. In fact, you won't have to come back here. Dr. Appleton should be able to check it and clear you. And you'll be back to jumping out of airplanes with your team."

Why did the doc sound positively giddy about that?

"Thank you, doc." Enrique didn't bother to shake his hand. "I'll let my CO and Dr. Appleton know." He had nothing else to say so he followed the doctor out of the exam room.

"Sounds good, Petty Officer Sanchez. Give Dr. Appleton my best."

Fat fucking chance of that. Fortunately, the other man didn't seem to care if he agreed as he headed on to his other patients in the VA hospital. Enrique was happy he could go. He made sure to square away all his medical records and have copies sent to his squad's headquarters, then headed out the door, feeling like he'd been set free.

He considered calling his CO to let him know the news, but figured they might be in the middle of their jumps in Sturges for Bike Week and it wasn't a pressing issue. It could wait until that evening when they were shooting the shit.

Instead, he spent time looking for Twice Tallied Treasures on his phone and mapped a route to its location. It sat right in the center of downtown and he got a chance to see the Depot again, reminding him of his first kiss with Suzie. Damn, just the thought of the woman made his dick harden until he could pound nails with it.

Focus, cabrón.

The last thing he needed was to show up at Suzie's best friend's shop with a tent in his jeans. He parked on the north side of the street and trotted across the crosswalk to the door of Twice Tallied Treasures. The building was made of red sandstone and had an actual turret at the top. *Good surveillance spot.* He pulled the door open to the thrift store and ducked inside out of the sun.

Enrique had poked around the thrift stores in his home town with his mom and *tias* growing up, but he'd always gravitated to the military toys and the old medals someone brought in to sell. It was the first time he'd seen actual awards for valor and strength. The shop in downtown Cheyenne held far more interesting things, like dishes, furniture and random art. There'd been a Velvet Elvis, Dogs Playing Poker, and even a stained glass piece that he thought were supposed to be poppies. But while he ostensibly looked for something to pick up for the wedding, in reality he browsed in hopes he could meet Seychelles Abernathy.

Suzie's best friend.

Without Seychelles' blessing, he'd have a much harder time making his relationship with Suzie last longer than the HALO jump. If his family and all their busy-bodiness had taught him anything, it was he needed the best friend's blessing before the father's.

"What can I do for you? Just browsin' or lookin' for something specific?"

The husky-voiced woman in a plaid shirt and jeans gave him a friendly smile as she worked on something behind the counter.

"Kinda both, actually." He matched her smile. "My name's Petty Officer Enrique Sanchez, and I was looking to find something for an upcoming wedding up at the Triple Star Ranch. I understand Dr. Suzie Appleton is a friend of yours and I wanted to make a good impression on her since we're both going."

She tilted her head. "Oh, so you're the petty officer she's been goin' on about. Nice to meet you, Petty Officer Sanchez. Are you really here to get somethin' for wedding? Or are you tryin' to get the goods on her?"

The look she gave him could've frozen the water all the way across the Atlantic. He laughed.

"To be honest, neither, ma'am. I'm here to talk to you. Now if I come home with something good for the wedding couple, that's icing on the proverbial cake."

She narrowed her eyes. "You know the couple gettin' hitched are Trip Colton and Henry Bright, right?"

He hadn't known who Trip was marrying, but he kept the surprise off his face. *Trip's marrying the young vet?* "Yes, ma'am. I was personally invited by Tom Colton and I couldn't show up without a gift."

"Right." Seychelles nodded slowly, gauging his reaction carefully. "Well, Trip and Henry both like music, horses, rodeo, and the occasional glass of wine, so you're welcome to look around."

"Thanks. I'll definitely take that under advisement." He didn't budge from his spot. "But I mostly wanted to talk to you because I like Suzie and I want to keep seeing her, even after I heal and go back to work."

Seychelles raised an eyebrow. "Have you talked to her about it?"

"First topic of conversation when I see her tonight. But I had to come into town for my follow-up appointment and Tom Colton told me about your store."

"Why are you talking to me?"

"Come on, the best friend holds a lot of sway with someone. After growing up with a lot of women around me, I definitely learned that. And Tom said I needed to talk to you, too."

To his surprise, she laughed. "Tom's pretty smart, and

if you're listenin' to him, you must have some smarts of your own." She leaned forward on her elbows. "All right, Petty Officer Sanchez, what do you want to know?"

Enrique shook his head. "Only what you want to share because most of this I'll be able to learn from her. What I'm really after is your blessing. Best friends have a lot of power and they can derail a relationship if they're not sure about a guy. So maybe I should be asking you what do you want to know?"

Seychelles sat back and laughed. "Definitely smart. All right, let's take it from the top. Suzie is big on honestly, compassion and kindness to those beings who are weaker, and family before job. She also believes in doin' what's right even if it's more difficult. So where do you stand on those issues?"

She'd given him a list and an objective. There was nothing a SEAL liked more than a clear path marked with stepping stones.

"I joined the Navy to protect those who couldn't protect themselves, though at the time I didn't realize it meant animals as well. Working at the Triple Star has given me perspective that the four-legged people are just as important as the two-legged. It's made me expand my understanding." He paused as he gathered his thoughts on how to address the other points. "I'm always honest and forthright to the people who matter most to me, as long as the information isn't classified, and my family is the reason I do what I do. While I'm in the service, my job is my priority. There's nothing I can do to change that as I've taken an oath and my integrity depends on me upholding it, so in that case my job comes first. But in serving my country, I serve my family and loved ones. And there's a saying we in the Navy SpecOps world have and it's "the only easy day was yesterday." I rarely do what's easy in my efforts to do what's right."

He stopped and scanned her expression, trying to

gauge how she took his answers. She had a damn good poker face, though her hands had stilled as she gave him her full attention.

"Does that apply to all things, or just your job?"

"All things. Frankly, relationships are harder than my job, and take a lot more work and maintenance because the goal posts move. There's a high level of divorce and dissolution of relationships in my profession because of that."

"And what about you? What will you do to combat the dissolution of your relationship with Suzie?" Seychelles held up a hand to make him wait to answer. "My goal here, Petty Officer, is to make sure my friend invests her heart wisely. I can't tell her whom to love because that's all up to her. But I don't want to throw my support into someone who is either looking for a quick fling or doesn't have the ability to look at his relationship from multiple sides and find the common ground."

"It's a bit early for that, isn't it?"

Seychelles spread her hands. "Hey, you came to me, buddy. In every love story, the hero gets an impossible task from the start. He's either gotta go on a quest to retrieve something or fight something. What I'm askin' isn't impossible, but it does require a lot from you. I know Suzie. You're the unknown variable here. How important is she to you?"

This had gotten heavy fast and he wasn't sure he was ready for something so deep. *Then why did you come to talk to Seychelles, cabrón?* Because he wanted the chance with Suzie. She was the first women he'd met in a long time that made him think of more than his next jump or mission. As cheesy as it was, she made him think of happily-ever-after. *My sisters are gonna give me so much shit for this.*

"Before I came to Cheyenne, true love isn't something I would have believed in." He shot her a rueful smirk. "You might not believe this, but guys, particularly military guys, don't hang around and talk about true love and finding the perfect princess to marry when they get out."

Seychelles laughed. "What? Really? I can't imagine."

"No, no, it's true. Emotions make us run for the hills in most cases."

"Yeah, never experienced *that* before." The sarcasm oozed from her voice.

"Right? Now emotions like anger, excitement, cold calculation, fear, we're all over those, though none of us will admit to the fear." He smirked. "But love is scary and most of us aren't equipped to deal with it. It's not one of the training evolutions we get in the military."

"What? I can't imagine." She widened her eyes and pressed her fingers to her chest in mock surprise.

He snorted. "Yeah, not their goal. But *my* goal is to spend time with Suzie, and if she wants, to take this relationship beyond my recovery here at the Triple Star Ranch. She's special and I want to learn more about her. She's worth it to me. She's my *sueño hermoso*, and worth the emotional work."

He stopped speaking and waited. He realized he'd meant every word and he desperately wanted Seychelles support. Suzie was it for him. He recalled his father once telling him that when he met the woman who made him think of happily-ever-after, there'd be no one else for him. *Guess you were right, Papa.*

"What does *sueño hermoso* mean?" Seychelles narrowed her eyes.

"Beautiful dream, the brass ring we all hope to attain."

She nodded slowly and he swallowed down his anxiety. He was a Navy SEAL, for glory's sake. One of the best in the SpecOps community. He'd earned his confidence. But as he'd said, there was no training for missions of the heart in the military, and he was at the mercy of this woman for the go-ahead.

"You're serious about this?"

"Yes, ma'am. As a heart attack."

Seychelles grimaced, but her eyes twinkled with humor. "If that's the case, you should definitely have Suzie take a look at you and maybe get an echocardiogram. But in either case, you have my blessing."

To her credit, she didn't warn him not to hurt Suzie as if either of them were children to be looked after, but he had no doubt her support of his suit would be withdrawn if he did. *But what if she hurts me?* He might be a big bad SEAL, but his heart was made of spun steel strands – resilient, but fragile enough to the right kinds of blows.

"Thank you, ma'am." He grinned. "Now what would you recommend for a wedding gift?"

Enrique ended up coming home with two hip flasks with matching leather wraps. The leather had been stamped with various leaf impressions and remained secured by a leather thong wrapped around a silver button. They were elegant and masculine, and he almost bought a wrap for Bruiser, though he couldn't remember the size of his flask.

Overall it was a good day and he headed back to the ranch feeling hopeful. Seychelles was in his corner and he had a real chance to win Suzie's heart.

CHAPTER TEN

By the time Enrique returned to the Triple Star, it was early afternoon and he was ready to rest. It had been an emotional day and it was barely halfway through. But talking to Seychelles had given him insights into Suzie. Seychelles mentioned that Suzie very rarely took time for herself. She was always too busy caring for others. She also never made time for romance in her life and it was a good sign if she was spending time with him.

He thought it was a step in the right direction.

Enrique paused at the front desk of the lodge as Andrew frowned at the computer screen in front of him. A jar full of coins sat beside him with more piles of coins strewn around it. Enrique must have made a noise because Andrew looked up, his expression clearing. *I must be losing my touch if he heard me.*

"Hi, Petty Officer Sanchez. What can I do for you?"

"I just came back from my PCP appointment in town." He held up his nylon brace. "Got the cast off, but still have to be careful. Is Dr. Appleton still in her office or has she gone home for the day?"

"Oh, uh, let me check." Andrew clicked a few things on the screen with his mouse. "It looks like she's still here seeing patients. Do you want me to have her paged?"

Enrique shook his head. "No, sir, I'll find her." He paused and tilted his head. "What are you working on?"

Andrew lost his easy expression with a sigh. "Every year we set up a swear jar." He pointed to the jar full of coins. "And every year we do a contest to guess how many objects are in the jar. It's kinda part challenge and part goal to reach at the end of summer."

"That's cool. What's the problem?"

Andrew sighed. "This year, we have three people who guessed correctly and I dunno what to do. There's only one prize."

"You could always let 'em fight for it." Enrique grinned. "Or just offer more prizes."

"Like what?"

He shrugged. "Like a signed CD from Henry Bright?"

"That's a great idea. And it'll be a good way to give him a little publicity now that he's not performin' as much."

"Happy to help. Are you going to the wedding?"

Andrew nodded. "I have to. I'm an usher."

"Hey, me too. Way to go, *hermano*. If you can keep a secret, I'll show you the gifts I got in town for the couple."

Andrew shot a look around the lobby then up to the camera in the corner. "I'd love to, but since we've put in cameras, I'm afraid Trip or Henry might see it." He grimaced as he pointed to the small black cylinder in the upper corner. "What did you get? There are no mics on the cameras."

Enrique lifted the bag he carried and placed his back to the camera. "I found these really cool hip flasks with tooled leather wraps that go around them. They're really slick."

"Wow, those are sexy." Andrew craned his neck. "I think both Trip and Henry will like them. Good choice."

"Yeah, I almost got one of the leather pieces for my buddy, but I wasn't sure what size would fit his flask."

Enrique grimaced apologetically as his phone rang and he pulled it from his pocket. "Sorry, gotta take this." He pulled the bag off the counter as he set the phone to his ear. "Hey, Bruiser, what's going down? How's Bike Week?"

"Amusing." His dour and stoic teammate sounded anything but amused. "Drunk men and women as far as the eye can see. It's a sight to behold."

"Now you're just waxing poetic."

"Heh, it's better than the full extent of my thoughts." Bruiser chuckled. "The jumps have been easy, though. Not much wind or weather up here this time, so we got to do some extra shit to make it look cool."

Enrique squashed the envy as he pushed his way out the backdoor of the lodge. He'd return to his team soon enough and that meant he'd be away from Suzie. He liked that feeling even less than he liked being separated from his crew. He'd grown fond of the Triple Star Ranch with the duck pond and the therapy horses.

Be honest: It's Suzie you're fond of.

"Glad to hear it. Of course you got the easy weather. And it's a good thing since I'm not there to save your asses." He paused beside a bench facing the pond and set down the bag.

"Yeah, Yeah, you keep tellin' yourself that, Sanchez. Whatever helps you sleep at night." Bruiser snorted. "But we have some bad news."

"Lay it on me, Chief." Enrique settled on the bench.

"There's no way to find the shooter once they left the park. There are no cameras in the parking lot or even in the Old Frontier Town. And there's nothing along the streets beyond the park."

"Not even traffic cams?"

"Nope. Except for Frontier Days, that part of Cheyenne doesn't get enough traffic to require them."

"Shit."

"Yeah. We got nothing and no leads to go on."

Enrique tried to think of anything they could use to identify the person who'd shot at him, but a grainy picture of someone in a hoodie didn't make a good ID. He leaned back on the bench and let his mind drift, hoping he'd see a path they hadn't taken yet.

Movement at the corner of his eye made him turn his head as the door to the Bunkhouse opened. A small woman dressed in the cleaning staff uniform pushed a laundry cart out onto the walkway. She had dark hair pulled into a severe bun at the back of her head and Latina features. She walked with a little bit of a limp, favoring her left leg. She didn't acknowledge him as she pushed her cart toward the laundry facilities behind the Bunkhouse and Enrique grimaced in sympathy. He turned his mind back to the conversation.

"Fuck. I can't think of anything we could try."

"Yeah, me either." Bruiser's voice had grown rough. "Cheyenne PD said they'd keep after it but they think it was a one and done event. Probably one of those anti-military whack jobs who needed to make a statement."

Enrique snorted. "You don't believe that, do you?"

"Not a fucking chance. But without any other evidence, we got shit to go on."

"Yeah." Enrique sighed. "You guys watch your sixes. My gut's telling me this isn't over yet."

"Yeah, mine is too. Keep your eyes and ears open. The shooter might still be around down there. The security is a little tighter up here after they heard about the shooting, but they have their own set of problems with drunk bikers and weapons."

"Copy that. Let me know if you find out anything new. Otherwise, fair winds, clear skies, and easy jumps."

"Roger that. Keep in touch and watch your back."

"Copy that. Later, Bruiser."

Enrique ended the call and gathered up his things. His gut said the shooter was still around and might make another play, but the question about their target bothered him. Were they aiming for any SEAL jumping out of the plane? Or were they coming for him specifically? And if it was him they were targeting, what was their motivation? Did he have an old enemy coming to look for him or was the goal to finish what they'd started at the rodeo?

The questions followed him into his room and hounded him through his shower, but the answers remained stubbornly absent.

****

"So I got a visit from a Petty Officer Sanchez today." Seychelles' voice sounded smug. "You didn't tell me how drop-dead gorgeous he is."

"That's because I didn't want you to start drooling over him." Suzie rolled her eyes even if her friend couldn't see. "I know how you feel about Latino guys." She chuckled. "Why was he there?" She scrubbed her head one-handed with the towel, trying to soak up the water out of her hair.

"He came in to find a wedding gift for Trip and Henry. Or at least, that's what he started with."

"Started with?"

"Yeah, he actually came in to talk to me. He figured he needed to get to know the best friend if he wanted to have a relationship with you.

"What, like asking my father permission to marry me?"

"Yeah, kinda, except he recognized that a woman's best friend has a lot of pull on her opinion of a guy and he made it clear that he understood and wanted my support in his dating you."

Suzie stopped in the middle of her bedroom. "And what did you tell him?"

"Hold your horses there, honey. I'm gettin' to that."

"Don't you use that old Wyoming tone with me, missy. This is my life you're talkin' about here. I need to know how hard you're gonna make it for me." Suzie snorted.

Seychelles laughed. "Actually I made it harder for him. I asked him where he stood on issues you believe in, and he told me he wanted to pursue this relationship even after his recovery. He said you're worth it for him to put in the effort."

"You didn't threaten him with something like, 'if you hurt her I'll gouge your eyes out,' did you?"

"No ma'am. You're a big girl and can take care of yourself." Seychelles paused. "But I think he means it and he's aware of the risks. He knows he's at the mercy of the military and where they send him, but he said his priority after his service is to making his connection to you strong."

Suzie bit her bottom lip as her excitement rose. "And what did you tell him?"

"I told him I couldn't tell you whom to love, but he didn't strike me as a guy who's giving us a line about his efforts, and I gave him my blessing to impress you."

Suzie dropped the towel on the bed and sat down beside it, staring at her bare toes. *I need to paint them soon.* "I like him, Sey. I like him a lot. He's sexy, and funny, and handsome, and masculine without being a dumb guy, you know?"

"Yeah, I think I know what you're talking about." Seychelles sighed. "I'd love to find a guy like that myself. But in the meantime, I'll continue living vicariously through you. I think you should take this chance, Suzie. He seems like he'd be worth it."

"Even if he's a SEAL who jumps out of airplanes for a living? Not exactly safety first."

Seychelles snorted. "I think you and he have different levels of what constitutes safety. He takes all the precautions humanly possible, and some inhumanly possible I suspect, to allow him to do the job for which he was hired. Getting shot at wasn't his fault this time."

This time. She had to remember Enrique wasn't the typical cowboy who worked all day and came home safe at night. Hell, he wasn't even like the military guys around Cheyenne who worked on base and went home at the end of the day. He could go "wheels-up" at a moment's notice and disappear for a while. He might have been stateside doing celebratory exhibitions, but he was a real SEAL and if the SpecOps community needed him, he'd be gone in a heartbeat.

"I can hear that big brain of yours churning over the reasons to back away and I'm telling you to give him a chance."

Suzie chuckled. "That's why he stopped by today, right? So you'd advocate for him to me."

"Hell yeah." Seychelles laughed. "But I'm not just doing it for him. He makes you happy, Suzie. Happier than I've seen you in a long time. And I'm not the kind of person who'd tell you to go for any hot guy who happens by. I want you to be happy and Enrique does it for you. Do yourself a favor. Grab onto him with both hands and don't let go."

"That's your expert advice, is it?"

"Yes, ma'am. I've known enough deadbeats that I can recognize a good guy when I see one."

Suzie grinned. "Yeah, I have to give you that. Thanks, Sey."

"You're welcome, honey. All right, I have to go and label some of the stuff I got from a recent estate sale. Glory, my life is exciting." Seychelles chuckled.

"Shut up. You know you love that stuff. It's like pulling teeth to get you to come out for a drink when you get a shipment in."

"Touché. And right now, it's calling my name. So I'll talk to you later, Doctor Lady."

"Later, Sey. Love you."

"Love you too."

Suzie hung up the phone and stretched as she shot a look out her windows. The day had turned out to be mild and she hadn't visited Painted Dog Tired in a couple of weeks. She grimaced and threw on an old t-shirt and a pair of faded jeans. *That poor horse has probably thought I've forgotten him.* She needed to get out as much as Painted Dog. Sometimes the problems of the world seemed to fade while on the back of a good horse.

She pulled her hair into a low ponytail, shoved her feet into her boots, and stuffed her Gambler's hat on her head before grabbing her keys. She brought the phone, too, but she made it go to silent. *I don't really want folks find me if it's not an emergency.* But the doctor in her made sure she could be reached.

She locked her bungalow and strode for the barn, letting her worries blow off toward Nebraska in the Wyoming wind.

CHAPTER ELEVEN

The frustrating news of the afternoon drove Enrique out of the Bunkhouse. Since he'd been cleared to run, he thought it would be a good idea to release his anger at their inability to find the shooter before he saw Suzie that night. He threw on some workout shorts and a tank top before he stretched his legs and torso, testing his pain tolerance around his ribs. They give a twinge, but nothing debilitating and satisfaction settled into his chest. *Not nearly broken anymore.* The lighter weight brace helped too.

He set off at a smooth jog around the duck pond, easily moving around slower pedestrians as he allowed his body to warm up. Ahead of him, the Latino cleaning woman appeared out the door of the lodge and moved to a nearby bench for a cigarette break. Again, her limp and her studied disinterest caught his attention, but he dismissed the warning as a result of his frustration and impotence. The shooter needed to be caught and he hated waiting for intel.

Instead, he stepped up his pace and tried to find a rhythm that allowed him to feel the burn without hurting. He headed past the barn toward the river, letting his mind go over the things he'd done that day. While the doctor's appointment was a success, he couldn't help wondering at the odd comments Lyttle threw at him. Something was off with the guy, but he was no longer a concern. Once Suzie signed off on his completed therapy plan, Enrique would be back with his team. *At least until we have holiday leave.* The exhibitions were only in the summer and the rest of the year he and his squad spent their time training, and keeping up their other skills. Each man in his squad came for a three year tour before they returned to their usual Teams. Because they were stateside and had performances up until December, they often got to spend the holidays with family.

I'd like my family to be here in Cheyenne. All he had to do was convince Suzie. *At least I have Seychelles' blessing.*

The idea gave him a little extra bounce to his step as he found a wildlife path along the creek. It was just wide enough to give him space to stretch his strides and the old familiar feeling of running euphoria set in. He still had two years on his tour as a Leap Frog and it would carry him to the end of his current enlistment.

He'd never questioned if he wanted to be a SEAL. He'd never had a reason to be anything else. But meeting Suzie and recuperating in Wyoming gave him a new perspective and an additional desire. He wanted to spend more time with Suzie, and her home was here. Being in the Leap Frogs helped because he was stateside and could communicate with her no matter where he was much easier than if he went overseas. He'd definitely see her during Cheyenne Frontier Days.

That's if she's onboard with a long term relationship that includes long distances.

Enrique grimaced and his breathing sped up, but he forced his strides to slow a little. *No use borrowing trouble, hermano.* No, and he wanted to make their relationship a success. He'd go the extra mile to make it work. He'd meant what he told Seychelles. *The only easy day was yesterday.* And he'd put in the same effort for working things out with Suzie as he did into his training for parachute jumps.

His thoughts carried him into an open field beyond most of the bungalows and movement toward the setting sun caught his attention. A horse and rider galloped through the amber light, the rider's hair and the horse's tail streaming behind them. The sight captured his attention and made him follow as if he could catch the flying horse.

When the pair reached the creek, the horse pivoted like rounding a barrel and came charging up the wildlife path. He immediately moved to the side and slowed to a jog, giving the horse and rider space. But the rider saw him and pulled her mount into a sliding stop worthy of a blue ribbon in a reining competition.

"Enrique." Suzie's sultry voice settled into his chest and hardened his dick at the same time. "Whoa, easy, Painted Dog." She patted her paint horse's neck and the animal blew out, catching its breath.

"Is this your championship barrel-racing mount?" He kept his distance until the horse settled.

"Yes, sir. Painted Dog Tired gives one helluva ride." She slapped the horse's neck with approval. "I'm glad we won the championship this year, and I'm glad it was our last competition, but it's good for us both to come out and ride."

Enrique agreed. And it helped that she looked beautiful doing it.

"You look good on that horse, Suzie. *Muy bonita.*" He approached the big animal and laid his hand on the warm shoulder. The pungent scents of horse and leather filled his nose, bringing back memories of working in his parents' barn. He ran his hand over her denim-covered thigh as he gazed up at her. "It's good to know I was rescued in the rodeo by a real *caballista.*"

She tilted her head. "What does that mean?"

"Horseman."

She grinned. "I am that. Well, horse*woman*." She nodded at him. "Were you cleared today to go running?"

He nodded. "Didn't Dr. Lyttle tell you?'

She shrugged. "He might have sent an email. I haven't checked since I left the office today." She grimaced and he empathized with her, glad his interaction with Lyttle was done.

"How is running? How do your ribs and lung feel?" Suzie morphed into the doctor right before his eyes and he mourned the loss of her relaxed self.

"It's good. No pain, just a little stiff and tired." He waved her questions away. "But it was a treat to see you riding. What are you going to do now that you don't compete? Isn't it hard to just go back to pleasure riding?"

He wanted to know her answer, but in the back of his mind was the question of his own retirement from the SEALs. What would he do if he wasn't jumping out of airplanes or rescuing their stranded forces? He didn't want to lose the skills he'd paid so dearly to acquire.

"It could be if barrel-racing was all I did." She nodded. "But I have being a doctor and that takes a lot of other specialized skills, too. I won't lose my skills, they just might get a little rusty. It's more unfair to Painted Dog. I should probably consider selling him to someone who will use his skills for their own barrel-racing dreams. But he's my buddy and my friend. Sending him to someone else would be like cutting part of my heart out."

She patted the horse then narrowed her eyes at him. "Are you thinking about what to do when you get out of the Navy?"

Damn, the woman was like a mind reader. "It was something that had crossed my mind while I was injured. I have two more years on my tour, but what would I do if I was medically discharged? What would I fall back on? I have these skills and they're pretty specific to what I do now. But eventually my body's not going to put up with that kind of punishment."

Suzie nodded. "With two years left in your tour, you have time to decide if you need to retire and what you'll do. It's good you're thinking about it now, but the decision doesn't have to be made tomorrow."

He nodded, but grimaced. "Yeah, I know. I guess I started to wonder what I could do after if I'm not badly injured, and if there'd be anyone waiting for me."

He realized what he'd implied the moment the words left his mouth, and he swallowed hard before meeting her gaze. *What the hell is she thinking?* She sat silently on her horse, the paint standing relaxed with one hind foot cocked, but her whole body had gone still. *Damn, I think I've stepped my foot in it.*

"What are you saying, Enrique?"

Time to man-up or ring out. "I don't want to be alone when I make this decision. A SEAL's only as strong as his team and I want you to be part of my team when it's all said and done." He held up a hand, though she hadn't said anything. "I don't need you to promise anything, I just want to know we have a chance at more than a recovery fling." He took a deep breath and met her gaze. "I'm saying I'm in this for the long haul and I hope you are too."

Again she said nothing for a long time and he thought his heart would shrivel.

"Is this why you went to talk to Seychelles today?"

He rubbed the back of his neck. "She called you, huh?"

Suzie nodded with a little smile. "She told me she gave you her blessing because she felt you meant what you said and you made me happy."

"Do I make you happy, Suzie?"

A mixture of anxiety and excitement filled his chest and stopped his breath. It was the same feeling he experienced just before he launched himself out the back hatch of a plane, and he suspected the result would be the same as having no parachute if she said no.

She leaned down and extended her hand to him. "Yes, Enrique. You make me very happy. Come home with me?"

She didn't have to ask him twice. He grinned and grasped her hand, using her left foot as a step to swing his leg over Painted Dog's rump. He settled behind her and wrapped his arms around her waist, and just barely resisted dipping his nose into her ponytail. *Glory, she smells good.* The soft heat of her against his chest made his cock rise, which made riding behind her challenging. But he wouldn't trade his position for the world.

"Comfortable?"

No. "Yeah, I'm good."

She clicked to her horse and the animal's motion rubbed the saddle's seat against his hardening flesh. He gritted his teeth and hoped he didn't get blue balls from her scent and the ride. Fortunately, they weren't far from the barn, but by the time they got there, he was ready to get off. *In more ways than one.*

She helped him swing down and he held Painted Dog's bridle as she dismounted with far more grace. She nodded to him in thanks and led the paint into the barn. He followed, his gaze glued to her ass in the faded jeans, and his cock saluted the thought.

"I need to rub him down before we go anywhere else. Would you help me take care of his tack?" Suzie swung her gaze toward him and Enrique jerked his attention up to her face.

"Yeah, I can do that."

She grinned as she caught him staring but instead hooked Painted Dog up to the crossties and went to work loosening the girth. Instead of handing him the saddle like he expected, she pulled the bridle off and gathered up the reins.

"Take this, I'll get the saddle." She thrust the bridle into his hands.

"I can take the saddle—"

"No, your arm doesn't need the added weight. Besides, I don't want you to hurt yourself more tonight. I have other plans for you." She winked as she hauled the saddle off her horse in one heave.

He couldn't argue with that though everything inside him screamed to take the heavy stuff from her. Not that she couldn't handle it, it was the courtesy that his *papa* and *abuelo* drilled into him. *And probably sexist as hell, knowing them.*

It didn't take them long to rub down the horse and put him in his stall. Enrique made sure he had grain and hay while Suzie filled the water bucket. But he kept thinking of her ass rubbing his belly as he rode behind her and his need hardened his cock again. *Shit, I gotta think of something else or everyone's gonna know where my mind's at.*

He tried to shift his thoughts, but his mind kept going back to her full breasts and her round hips, and his hardon persisted.

Suzie turned off the hose and shot him a smile. "Ready?"

Fuck yeah.

"Yes, ma'am." He couldn't be more ready.

He followed her out of the barn, enjoying the sway of her hips in those jeans. Damn, he'd start to drool if he wasn't careful. He caught up to her and caught her nearest hand, weaving his fingers through hers. She glanced down at their joined hands then back up at him with a smile. It damn near made his heart burst and he wanted to fist-pump the sky.

He didn't remember much of the walk to her bungalow. He was concentrating too much on keeping his hardon from tearing his running shorts. But once she let them inside the cool building, she slammed the door shut, pushed him up against it and knelt at his feet.

"What are you doing, Suzie?"

"What I've wanted to do all day today." She dropped her hat to the floor and reached for his shorts, curling her fingers over the waistband. "I'm gonna suck your cock until you can't hold back."

"*Dios mio.*"

She pulled his shorts down and exposed his cock already hard and dripping pre-cum. She hummed with approval as she ran her hands over his hips. She trailed her fingers down the crease between his balls and thighs, and he saw fuckin' stars. He loved her take-charge attitude and if this was how she'd greet him every time he came to visit, he might never leave.

She tilted her head and ran her nose over his scrotum, her breath tickling and sending erotic sparks through him. He loved her teasing him and his cock flexed with each stroke of her nose. But he gasped as she grabbed his shaft and licked up the length of it before she kissed the crown of the head.

"Show me that fantastic SEAL stamina, Enrique. I want to know how long you can hold out."

Holy shit. That sounded like a challenge and knowing her talented mouth as he did, he wondered if he'd fail. He swallowed hard and gritted his teeth as she set to work on his cock.

Slick heat engulfed his shaft and he tightened his hands into fists to keep from giving into the delicious pleasure. Suzie had a way of igniting all his nerves with erotic fire just using the heat of her mouth. Every pass of her tongue over the edge of his glans made him moan and sparkles danced behind his eyes. His release threatened every time she took him deep, her lips sliding to his base.

Gotta hold back.

She settled into a rhythm sliding along his shaft and using her teeth to scrape the edge of his head. He listened to the wet sounds of her enjoying her treat and thanked his lucky stars she did. It was just one of the things he loved about her.

Whoa, love? Real love?

He hadn't been kidding when he told Seychelles he wanted a chance with Suzie, but he also had been talking about love in an abstract term, something they'd build over time. He already knew he enjoyed being with her and the sex was fucking awesome, but sex wasn't love. Love took years, didn't it?

But as he stared down at Suzie working his dick with her mouth, her tongue wreaking havoc on his sensitive flesh, he realized he wanted more moments of sharing her time in the kiddie pool while they watched the storms roll in. He wanted more time to make leisurely love with her, pleasuring her until she screamed his name. He just wanted more of her.

The depth of his understanding helped focus his mind into holding back the impending orgasm. She wanted stamina? He'd give her that and more because he had a new goal—making her tremble in his arms from his love.

But Suzie slid her hands up his thighs to caress his hips, distracting him as one dropped to fondle his balls and the other followed his happy trail up to his belly. The combination of her soft touches along with her hot mouth splintered his attention and his focus slipped.

"Aw fuck, *querida*, you have to stop or I'm gonna come."

But Suzie was taking no prisoners and increased the pressure around his cock. Her eyes sparkled when he glanced down at her and he knew she wasn't going to stop. That determination combined with her teeth on the edges of his cock head sent his release boiling from his balls to shoot down her throat.

"Oh, yes. Aw fuck, yes, *querida*. Suck my cock hard and take my cum. *Dios mio!*"

She sucked him down, moaning her own pleasure as he pumped into her mouth, his hands tangled in her ponytail.

Hot jets of cum shot down her throat until he couldn't see straight and slumped against the door at his back. She swallowed his cum and polished his dick until he was clean, giving him one final lick as she sat back on her heels and smirked at him.

"How do you feel, Enrique?"

"Fucking awesome."

She grinned. "Mission accomplished."

He laughed as she rose and settled in the chair beside the door to remove her boots. That gave him time to recover and plan his attack. Because he could smell the musky scent of her arousal just leaning next to her and there was no way he'd forego giving her what she needed.

Once she had her boots off, he'd recovered sufficiently to stand. He tried to step out of his shorts until he realized he still wore his running shoes. *Damn, she didn't bother to take anything off but my skivvies.*

He bent over, his naked ass against the door, and untied his shoes before toeing them off and stepping out of his shorts.

"You have a nice ass." Suzie cupped it with her hand and squeezed gently, making his cock rise again. "I could watch your ass for hours."

He laughed as he pulled his shirt over his head and dropped it with the shorts and shoes. "I'd rather be watching yours, *querida*. But in the meantime, I'm gonna take you to bed and love you up."

"That's not necessary—"

"Oh, it's necessary." He took her hand and drew her against his chest as his cock slowly stiffened. "I'm going to make love with you, Suzie, until you're boneless with pleasure."

He drew her toward her bedroom, giving her the view of his ass just as she wanted. But she caught sight of the tattoo on his left arm and maneuvered around him until she could look at it when he stopped beside her bed.

"Wow, this is cool."

He glanced down at the American eagle clutching both the American and Mexican flags in its talons. "Thank you. It was my reward for having made it through SEAL training."

"Is your family from Mexico?"

He nodded as he set to work unbuttoning her jeans and sliding them off her hips. "My mother's family. My father's family has a papaya farm in Nicaragua, but my father didn't want to be a farmer. He's a *caballista* through and through, especially when he saw the Andalusian horses in Spain. My mother was there with her father looking at connecting some of their horse bloodlines, and my father was smitten. Or that's how they tell it."

Suzie laughed as he unbuttoned her shirt. "Smitten?"

"Si, por su puesto. He tracked her down in California and found out her family bred horses for dressage. That clinched it for him and he made efforts to woo her."

"If she lived in California, why the Mexican flag?"

"Because her family has been on their land long before it was called California, when it was still Mexico. And I'm proud of my heritage. Ahh." He opened her shirt and took in her large breasts held in utilitarian cotton. "You are *muy bonita*, Suzie, and I am smitten." He raised his gaze to hers and hoped she could see the truth in his eyes.

****

Suzie liked the look in Enrique's eyes. He meant his words and pleasure bloomed through her. She wasn't young or pristine anymore, and she certainly wasn't in the kind of shape required for a Navy SEAL. But from his expression as he peeled off her shirt and unhooked her bra, that wasn't what he was looking for.

He really is smitten.

"Lie down, *querida*. Let me show you just how smitten

I am." He drew her to the bed and let her slide onto it to lie on her back. "There's nothing as beautiful as an aroused woman except maybe a satisfied one. I aim to make sure you're the latter."

"Oh yeah?" She grinned as he crawled onto the bed and crouched over her. "How will you do that?"

"First, I'm going to kiss and lick my way down your body like this." He dropped his head and laid a kiss on her sternum between her breasts before dragging his lips over to one nipple. "Mmm, so sweet."

He sucked on her, rolling the sensitive tip between his lips with his tongue, and her pussy clenched with desperate need. She hadn't expected to get so turned on by sucking him off, but his moans and evident delight lit her fire. He moved over to the other breast, plucking her abandoned nipple with his callused fingers.

"Oh, glory, I love that."

He chuckled as he moved lower, kissing her until he arrived at her mound. There he paused to inhale deeply, his smile broadening.

"Oh, *querida*, you have the sweetest smelling pussy." He nuzzled her nether lips, blowing hot air on her sensitive flesh. "I could spend hours feasting on you right here."

"I don't think I could last that long."

"We shall see, yes?"

She started to laugh but it was cut off by his mouth fitting over her slit and his tongue swiping through her folds. Her arousal ramped up until she whimpered and writhed in his grip. She didn't know if she needed him to lick her faster or if it was too much. Enrique hummed his own approval and clamped his hands to her hips, holding her in place.

He settled in between her thighs and did what he'd promised. He feasted. His tongue found every fold and nerve, lighting up her senses and shattering her as the pleasure built. She tried to hold back, to feel everything but the building ecstasy, but Enrique was relentless, and soon she could do nothing but fly at his hands.

"Oh sweet glory! Oh my gloooorrryyyy!"

She cried out in delight as she flew away from herself. He kept up his ministrations while she soared behind her eyes, letting the pleasure wrap her in soft clouds. When she came back to the room, she found him wiping his mouth and grinning, proud of himself.

"You think you're all that and a bag of chips, don't you?" She tried to sound snarky but she was much too breathless.

"*Sí, señorita.* I know I am." He crawled up her body and reached into her beside drawer to pull out the condoms. "And now I'm gonna prove it to you."

He quickly sheathed his hard cock and positioned it at her pussy entrance as he studied her. She hadn't quite caught her breath after her last orgasm when he pushed his cock into her still-spasming body.

They both groaned as the ripples of her inner muscles caressed his hard shaft.

"*Dios mio, querida,* you are so tight and hot." Enrique braced himself over her and gave her a warm smile. "You feel so good to me, Suzie. Now I'm gonna fuck you slow and deep, and prove to you I'm all that."

"And the bag of chips?"

She huffed a laugh as he pulled his body from hers, but it changed to a moan when he pushed back in.

"*Sí, querida.* And the bag of chips."

He rocked his hips, his cock sliding along her inner walls and brushing her clit with every pass. His gaze never left hers as he thrust in a maddening rhythm, not too fast but with enough speed to tantalize her body.

"Look at me, Suzie. I want to see you when come apart beneath me."

"But I need—"

"I know what you need, *querida,* and I promise to give

119

it to you." He snapped his hips forward and buried himself to the hilt.

Suzie gasped and clutched his hips. "Yes. Just like that."

"Keep your eyes on me, *preciosa*. I want you with me when we come."

It was so hard to do as he asked. She struggled against showing him her true self and the vulnerability that came with it. But his presence commanded her attention, from his thrusting cock to his taut abs as he moved. *He's so fuckin' beautiful.*

"Oh, *querida*, you're so hot and sexy. I want you to take pleasure from me." He grew breathless as he sped up his thrusts. "Let me take your breath away. Oh glory, *querida*, I'm not gonna last. Come with me."

He thrust harder and faster and her body followed his lead without conscious effort. She whimpered each time he sheathed himself and moaned when he withdrew, her body desperately trying to hold onto his thick length. But he returned, strumming her clit with greater intensity. Her release swelled but she held back until he leaned down and teased her earlobe with his tongue.

"*Te amo, mi amor. Te quiero de aquí a la luna.*"

The words spoken in his sexy, silken voice sent her over the edge of ecstasy once more, setting fire to her world. The pleasure shot her among the stars and his erotic mumblings in Spanish accompanied her until he shouted his own release and stiffened above her.

As requested, she kept her gaze on him and a sense of coming home hit her straight in the heart as she floated in euphoria. This was the man who would fill her nights with delight and her days with joy. She wanted him and wanted to give him somewhere to go when his tour of duty let up. Yes, she was busy and yes, he traveled a lot, but at this moment her heart said he was meant to be hers, and she would fight to keep him.

At last he came down from his release, his body still braced above her. His head hung as he tried to catch his breath and she ran her hands over his sides, enjoying the supple skin and the strong muscles.

At the last moment, it occurred to her that he might be feeling pain and she tensed.

"Are you all right?"

He lifted his head and gave her a tired smile. "*Sí, Querida. Soy muy bien.* I'm very good. No pain." He pulled back, holding the condom to his shaft. "Let me clean up."

She let him go and heard him in the bathroom while she drifted in pleasant exhaustion, letting her revelation settle into her bones. She wanted him and wanted the chance to see if they could make this last after he returned to his job. *He's the one.* The one she wanted to try with. No one had made her feel like putting effort forth until him.

When Enrique came back to the bed, he lifted the covers for her to climb under and slid in beside her. Then he wrapped his body around hers, cradling her to his chest.

Instead of feeling smothered, she felt cherished and wanted. Loved even, though he'd never said it aloud. At least, she hadn't heard him say it. But it was in his actions and his arms around her. This was where she wanted to stay, and she'd do her damnedest to make sure they did.

CHAPTER TWELVE

Morning yanked Suzie out of sleep with the incessant buzz of her alarm. She stretched her body, scissoring her legs under the sheets, and realized she was alone. She opened her eyes and glanced around, finding the room empty. Disappointment bounced around inside her as she slid her feet to the floor and padded, naked, into the living room. The coffee machine held a full carafe of black gold and a bouquet of wildflowers sat on the table with a folded note beneath them.

DEAR SUZIE,

MY TIME WITH YOU LAST NIGHT WAS AMAZING. I'M SORRY I COULDN'T STAY LONGER BUT I PROMISED TOM I'D HELP OUT WITH THE WEDDING AND I NEED TO PRESS MY UNIFORM. I MADE COFFEE AND I HOPE IT'S STILL WARM. I LOOK FORWARD TO SEEING YOU AT THE WEDDING TODAY. PLEASE SAVE ME A DANCE. AND MAYBE WE CAN PICK UP WHERE WE LEFT OFF LAST NIGHT.

LOVE, ENRIQUE

Her disappointment dissolved and she picked up the

flowers, delighted with the idea that he took the time to find them for her. A smile curled her lips at the memories of their lovemaking and she set the flowers in a glass with water to save their blooms.

But Enrique wasn't the only one who needed to get ready for the wedding. She'd offered to help out where needed. Mrs. Guthrie had most everything well in hand, but everyone promised to chip in to make sure the decorations in the arena were set up, including the tables and chairs. The Knights from the neighboring ranch were bringing in straw bales to provide seating and extra tables and tablecloths for the reception. It was all hands on deck and they'd be waiting for her.

Suzie ducked into the shower and got ready in record time, foregoing the makeup until later after she'd helped with setup. She did stop long enough to turn on her computer and check her email just in case any emergencies came in from the night before.

She found an email from Tom about some incoming patients that had some special care needs and one from her dad with humorous memes. *Thank goodness he's figured out the internet.* She mentally rolled her eyes at all the emojis in the subject line. But the last email was from Dr. Lyttle about Enrique.

She narrowed her eyes, some of her pleasure from the morning draining away, but her phone dinged with a new text message and she shook her head. She didn't have time to look at the email now. She'd get to it after the wedding festivities. She shut down the computer, grabbed her coffee, phone, and keys and headed out into the cool morning. *Fall's coming.* They might have an early winter given the scent of water in the air.

The text had been from Seychelles saying she'd meet Suzie at the lodge's kitchen with muffins from The Bread Basket. While Suzie loved their muffins, disappointment filtered through her thoughts that the text hadn't been from

Enrique.

Get over yourself. He left you a note.

Shaking her head at her silliness, she hurried her steps toward the lodge and the muffins promised by her best friend. But she couldn't help but shoot a look at the Bunkhouse as she passed by. Most of the patients had the day to themselves because of the wedding and she suspected they were taking advantage of the time to sleep in.

Suzie pushed into the lodge and the quiet of the morning disappeared in a wall of energy. Staff members and stable hands moved to and fro, carrying decorations and totes full of items for the wedding and reception. In the center of it all, Mrs. Guthrie directed her troops like a general, her orders sharp and clipped with efficiency. Suzie had to admire the older woman's gumption.

She'd known Adele Guthrie had been sweet on Trip Colton for years and the discovery that he'd given his heart to Henry Bright, his junior by almost thirty years and a man, hadn't gone over so well. Their row had made the rounds and Suzie suspected Adele had been behind Trip and Henry's breakup last Thanksgiving.

But looking at her now, preparing for their wedding, the older woman appeared to have made peace with their relationship.

"Ah, Doc Suzie, I'm glad you're here." Adele waved at her. "I need you to take my friend Sage and her son Adam to the arena where they'll be helping set up tables and hay bales. Tom and Amber are already there. Amber's looking after Emerald and she'll watch Adam too."

The curvy woman with brownish-red hair and pale hazel eyes smiled and nodded as she shook Suzie's hand. "Nice to meet you, Doc Suzie."

"Same. You sure you're okay helping with tables and straw bales?"

Sage nodded. "Yes, ma'am. I grew up on a ranch so

I've never had much trouble with that. Although Mrs. Guthrie mostly wants me to make sure the boys get the tablecloths and chair covers right."

Suzie laughed. "That sounds like her. Just let me make sure I find my friend so she knows I'm not ducking out on her and we'll head over."

"Mom, I'm hungry." The little boy with red hair, a constellation of freckles across his nose and sharp brown eyes tugged on his mother's sleeve.

"I know, Adam. But we have to wait just a bit longer before we get something." Sage's voice held the patience of a mom.

"Hi, Adam, I'm Dr. Suzie. If you can be a little patient, I'm sure my friend Seychelles will have an extra muffin or two you can have."

The boy sized her up, his expression telling her he weighed the truth of her words. "Promise?"

Suzie bit back a laugh. "Yes, I promise." Even if she had to give him hers.

"Okay." He nodded but she didn't think he believed her.

Damn, this kid is a tough audience.

Her phone pinged with another text message and she pulled it out. "Looks like my friend just pulled up to the lodge. We'll get those muffins and conscript her to help us with the straw bales."

Sage laughed. "Good plan."

They headed to the foyer of the lodge where Seychelles bustled in swearing and growling as she carried a box of muffins. Suzie raised her eyebrows.

"Sweet glory, honey, who put the burr under your saddle this morning?"

"Don't even start with me," Sey snapped as she set the box down on the reception desk. "I had to take my neighbor's dog to the vet this morning because the stupid beast decided that a paper wasps nest would be a fun chew toy. His face swelled up like a friggin' volleyball and he damn near stopped breathing."

"Where was your neighbor?"

"She works the nightshift at Walmart and I couldn't let her lose her best friend. He might be dumb, but he protects her and is her world right now." Sey shook her head.

"Maybe he was protecting her from the wasps." Adam's suggestion sounded reasonable.

"Right, like a natural protector." Suzie nodded.

"Oh, he's a natural, all right. A natural disaster." Sey scowled. "But after that, I managed to follow the car who hit a friggin' skunk on the highway. Guts and fumes everywhere. That damn skunk stunk for six miles! Now my car is gonna need a bath in vinegar or it'll stink for the next six days."

"So it was a good morning, then?" Suzie smirked.

"Shut up." Sey rolled her eyes. "The good thing is I brought muffins and they're worth the wait."

"And don't smell like skunk." Suzie grinned.

"Yes, thank goodness." Sey turned her attention to Sage and Adam. "Hi, after all that drama, I'm Seychelles Abernathy." She held out her hand.

"Nice to meet you. I'm Sage and this is my son, Adam. We're friends of Mrs. Guthrie. She drafted us to move straw bales and set up tables for the wedding."

Seychelles snorted and held out the pastry box. "Then you better take some muffins because it's going to be a long day. I promise they don't smell like skunk."

They all took a treat and headed out the backdoor of the lodge. Seychelles led the way, talking a mile a minute to Sage and Adam as if she'd known them for years. It was one of the things Suzie had always liked about her best friend. She'd never met a stranger.

When they entered the arena the place had already started to transform. The stage flooring had been put down and linked together to cover the far half of the arena where the ceremony would take place. The tables would be set up in the straw-covered dirt with folding chairs. Straw bales had been positioned around the outer edges of the arena for extra seating and some of the stable hands were draping brightly colored cotton blankets over them for comfort.

"Well, hell, it looks like we're a bit late. Let's get started on the tables and chairs." Seychelles headed for the folks bringing in the folding furniture.

Suzie followed along, looking for Enrique among the men working to get things set up, but since most of them wore cowboy hats, she couldn't see his face. They got straight to work, helping unload the tables and setting them up. Adam helped with the chairs and had good ideas about placement of the tables to leave an aisle up the center of the arena for the procession. As he warmed up to them, he grew snarky and had them laughing. Seychelles laughed the most.

By the time lunch rolled around, the arena looked like something out of a shabby chic photoshoot for a wedding magazine. Old fashioned railroad lanterns sat on the tables with wicker woven place mats. Mason jars were used as glasses and the silverware had a darkened bronze patina. Bronze napkin rings with the initials T&H below the Triple Star Ranch brand and the date held each guest's napkin and were meant to be taken home at the end of the night.

The ceremony would take place on the flooring and then it would be converted to a stage where Henry's old band buddies would play music for the celebration. Henry wanted to sing the song he'd written for Trip when they'd had their breakup, but then he'd leave the performance to his friends.

"Wow, this place turned out nice." Amber appeared beside Suzie with her dog Nimbus and Emerald on her hip as they gazed at the venue. "You'd have to look hard to see it's a livestock arena."

Suzie raised an eyebrow. "Didn't they do this for your

wedding to Tom?"

Amber shook her head. "Nope. I didn't want the rigamarole. Tom and I did a small service one holiday weekend with just family and then took off to a friend's cabin in the Grand Tetons. This is the first wedding we've had at the Triple Star."

Suzie had been away that weekend for a medical conference in Texas and missed their nuptials . Amber sounded a little wistful now and Suzie could understand. She didn't want a huge production either, but she loved the beauty and elegance of the celebration. *Maybe I could just have a party for friends and family here at the ranch like this, too.*

The question was, who would she be marrying?
Petty Officer Enrique Sanchez.

She snorted aloud and Amber shot her a surprised look. "Something funny?"

"Oh, I just had a silly thought and had my "yeah, right" moment aloud." Suzie shook her head with a rueful smile. "How are you and Emerald doing?" She smiled at the pretty little girl riding her mother's hip, and again tamped down on the need to hold her.

"Good. The breastfeeding seems to be working well and my nipples aren't as chapped." Amber stopped and a blush rose to her cheeks. "Sorry, that was probably TMI."

Suzie laughed. "Since I'm your doctor as well as your friend, I don't think it counts. Now I might hesitate to hear how you and Tom are getting on sexually, but in terms of babies and postpartum health, I'm all ears."

Amber's blush grew. "Yeah, I'm not gonna tell you about that."

"Good." Suzie grinned. "I actually have to get back to the kitchen to help with the food. Are you going that way?"

"No, I'm actually headed home to take a nap and hopefully build up my stamina for tonight. I want to help celebrate, but I only have so much energy to mind this little one and attend the wedding." Amber ruffled her daughter's hair, making envy surge in Suzie's gut. "Besides, she needs a nap, too, or she'll be hell on wheels later. Plus I have to look after Mrs. Guthrie's friend's son."

"Adam, yes. He's a smart kid. Sharp."

"Good to know. Hopefully he won't be too bored during the ceremony and party."

"He might be really entertaining. He's got snark and his jokes are right on. You might have a ball." Suzie patted Amber on the shoulder. "I have to get going. Have a good nap."

"Thanks, Suzie."

Suzie jogged back to the lodge and found the kitchen full of women. Adele had everyone doing a separate job and it looked like they'd have more than enough food for the wedding guests. Seychelles worked on the mini kababs, Adam helped Sage arrange the little paper cups full of meltaway mints, several other women put together casseroles and salads, while Adele presided over a hearty eight bean and ham soup.

The caterer spent time doing the last decorations of the cake under Adele's watchful eye, creating an elegant set of three-tiered cakes decorated with stars and music notes. The last tier would be for the grooms alone with a topper of two horses, noses together. The beauty of the cakes took her breath and momentarily made tears start in her eyes.

"Doc Suzie, I'm glad you're here. Would you put together the cider, please? We need to heat it up and add the cinnamon sticks and cloves."

"Yes, ma'am." She cleared her throat and threw herself into cider prep.

Laughter and creativity abounded, and Suzie enjoyed herself preparing for Trip and Henry's celebration. Some of the tension around Adele's eyes had faded now that the special day had arrived and everyone worked like a well-oiled machine. An hour before the wedding, Adele shooed everyone out of her kitchen, pronouncing the meal ready to go.

"Thank y'all for your help. I'll meet most of you back here just after the end of the ceremony and we'll haul it all over there to set out on the banquet tables." She swung to look at Sage. "They set them up at the back of the arena, right?"

"Yes, ma'am. Should be good to go."

"Okay, then." Adele waved them out and Suzie headed out the back toward the Bunkhouse.

She had just enough time to shower, do her makeup, and change before she had to be back for the wedding. She figured she'd help tote some of the food to the banquet tables or at least to the arena so it wouldn't be left just to Adele. But she also hoped to see Enrique and get at least one dance with him. That put a spring in her step as she headed back to her bungalow.

****

Enrique sighed as he shrugged into his service dress blues jacket and tugged the sleeves. Technically, this uniform was a bit too casual for a wedding, but since it was all he had on hand and he still looked pretty sharp, he didn't feel too bad about being non-regulation. The double row of gold buttons down his belly needed little polish and his Budweiser, wings, and fruit salad all stood out against nearly black wool. He straightened his tie, rubbed a last minute scuff off his shoe, and set his cover on his head.

Looking sharp, hermano.

It reminded him of the few events where he'd needed to dress up with his team, and he felt a little naked without them around him. He'd called them this morning after he'd gotten back to the Bunkhouse. He'd needed to find out if they had new intel and to report he'd been cleared for exercise. But he also needed to talk to Bruiser about an idea that had formed after he snuggled up against Suzie's hot body last night.

"This is Kent."

"*Buenos dias*, Bruiser. You boys making it okay without me covering your asses?"

"Whatever, Sanchez. We're not the ones with broken ribs. How's it going out there in the cowboy state?"

"Good. The doc cleared me for running and exercise, saying my lung and ribs are good to go. Two more weeks and I should be ready to get back to the team."

"Fuck yeah. That's great news." Relief underpinned Bruiser's voice. "How's the other thing been going? The cops find anything?"

"No, and nothing's happened around here. But my gut says it's not over."

"You think the shooter is still there in Cheyenne?"

Enrique had grunted. "That's what my gut says. Got no proof but things don't seem settled yet."

"All right, keep your eyes open. We haven't had any problems at all, so you might be right. Seems like it's personal if the shooter is still hanging around, though."

"Yeah, but I can't think of anyone who'd come gunning for me specifically."

"Yeah, we never do until they show up." Bruiser took a deep breath. "So, when are you going to head back to the team?"

"As I said, two more weeks to get myself back up to speed. When's the next show?"

"We're heading to Virginia Beach next weekend, but we should be heading back to California about that time. Think you can get the docs to sign off on sending you out by then?"

"Yeah, I think that's doable."

"Good. We'll get our flights routed through Cheyenne to come pick you up."

"Roger that." He'd paused and took a deep breath.

"Hey, Bruiser, I gotta run to help set up for a wedding, but I wanted to talk to you about something for retirement when you got time."

"Retirement? Don't you still have two years on your tour?"

"Yeah, but it's always good to have a plan."

Silence had echoed on the other side of the phone as Bruiser took in his words. "It's the lady doc, isn't it?"

"What?"

"The cowgirl in the arena who saved your ass. She's the one makin' you think about retirement, isn't she?"

Damn, he'd forgotten how perceptive Bruiser was. He always looked like a big, slow thug, but he was one of the most intuitive men Enrique had ever met. And why they were best friends since they joined the same team.

"She's the one making me think about a future after the Navy." He'd paused, chewing on his lip. "I like her, Bruiser. She's smart, doesn't take anyone's shit—"

"Roger that." Humor laced Bruiser's interruption.

"—she's funny, compassionate, gorgeous, and strong enough to put up with SEALs. She's worth figuring out a way to stay close to her."

"Holy fuck. You found The One, didn't you?"

His teammates had ribbed him hard about his belief in the ultimate One True Love. His father and paternal grandfather had talked about it, and neither of them had waited long to marry their respective loves. Of course, the previous generations hadn't had to learn much more than their women's names, appearance, and fathers' permission before they'd married, but they always maintained they knew their love the moment they saw them.

"Yeah, *hermano*, I think I have."

"Fuck. And you like Wyoming?"

"I like her. If she's in Wyoming, that's where I want to be." He'd sighed knowing his friend thought him crazy. "Look, I gotta go, but I'll give you a call later to talk about an idea I've got. Copy?"

"Yeah, copy that. One last question. Have you told her about The One shit?"

"No, not yet. But I plan on doing it tonight after the wedding."

"Who's getting married?"

"The ranch owner. His son asked me to be an usher."

"Well look at you bein' all neighborly and all." Bruiser had laughed. "All right, Sanchez. I'll catch you later, and you better let me know what she says."

"Roger that."

He'd ended the call then hurried over to the arena to help Tom and the other stable hands put together the floor and straw bales. No one gave him shit for being a little late, but after having spent the night with Suzie and realizing she was The One, he couldn't have been happier. His ribs and arm weren't as thrilled with him by the time they'd gotten everything set up, but his good mood had persisted. Especially when he'd caught sight of Suzie.

She'd been helping another woman with a kid set up tables and chairs, and covering them with white cloths. She'd laughed and it had echoed throughout the whole arena. He'd damn near dropped the straw bale on his foot when it flowed over him.

That was the moment when the realization that she was his One was verified. *Sweet glory, I want her forever.* He wanted to spend all his on-leave mornings in bed with her, and soak his feet in her kiddie pool at night. He wanted to watch her laugh with her friends as she helped set up for her own wedding. Her wedding to him.

He'd stood there like a deer in headlights until Tom had clapped him on the shoulder and asked him if he was all right. He'd nodded and said his arm was bugging him a bit to deflect questions, but had gone back to work. His mind wouldn't let go of the idea of their own wedding and he'd wondered how the hell he was going to say anything to Suzie about it.

You're not, dude. You're gonna wait until you're both ready and then pop the question.

He stared at himself in the mirror, looking sharp in his uniform, and wondered if she felt as deeply about him as he did about her. In the grand scheme of things, he hadn't known her long. But his heart had taken the short weeks they'd been together and created a strong foundation on which to build something more. He sighed, straightened his shoulders, and nodded sharply.

Time to get this show on the road.

He pulled his cover off and tucked it under his arm as he grabbed his keys, his phone, and stepped out his room door, scanning the halls of the Bunkhouse out of habit. He caught movement at the end of the hallway. *That's the cleaning lady I keep seeing.* He frowned. Tom told him the staff had the day off because of the wedding and the guests knew they'd have to suffer with dirty sheets for one extra day. What the hell was she doing here?

He strode down the hall to catch up to her, but by the time he got to the stairs, she was already gone. He heard the door to the outside close and shook his head. Why did he keep seeing this woman? And why the hell was she in the Bunkhouse?

The question bugged him all the way down the stairs and outside. He automatically looked around, but there wasn't anyone near the building. He tugged his cover onto his head and turned his feet toward the arena, but he scanned his surroundings, the hair on the back of his neck standing up with unease. It didn't feel like he had a gun aimed at him, but someone watched him. His shoulder blades itched and he kept waiting for someone to make a move.

I wish I had a weapon.

When he reached the arena entrance, he put his back to the wall and let his gaze pass over the grounds. Nothing

caught his eye or tripped his warning system, but he
remained on edge until Tom appeared beside him. A few of
the incoming guests gave him a curious look, but other than
cataloging them as non-threats, he didn't respond to their
expressions.

"Hey, everything okay, Enrique?"

He gave a sharp nod to Tom's question. "Yes, sir."

"You look tense, is all. You don't have to be nervous.
You're not the one gettin' hitched." Tom smirked and
Enrique let some of his tension go.

"No, sir, I'm not." *Not yet.* He adjusted his shoulders
as the feeling of being watched dissipated.

"You are lookin' sharp, though. Damn, the guests will
be fightin' over who gets to be seated by you."

Enrique chuckled as Tom grinned. The cowboy had
cleaned up pretty well, too. He wore a white button down
shirt with a tie and black brocade vest over crisp blue jeans
and black cowboy boots. A championship belt buckle
closed his belt.

"I'm not the only one the guests will be sighing over,
hermano. You're probably everyone's cowboy fantasy
come to life."

Tom raised an eyebrow. "How would you know about
cowboy fantasies?"

Enrique snorted. "I have two sisters who love to read
romance. And they have friends. It's insane what all I know
about those books."

Tom laughed. "Good to know. In the meantime, you
can start takin' guests to the folding chairs on the dance
floor. When the ceremony's over, we'll move all the chairs
off to the racks behind the stage so we can have dancin'
and stuff."

Enrique nodded. "Roger that."

The first person he approached was an older woman
around his mother's age. She was spritely and her eyes
brightened when he offered to take her to her seat.

"My, aren't you a handsome man. Are you on active duty?"

"On medical leave, ma'am, from the Navy." Enrique smiled as he led her inside. "Trip or Henry's side, ma'am?"

"Trip's." She stood a little taller. "I was a USO girl and I danced a mean Two-Step back in the day. You save a spot for me on your dance card, y'hear?"

He chuckled as he led her to her seat. "Yes, ma'am." He returned to the entrance trying to smother his smile.

His next charge was a younger woman with an hourglass figure á la Dolly Parton. She even wore the short summer dress and the cowboy boots. Her hair wasn't quite the bouffant Dolly used to sport, but if she'd been going for a lookalike contest, she would've been in the running.

"Let me show you to your seat, ma'am. Trip or Henry's side?"

She giggled behind her hand as she took his arm. "Goodness, I'm too young to be a ma'am. And I'm a friend of Tom's."

"Just a term of respect, ma'am." He tugged her toward the folded chairs on the left.

"I just love weddings, don't you? Everyone's all dressed up so nice and lookin' good." She leaned in to not only give him a good look down her cleavage but to rub her breasts against his arm. "Nice to see old friends and meet new ones. Like you." Her smile widened. "My name's Cathy."

"It's very nice to meet you, Cathy." He removed her hand from his arm and handed her into her seat with a polite smile. "Enjoy the wedding."

She opened her mouth to say something but he smoothly turned on his heel and headed back to the entrance, amusement filling his chest. *Oh, that one is on the hunt for a husband.* He expected she'd be trying for his attention the whole night. The uniform did funny things to women. He shook his head and looked up for his next charge.

A stocky young man about his age waited near the doors. He stood a little shorter than Enrique with short blond hair and brown eyes, but the way he watched the people around him and the entryway suggested he'd been in the service.

"Good afternoon, sir. May I take you to your seat?" Enrique gestured inside.

"Yeah, that'd be good, and you don't have to call me sir. I worked for a living." An easy smile curled the man's lips.

"An enlisted man. Which branch?"

"Marines. You know, the best of the best." The smile widened.

Enrique nodded with his own smile. "Yeah, that's what I've heard them say about themselves."

The man laughed as he limped a little down the aisle. "Damn straight, Petty Officer…"

"Sanchez." He held out his hand to shake and the man's weapon roughened palm engulfed it.

"Good to meet you, Sanchez. I'm Brian Calvert, USMC retired."

"A pleasure, Mr. Calvert. I forgot to ask, Trip or Henry's side?" Enrique gestured to the front.

"I'm here for Henry."

"Right." He led Brian to a seat near the aisle that had both easy access and easy escape. "Thank you for your service. And just between you and me, I'm glad the Marines are on our side."

"Oh yeah?" Brian grinned. "Because we'd take you down hard?"

"Nah, the Navy SpecOps guys would still beat you, but it'd be a helluva fight."

Enrique touched two fingers to the brim of his cover as he left Brian laughing in his seat.

He swung his gaze around the room, noting some of

the women had brought in food and drink items and set them on the banquet tables in the back. He looked for Suzie but didn't see her and stuffed his disappointment down as he returned to the entrance.

Where the world came to a grinding halt.

Suzie stood waiting for an usher as she spoke to Tom. She wore a sundress with orange and red poppy flowers against a white background. The bodice cupped her full breasts enough to make him drool and the skirt flared around her knees. She damn near dropped Enrique to his knees. Short black heels made her calves and ankles stand out and he had the overwhelming urge to run his hands over them just to test the softness of her skin.

One of the other guys ushering folks to their seats tried to take her arm and Enrique had to tamp down a snarl. He didn't want anyone else to have that honor and he lurched back into motion to reach her side. But Suzie smiled and waved the other man off as she turned back to Tom.

"I'm so happy for your dad and Henry." She laid a hand on Tom's arm and Enrique's inner Neanderthal rumbled a warning. "And just to let you know, Amber was a little wistful this morning while we were setting up. You might think of having a first anniversary party or something so she can have a similar celebration."

"Yeah?" Tom looked thoughtful.

"Just a suggestion, but yeah, I think so." She patted his arm and turned her attention to Enrique. Her eyes widened and she froze. "Sweet glory, Enrique. You're very handsome today."

He'd never felt the need to preen before, but Suzie's rapt attention on him made him straighten up even more than usual.

"Thank you, Dr. Suzie. May I take you to your seat?" He offered her his arm and ignored Tom's knowing smirk.

"Uh, yes. Thank you." She took his arm and stepped away from Tom, who grinned wider.

"Told you you looked sharp, Petty Officer."

Enrique didn't bother to answer as he laid his other hand on top of Suzie's. He leaned closer to her but resisted kissing her cheek.

"I missed you this morning."

A flush of pleasure stained her cheeks. "Me, too. I looked for you in the arena earlier but didn't see you."

"Oh, I was there. I spent most of my time trying to catch a glimpse of you. Almost caught my hand between the planks a couple of times because you were so sexy."

She raised her eyebrows. "Sexy? In my T-shirt and jeans?"

"Yeah, I couldn't keep my eyes off your ass." He grinned as her flush deepened. "You know you're the most beautiful woman in this room, right, *querida*? If I could, I'd spend the whole wedding with you." He led her to one of the front seats on Trip's side. "Save me a seat beside you, will you?"

Suzie nodded and her smile settled into something more seductive. "And at least one dance."

He grinned. "If I have my way, I'll have them all." He kissed her hand before he strode back to the entrance to continue his task. But his heart filled with excitement over the prospect of sharing this celebration with her.

And that's because I want to share a wedding with her.

Yeah, he still had time for that one.

CHAPTER THIRTEEN

Suzie wished she'd remembered to bring a handkerchief to wipe her eyes as the wedding began. Trip Colton stood up so tall and proud beside his younger groom. He wore a silver brocade vest and a burgundy tie, while Henry wore a burgundy brocade vest and a silver tie. Byron Abernathy, Trip's best friend and Seychelles's dad, held out a rose and white gold braided ring for Trip to slide onto Henry's finger. Tom stood beside him, grinning with pride.

Trip stumbled over his vows a little, all choked up with love and joy, and Suzie lost her fight against the tears. She tried to wipe them away gently, but she couldn't catch them all. *Great, now I'm gonna look like a raccoon.*

Before she could do more than sniffle, a cotton handkerchief appeared in her line of sight.

"For you, *querida.*" Enrique gave her a tender smile.

"*Gracias.*" She smiled back and made sure to catch her tears, half of them from his sweetness.

He wrapped an arm around her shoulders and snuggled her up against his side. She hadn't felt so cherished since her father tucked her into bed each night and read her Louis L'Amour stories.

Then it was Henry's turn to swear to love and cherish Trip for all the days of his life, and his experience as a performer showed. He never missed a line or got choked up, but he grinned the whole time like he had just gotten the best Christmas gift ever. Trip's ring was a brushed silver titanium band that fit in with the rough old cowboy he was. Ransom Knight, the owner of the Fantasy Ranch next door, stood in as Henry's best man and handed over the ring so Henry could slide it on Trip's finger. Then he pulled Trip's hand up to his mouth and kissed the ring.

There wasn't a dry eye in the house.

"Then by the power granted to me by the State of Wyoming, I now pronounce you husbands and partners for life. You may now kiss the groom."

The Justice of the Peace stepped back as Trip wrapped his arms around Henry and they kissed under their cowboy hats, one black and one white. It was sexy as hell and the crowd broke into cheers.

Suzie caught movement out of the corner of her eye and turned to look at Enrique. He gazed at her with a combination of tenderness and desire she'd never seen before. While the cheering continued she stayed lost in the love blazing from his eyes.

I want this with Enrique.

The urge to lean forward and kiss the living daylights out of him right there in the front of the wedding ceremony gripped her. She almost gave into it but the wedding party moved down the aisle and Enrique turned to watch. She bit her lip before it morphed into a smile for Trip and Henry. Enrique squeezed her hand before he put his hat back on his head.

Damn, he's so sexy.

"I have to help usher people and clear the chairs. I'll see you at the table, yeah?"

She nodded and watched him direct her and the people in her row toward the back. He winked as she passed him and a warmth started in her chest at his smile. She sauntered toward the buffet tables, belatedly remembering she was supposed to help set out the food.

Off cloud nine, sister. She shook her head and hurried over to where Mrs. Guthrie was back directing her troops. It didn't take long to get the food set out with so many helping hands, and by the time Enrique and the other ushers had cleared away the folding chairs from the dance floor, everything was ready to go. She offered to stay and help serve the food, but Mrs. Guthrie waved her off, saying she had it well in hand.

So Suzie grabbed a plate and filled it with her dinner before heading to her assigned table close to the one for the wedding couple. Trip and Henry hadn't made it from the well-wishers yet, but they didn't seem in any hurry. They held hands as they shook those that came to speak to them. Suzie's heart swelled in joy and mild envy. Trip deserved his happy ending after all the years he'd been widowed. And Henry was his perfect match despite their age difference.

"Hey, what's got that sappy smile on your face, honey?" Seychelles settled into the chair on her left, her eyebrows raised.

"I'm so happy for Trip and Henry. They're so cute together and they deserve it."

"Yeah." Seychelles nodded. "My dad said Trip was afraid of how he'd react to him loving Henry, but dad's one of those rare old guys who doesn't care whom you love as long as it doesn't hurt someone else."

"Definitely a rare guy indeed." Suzie took a sip of her water out of the mason jar glass. "I'm very glad he's supportive of Trip." She let her gaze slide away to where Enrique gestured to folks to move toward the buffet tables. He looked so smart in his "crackerjack" uniform, she could barely keep her eyes off him.

"I see that dreamy smile on your face, missy."

Seychelles laughed as heat filled Suzie's cheeks, but she sobered. "He really makes you happy, doesn't he?"

"Yes, he does." Suzie bit her lip. "Oh, Sey, I think he might be the one and only for me."

"Yeah, I'm getting that impression." Seychelles laid her hand on Suzie's arm. "Personally, I think he's perfect for you. Not that there won't be things you'll have to work out, I'm sure. But I think he might be worth the work."

"He's definitely the first guy who's been worth it to make the effort."

"Oh, honey, I'm so excited for you." Her gaze slid back to the buffet line. "Here he comes. Damn, you do know how to pick the hot ones. There's nothing like a man in uniform to get the juices flowing."

Suzie snorted and raised an eyebrow. "You like a man in uniform?"

"Oh, yeah." Seychelles sighed dreamily. "There's something about a fancy suit and just the right hat and shiny shoes." She shot a wistful look in Enrique's direction. "It's hot."

They both smiled at him as he sat down on Suzie's other side and he raised his eyebrows at their matching expressions.

"If you're going for innocence, you're not quite pulling it off." He set his plate down and his sailor's hat on the table. "What were you two talking about?"

"Nothing," Seychelles said.

Suzie laughed. "We were remarking on how men in uniform are sexy."

"Suzie!" Seychelles actually blushed.

"Really? You think I'm sexy in my uniform, Seychelles?" He straightened up a little and shot her a cheeky smile.

"No, I said *men* are sexy in uniform, not you specifically." She raised her chin and straightened her shoulders. "I don't hit on my best friend's man."

"I didn't think you were hitting on Enrique, Sey." Suzie grinned. "But it's good to know a man in uniform might catch your attention." She shot Enrique a smile. "The rest of your team dresses up like this, too, right?"

"Yes, ma'am." Enrique sipped his water. "All of them. If you like tall, there's Petty Officer Second Class Avery Hightower. He's around six-five and has great dance moves, though not as good as mine." He winked as they laughed. "But if you're more into ninja computer skills, there's Petty Officer Third Class Aaron Chin. He's our communication and computer expert. Neither of them have romantic partners and they're always willing to impress women with their dress blues."

Seychelles narrowed her eyes and tilted her head. "Hmm, they'll be coming back here to get you, right?"

Enrique laughed. "Kinda. They're routing their trip through Cheyenne to pick me up on the way to our next show."

For the first time, unease slithered through Suzie's awareness. "When will that be?"

"Dr. Lyttle signed off on my return to duty in about two weeks, so the end of this month."

Two weeks. That's all she had left with him. Her heart quailed at the idea that he'd leave and possibly never come back.

Why would he come back? Cheyenne wasn't San Diego. Hell, it wasn't even as busy as Fort Collins or Denver. And he was in the Navy. Not much water in the intramountain west. He'd said he had two more years on his tour, so he'd be back for Cheyenne Frontier Days, but four days a year seemed hardly worth the effort.

"Hey, are you all right?" He grabbed her hand and squeezed. "Suzie, what's wrong?"

"Oh, no, nothing. Sorry, I just realized that you've been here that long. The time flew by." She tried to find her smile, but the sorrow remained. She took a deep breath.

"But this is good, right? You're almost complete in your therapy and you'll be back to what you do best with your team."

"Yeah, that's right."

He nodded but his gaze remained on her and she suspected he didn't miss her lack of enthusiasm. He opened his mouth to say more but Byron stood up to make a toast for Trip. Enrique squeezed her hand again and tipped his head to let her know he wasn't done talking, but she turned her attention to the speakers.

After Byron, Henry's best man, Ransom, gave his toast to Henry and Trip, about defying the odds, not only in love but in life. The words rang sweetly through the arena and everyone laughed and dabbed tears during it. Suzie's cheeks hurt from smiling.

Then Henry took the microphone and moved over to the stage portion of the floor. The members of his old band had set up while the guests ate and sat ready to entertain. Henry picked up a guitar waiting for him and slung the strap over his shoulder as he faced the crowd.

"I'm sure most of y'all know the story of how Trip and I got together." Henry smirked ruefully at the crowd when they laughed. "It wasn't easy or fun at the time, but it sure was worth it in the end. Hell, it got me writin' music again, and this is the first song that came to mind when I finally pulled my head outta my ass and tried to come home. This is for you, Trip."

The strains of a very popular country rock song filled the room and Suzie gasped. She'd heard the song a lot on the radio and loved the romantic side of the singer realizing his mistake. She had no idea it had been about Trip and Henry's love. She watched Henry sing to his new husband and there was no doubt in her mind that what they felt for each other was real and strong.

What do I feel for Enrique?

The question made her turn to look at him and she

145

found his gaze on her, a small, tender smile curling his lips. It warmed her heart and made her shiver with excitement and pleasure. She wanted him, but not just for sex. She wanted to listen to him tell her stories about his day and the exciting things he'd done. She wanted to share her accomplishments and funny incidents being a doctor. She just wanted to spend more time with him.

I have two more weeks. It would have to be enough.

The song ended and the crowd clapped as Trip rose and wrapped Henry in his arms, love beaming from his face. That kind of love was what she wanted with Enrique and she'd use her two weeks to find out they had it.

Trip and Henry moved over to cut the cake and feed each other pieces with the utmost love and respect. It was sweet and Suzie squeezed her hands in her lap, forgetting she had Enrique's until he squeezed back. She shot him a giddy smile as he rose to get them both a piece of the cake.

"Stop it. You look like you're at your own wedding." Seychelles leaned close and bumped Suzie's shoulder. "You're gonna give me cavities you're so sweet."

"Shut up." Suzie couldn't help her grin. "I'm just so happy for Trip and Henry. They deserve they're happy-ever-after. And I can't help but be a little envious. I want one, too."

"What the hell do you think you got goin' on with that Leap Frog over there? Sweet glory, woman. I'd say you're well on your way." Seychelles rolled her eyes.

Suzie nodded, but refused to give voice to the hope that Sey was right. Could Enrique be the one she'd work to keep in her life despite all his travel and her odd doctor's hours? She turned to watch him accepting some cake and her heart leapt in anticipation.

Yes, he could.

She didn't want to take the careful path anymore. She wanted to work for her own HEA with him. He was honest, kind, strong, funny, smart, and skilled, but he also made her feel good and liked her without wanted her to change. A rare man in her experience.

"Don't let him go back to his team without telling him how you feel, Suzie." Sey's voice had grown serious as she met Suzie's gaze. "Seriously. He said he's in it for the long haul. Let him know you are, too."

Suzie only had time to nod when Enrique returned with two plates of cake.

"They had chocolate and yellow cake, but I didn't know which you'd prefer, so I got one of each." He held up each plate.

"Yellow cake, please." She took the plate and he sat down with a grin.

"Oh good, I prefer chocolate, but didn't want to take it before you chose."

"Thanks." She glanced at Seychelles and met a 'see?' look before Sey stood.

"I'm gonna to check on Mrs. Guthrie to see if she needs me to do anything before the party really gets going. I'll even bring back some coffee if you'd like some."

"Oh, I should do that, too—"

"No, you stay here with Enrique and enjoy your rare time off. We got this." Sey shot her a meaningful glance before she smoothed her smile. "I'll see you in a little bit."

"What was she trying to say before she walked away?" Enrique took a bite of cake as he raised an eyebrow.

Suzie sighed and rubbed the back of her neck. "She just wants me to be happy."

"We have that in common, her and I." He gave her a soft smile as he scanned her face. "Suzie, I want to talk to you about something, but I don't know if now's the right time with all this." He waved to the festivities around them. "Going on. But can we talk this evening after the party?"

She bit her lip. "It's too serious to talk right now?"

He shook his head, his smile widening. "No, well, yeah, kinda. But I don't want either of us to be distracted.

It's *that* important."

Hope and fear and excitement bubbled up in a churning morass of emotion, but she swallowed hard and nodded.

"That's a good plan." She ate some cake to calm her nerves. "I can do that."

"Good." He licked some of the frosting off his fork and she shivered with the memories of him licking her pussy.

"Ladies and gentlemen, make way for the grooms and their first dance."

Trip led Henry onto the dance floor then stood beside him a couple of feet apart. They both dropped their heads so the audience could only see the tops of their cowboy hats, and Suzie had to admit it was pretty damn sexy. The music started, an up-tempo country rock piece, and both Trip and Henry moved in sync, like line dancers. The crowd whooped as they moved around the floor, the older man moving as well as his younger husband.

They swayed their hips, slapped their thighs and ankles, and twirled in step to clapping and cheering. Suzie laughed along with the rest until Henry and Trip came together to slow-dance. At the end of the song, Trip dipped Henry, and kissed him, making the crowd roar. Suzie put her hand over her chest and fought tears while Enrique grabbed her other hand. Trip and Henry's love was so beautiful and her heart ached to see it.

Something else took that moment to ache and she squeezed his hand. "I have to run to the ladies room."

He nodded and rose with her, pulling out her chair. "See you soon."

Her heart fluttered but she made her feet walk away. She did need to use the restroom, but mostly to clean her face and settle herself. She ducked through the doors of the bathroom and took a deep breath before she used the facilities. When she got to the sink she stared at herself in the mirror, studying her face.

"Deep breath, honey. Just tell him how you feel and let the chips fall where they may."

Easier said than done. "But nothing worth doing is ever easy." She said her father's words aloud to get herself out of her head. "And the SEALs say, the only easy day was yesterday. Yeah, they're right about that."

She washed her hands and her face, patted everything dry, and nodded sharply. She could do this. She could take a chance on what she wanted, and win in the end. She squared her shoulders and pushed out of the bathroom as the band struck up a new tune. Trip and Henry wandered around the room, talking to people while other folks took up the space on the stage to dance. Mrs. Guthrie had her troops marshaled with Seychelles and Sage trading the big food dishes out for bins of water in ice and coffee. Sage's boy Adam had found a new friend in the stocky blond man who'd sat on Henry's side. It warmed her heart to see both of them focused on each other.

*Speaking of focus…*She swung her gaze toward the table where Enrique sat but stopped short in dismayed surprise. A buxom blonde woman reminiscent of Dolly Parton sat beside Enrique, drunkenly leaning on him and pawing at his crotch. Anger scorched a path up Suzie's back and made her fists clench at her side. *What the everloving hell?* She managed to push the anger aside enough to recognize Enrique didn't appear to be enjoying the woman's attention, but the Dolly lookalike refused to be deterred.

"Oh, come on, sailor boy, I promise to make it worth your while." The woman tried to give him a come-hither smile but it looked like a lopsided grimace and she wobbled in her seat.

"Your offer is kind, Ms. Cathy, but I'm just here for the wedding." He gently disengaged her wandering hands.

"Yeah, me too. Weddin's are for hookups, right?" She leaned forward, the view down her cleavage as wide as the

Grand Canyon.

Sweet glory. The woman is six sheets to the wind.

"I've heard that, yes, but I've come with someone so I'm not available."

Enrique again caught her hand moving toward his groin and moved it away. He turned his head and caught sight of Suzie, his expression shifting to dismay.

Cathy snorted and pouted. "I don' believe that, honey. I saw you come in alone so I know you're just playin' coy. But you don' have to do that wi' me. I promise to be a good lay."

She lurched toward him as he started to get up, but she misjudged where he was and went sprawling into the dirt between the tables. She landed hard before anyone could catch her and she cried out when her arm collapsed. Enrique swore and knelt beside her, trying to get her up. Suzie joined him just as huge tears started down the blonde's face.

"Ow, somethin's wrong. My arm hurts." Her wailed words made most of the guests look over.

"Let me see, I'm a doctor." Suzie tried to keep the annoyance out of her voice, but given the sharp look Enrique gave her, she'd missed the mark.

"Ow, ow, ow, it hurts." Cathy whimpered as she snuggled against Enrique's chest.

Suzie gritted her teeth while she slid her hands along Cathy's arm, trying to focus on the bones rather than backhanding her.

"I don't think it's broken, but we should get her an ace bandage and a sling. I have them in my office." Suzie rose and helped the woman up, trying not to gag at the overwhelming scent of bourbon wafting off her. "Come on, Ms. Cathy. We'll get you fixed up."

"I'll help bring her." Enrique helped woman up though she slumped against him.

"What's going on?" Seychelles appeared beside them,

her expression worried.

"Just a little tumble, but I think she needs a sling to keep that arm out of the way, and she's pretty hammered. We're just taking her to my office in the clinic." Suzie gestured for them to leave, disgust and anger trying to push through her doctor's façade.

"I'll come with you and find out where she's stayin'. We can get her to her room after. Do you know who she came with?" Sey helped guide them through the tables toward the door.

"No idea. Maybe Mrs. Guthrie knows."

"I'll ask her on the way out and join you in a minute." Sey held the doors to the arena open so they could drag Cathy into the afternoon sunshine.

"My arm hurts." Cathy's moaned words made Suzie want to roll her eyes, but she had to keep up her professional reputation. She'd seen enough addicts in her years as a doctor to dismiss the whining.

Yeah, but none of those addicts had hit on the man I really like.

Enrique didn't say anything as they marched past the duck pond to the lodge, just stoically helped Cathy along. Suzie tried to calm her anger. Enrique hadn't responded favorably to Cathy's come-ons and he'd been actively trying to avoid her. *So why am I so pissed off?*

She hadn't come up with an answer when they entered the clinic reception area. She pulled out the keys to her office and she had to resort to brutally shoving her anger away to concentrate on the patient in need. *Remember the Hippocratic oath.*

"Here we are. Just a moment now and we'll get you that bandage and sling." Suzie reached for her door to unlock it, but the knob turned without much effort. "What the...?"

"I don't feel well..." Cathy moaned as Enrique leaned her against the wall.

"What's wrong, Suzie?" He stepped up beside her.

"I never leave my office unlocked." She wrinkled her nose just as Seychelles caught up to them. "Do y'all smell something?"

She had to shove the door open hard as something had blocked its path. Hot and fetid air hit her nose when she got it open and she damn near gagged on the stench. Drawers lay at haphazard angles. Cabinet doors stood open into the room and the floor was covered with papers and broken containers. The shelves had been cleaned off as if the vandals had been looking for something specific.

Suzie stared at the mess in dismay, the unfamiliar fear creeping up her throat from her gut.

"Hey, Cathy is Clair Knight's friend and should be— Holy shit, what the hell happened in here?" Seychelles gaped at the debris-lined floor.

"Stay here." Enrique slid past them.

Suzie nodded dumbly, her gaze flitting over the damage. Despite the mess, Enrique made no noise as he moved through the room, his sharp gaze taking in blind corners and shadows. He disappeared into the connected exam rooms and Suzie's gut cramped.

Don't be silly. He's a Navy SEAL. But even SEALs were human and could be surprised.

"What's that smell?" Seychelles wrinkled her nose.

Suzie carefully inhaled again. Under the scents of spilled herbal remedies as well as essential oils, something rank and rotting permeated the air. She tried to see where the smell originated, but the piled papers covered everything. Enrique hadn't returned yet, but nothing moved in the office.

"Let's see if I can find whatever it is." She often used her nose for things like cooking and cleaning out the refrigerator – the latter not nearly as fun – but rarely did she use it in the office.

"It smells like something died in here." Seychelles

squatted and gathered some of the scattered papers. "How are you going to know what papers go in which files?"

"I have a system." Or she did before someone destroyed it. Hopefully, her computer had survived, though she did have backups of all her records on a cloud server. "Keep an eye on Cathy. I don't want her to get into this mess." She stepped around the worst of the broken glass. "I'll gather the papers later and I'll go through them when I have time. Whatever that smell is has to be cleaned before it makes us all sick."

She lifted papers and straightened them into piles, stacking them to the side as she picked her way through the room. Broken glass from jars and beakers crackled under her feet as she moved carefully through the debris. She didn't touch the drawers or cabinets, having seen enough forensic shows. The cops would need to dust for prints. The stench increased closer to the back of the room and by the time she reached her desk, her eyes were tearing.

"Sweet glory." She moved her chair and covered her nose and mouth with her arm. Blood stained the edges of the desk and floor, and smeared across the seat of the chair. "Oh, hell."

"What is it?" Seychelles left Cathy and moved to her side, gasping. "Is that a dead cat?"

Suzie squinted. "I think so. Or what's left of it."

"All the other rooms are clear." Enrique reappeared. "Are you all right?"

She shook her head and hurried over to the nearest window to throw it open. The smell was overriding her aversion to vomit and she had to get fresh air in the room.

"Suzie?" He stood behind her, his strong body taut and tense, concern leaking through his usual stoic-warrior expression.

"I'm just trying to rid my nose of that stench. I'm okay. We should check on Cathy."

He wrapped his arms around her from behind, his body

warming her suddenly cold core despite the summer temperatures outside. He didn't give her any false platitudes or empty words, he simply lent her his solid presence and it calmed her more than any words could.

Who the hell would do something like this? Most of her patients had suffered some form of PTSD, but they'd never trashed her office before. And no one left a mutilated animal for her to find.

"We have to tell Tom. Maybe Ethan can find something on the security cameras from last night or early this morning." Suzie tried to find some sort of order in the chaos around her as she turned in Enrique's arms. "I need to get this place cleaned up."

"No, *querida*. We have to call the police before we let the stable hands in here to help." Enrique squeezed her gently. "Who's Ethan? I could talk to him."

"He's the security guy Tom hired after Amber was abducted. He might have seen something." She ran her hand over her face. "But I can't let the stable hands do this. These are private records of the patients here. They're confidential."

He nodded. "I know. Once you get the papers all gathered up, we'll get the men in here to do a thorough cleaning. It's gonna take a while to air out."

"Oh my glory!" Seychelles's exclamation had them turning toward her. "I think...I think there's a note attached to the carcass."

"What?" Suzie's stomach rolled as Enrique moved to Seychelles's side and looked down. "Seriously?"

He bent out of sight to reach for something, only standing when he lifted a bloodstained piece of paper and the scalpel that had pinned it to the body. He scanned the note and his expression hardened into banked anger.

"What does it say?"

Seychelles frowned and shook her head. "I don't know. It's not in English. Spanish, maybe?"

Enrique gave a sharp nod and moved toward the door, note in hand. "Stay here. I gotta make a call."

"Enrique—"

But he was already gone. Suzie looked at Seychelles who shrugged.

"Let's see if we can find a sling and that ace bandage for Cathy."

"Right." Suzie moved to the next window and threw it open to let in the fresh air. *Thank goodness for the Wyoming wind.*

"Ugh. I'm gonna be sick." Cathy's voice drew their attention to the door just before she heaved her bourbon soaked dinner all over the papers in front of her.

"No, wait!" Seychelles tried to get to her, but it was too late.

Sour vomit hit the paper-strewn floor, adding to the noxious mess.

"Aw hell." Suzie closed her eyes and begged whichever deity was listening for patience.

CHAPTER FOURTEEN

Enrique headed back to the arena to track Tom down but he stopped at the front desk to get a tissue to hold the note. If someone wanted to do forensics on it, they'd have to get elimination prints from him and Suzie. He didn't want to add more to them.

He pushed out the door of the lodge and jogged to the arena, his gut tight. The message in the note made it clear he was the target of the shooter.

"I will trap you like a cat in a box. You cannot get away from me. I will make you pay for my husband's death. I'm coming for you, pendejo, you and your puta."

Anger curled inside him as he pushed into the arena. This was a place of healing. That anyone would threaten the people here, the healers and the victims of PTSD, infuriated him. Especially since the tango seemed to be targeting him and Suzie.

It's the shooter from the rodeo. Of that he had no doubt as he caught Tom's gaze and motioned him over toward the tables with drinks on it.

"How is the woman who fell doing?"

"I don't know. She was pretty drunk and hitting on me hard, but that's not why I need to talk to you. Someone destroyed Suzie's office and left this pinned to a mutilated cat on her chair." He held up the note. "We need to call the cops and I need to get a hold of your security discs for the hallway outside the clinic and the waiting room."

"What the fuck?" Tom's eyes widened as he stared at the note covered in blood and flesh.

"Yeah, it's pretty sick and I have a feeling I know what it's about. Where's your security guy, Ethan?"

"Come with me." Tom waved at Andrew and all three of them stepped outside. "Andrew, I need you to call Ethan and tell him we're coming to check the security tapes. I'm gonna call the sheriff and get him out here. You said you think you know what this is about, Sanchez?"

Enrique nodded. "Yeah, but I'm not gonna talk about it out here. It's a security issue that we thought had been solved. Guess it hasn't."

"Yeah, I'd say that's accurate." Tom scowled as they headed back to the lodge. He punched numbers into his phone and held it to his ear as they stepped inside. "Yeah, I need to talk to Sheriff Taylor. This is Tom Colton at the Triple Star Ranch."

Andrew shot Enrique a worried look. "The security office is this way."

"Can you get me a plastic baggie or something? I don't want to lose any forensic evidence off this." Enrique held up the grisly note.

"Oh, yeah. I have some at my desk." Andrew ducked behind reception and pulled out a box of zip locking bags. "Will this do?"

Enrique nodded and shoved the note inside, sealing it before shoving it into his jacket pocket. "Yeah, that's perfect. Now where's the security office?"

"This way." Andrew hurried down the hall away from the clinic. "Did someone really trash Dr. Suzie's office?"

"Completely." Enrique scowled. "As soon as we talk to the security chief, I'm going back to her office and make sure she's okay."

Andrew nodded with a worried look. "We better hurry then."

They made it to the office and Ethan was waiting. "I don't know when the perp did the damage, but I think I know who." The young man with a buzzcut didn't bother with pleasantries.

"How did you not see it happening?" Enrique stood behind his chair and faced the monitors.

"I used the restroom. I wasn't gone longer than six minutes." Ethan cued up the security feeds. "There aren't any cameras in her office, just in the waiting room and hallway outside. The person who did this got in while I was gone."

"Did you see them leave?"

Ethan shook his head. "Nope. But the cameras did."

He backed up the video until it showed the time stamp 16:23.

"That's the waiting room outside the doctor's office." Ethan pointed to the monitor in the center. "This one is the entry way near Andrew's desk and the hallway past the clinic." He pointed to the monitor on the left. "And that one is the door out to the duck pond on the left. Keep an eye on the doctor's office."

Ethan started the video just as Tom came in the security office. "What are we watching?"

"This is the clinic waiting room." Enrique vibrated with nervous energy. Nothing appeared to be happening, but he reminded himself to be patient.

"What's that?" Andrew pointed at the screen. The time stamp read 16:25.

"Cleaning woman, I think." Ethan tilted his head. "Does she look familiar to you, Tom?"

Tom shook his head. "No, but I can't get a good look at her face. It's blocked by the cart. Does she ever show it clearly?"

"Yeah, on the way out. Check out the time stamps. She arrives at 16:25, and leaves…" He made the video speed forward until 16:33. "Here. 16:33. I saw her but didn't think anything of it. But she does look at the camera here." He stopped the video. "I don't recognize her, but I'm still new. Do you know her?"

Tom shook his head. "No. I didn't hire her, but my dad might've. We've been so busy with the wedding I haven't paid much attention." He frowned. "Where does she go after?"

"Through foyer." Ethan played the videos. "Check out the monitor on the left."

The cleaning woman left the office through the waiting room and appeared in the hallway just before she reached Andrew's desk still pushing the laundry cart. It seemed empty. She disappeared off the screen at 16:35. But she appeared in the video on the right heading out to the duck pond at 16:37 without the cart."

"What the hell happened to the cart?" Tom scanned the three videos.

"I dunno, boss. But I know where she goes after she left the lodge." Ethan clicked his mouse and brought up a view of the arena and the barn's parking lot. "Right there."

The time stamp read 16:42. The cleaning woman strode with a determined step toward the arena. She held her hand in her skirt as if using the fabric to conceal something. The hair on Enrique's neck stood up and he held his breath. Was she at the wedding?

She'd almost made it to the arena when someone came out. A couple of the guests appeared to be having a smoke and they gathered around the door. The cleaning woman shifted her course to bypass the arena doors and kept walking to the barn parking lot. She had to switch whatever was in her hand to dig out some keys and Enrique growled.

"She has a handgun with a suppressor."

"How can you tell?" Tom leaned forward.

"Run it back and zoom in if you can."

Ethan did as he was asked and enlarged the image as they watched again. The handgun wasn't large, but the barrel extended too far away from the grip to be all one piece.

"There. See it?"

"I'll be damned. And she hid that in her skirt?" Ethan shook his head. "I'm impressed no one saw it."

Enrique nodded. "Can you make a copy of the feeds in front of the doctor's office from 16:23 to 16:35 and the parking lot cam feed from 16:42 until 16:50?"

"Sure, why?" Ethan raised an eyebrow.

"I want to show the computer specialist from my team." Enrique met Tom's gaze. "I think this woman might have something to do with the events at the rodeo this year."

"You think this person might be the shooter?" Tom's eyes widened.

Enrique shook his head. "I won't know until Petty Officer Chin compares the surveillance videos. He's a wiz at this stuff and is great at identifying people."

Tom narrowed his eyes and stared at the frozen images on the screens as he worked through his thoughts. Enrique hoped he wouldn't have to find a way to get the videos without Tom's permission, but he'd get them to Chin come hell or high water.

"All right. Make two copies. I'm pretty sure we'll want to give all the surveillance to the sheriff when he gets here, too." Tom nodded and Enrique let out the breath he hadn't known he'd held.

"Great. Email it to this address." Enrique jotted down the team's general email address where all the teammates had access. "I'm gonna go check on Suzie. She's been in her office dealing with a drunk guest."

"Oh no." Tom scowled. "Who is it?"

"Someone named Cathy. Tried to hit on me and lost

her balance. She sprained her arm and Suzie was going to wrap it when we found the office." Enrique pulled out his phone to see he he'd gotten any messages. No notifications showed up, but he remembered the note. He tugged it out and set it on the desk, taking a picture of it. "This was pinned to a cat's carcass in Suzie's office. You should make sure the sheriff gets it when he arrives."

"Carcass?" Ethan's eyes widened. "There's a fuckin' dead cat in her office?"

Enrique nodded. "Yeah. The vandal wanted to be sure she got the message. From what it says, I'm pretty sure it was meant for me, too."

"Oh yeah?" Tom picked up the baggie with the note inside? "Is that Spanish?"

"Yeah. It says, 'I will trap you like a cat in a box. You cannot get away from me. I will make you pay for my husband's death. I'm coming for you, asshole, you and your bitch.'"

"Fuck." Tom shook his head. "I'll make sure the sheriff gets that, but it does sound like it might be connected to the shooting at the rodeo."

"Good. I'm gonna go check on Suzie."

Enrique ducked out of the security office and trotted down the hall to the clinic, keeping his eyes and ears tuned to any movement. His gut cramped at the thought of Suzie being alone when there was a shooter on the loose. The people at the Triple Star Ranch were supposed to be safe from shit like this. This kind of threat was more his line of work.

"The door to the office stood open, the stench of the dead cat mixed with something else, and Enrique wrinkled his nose.

"Suzie?"

No one answered him and his gut sank. Where the hell was she?

"Suzie?" He raised his voice as he leaned in the

doorway.

"In exam room two. Two doors down from the office." Her voice carried to him and he sighed in relief.

He retreated from the waiting room and moved down the hall, taking note of where the security cameras sat. He wanted to know how the cleaning woman made it to the clinic while avoiding them. He suspected she'd show up on more than the ones they looked at, but knowing where they were helped them pinpoint where she'd been.

He found Suzie and Seychelles in a room with a hospital bed. Cathy lay on the bed dressed in scrubs and an IV attached to her arm. Her other arm lay across her body wrapped in an ACE bandage and swaddled in a sling.

"What the hell happened?" He stopped beside Seychelles.

She grimaced. "Cathy decided she couldn't hold anything back and puked her meal all over the floor of the office. Whoever gets to clean that up will have fun. It ain't gonna be me."

Suzie shook her head. "Me either, frankly. But she was dehydrated so I have her on fluids and got her cleaned up as much as possible. She'll still need a shower when she sobers up." She raised her gaze to him. "How are you doing?"

"Good. Tom called the sheriff and the cops will hopefully be here soon." His phone pinged with an incoming email and he checked the screen. *Good, the surveillance videos.* He'd make sure Tae got a look at them. "We think the person who did this is the same person who took a shot at me in the rodeo."

"What?" Suzie blanched white. "They were – are here at the ranch?"

He nodded. "We think so. We'll have to do some comparison analysis on the two surveillance videos, but given the note stuck to the carcass of the cat, I'd say it's the same person."

"Are you serious?" Seychelles wrapped an arm around Suzie. "What did the note say?"

Before he could choose his answer, his phone rang. "Let me just take this. I'll be right outside the door."

He closed the exam room door and lifted the phone to his ear. "This is Sanchez."

"What the fuck am I looking at here?" Bruiser's voice rumbled across the line.

"That's surveillance video from the Triple Star Ranch. I think the shooter is here. Check the person in the videos against the security vids from the rodeo. Have Chin determine if they're the same person."

"Why do you think they're the same? That's a cleaning lady."

"Yeah, a cleaning lady that none of the staff at the ranch knows." Enrique scanned the hallway and headed back to the open office. "She trashed the doctor's personal office and left a note pinned to the carcass of a mutilated cat under her desk. I'm sending you some pics." He paused long enough to activate the camera on his phone and snapped a couple of shots. "The note read, 'I will trap you like a cat in a box. You cannot get away from me. I will make you pay for my husband's death. I'm coming for you, asshole, you and your bitch,' in Spanish. I'm thinking it's the same person."

"Fuck. It looks like an IED went off in there." Anger threaded Bruiser's voice. "All right, I'll get Chin on it. You got the local LEOs involved?"

"Yeah, the sheriff's been called. I'll clue him into the connection between this and the rodeo shooting." He paused and glanced back down the hall to the exam rooms. "Here's the thing. I've seen this cleaning lady all over the ranch lately. She was never looking at me, but she was always somewhere around when I was out and about. I think she's been reconnoitering for a while."

"Mudfucker. I'll get Chin on this ASAP and relay what

he finds. If the LEOs find anything, get word to us. Let's make this a team effort so we aren't caught with our dicks out. You better watch your six, Sanchez."

"Roger that."

Enrique ended the call and moved back closer to the exam room door. He glanced up at the cameras and grimaced. He'd suggest to the sheriff to look over all the videos from the last month to see when the cleaning lady showed up. That would give them a lead on where she went each day. But his gut said he wouldn't like what they found out.

****

Suzie rolled her head on her neck to loosen up the tight muscles as they waited for Enrique to come back. Cathy had fallen asleep so she went back to her office to look over the mess.

"I wouldn't go in there." Seychelles stood to the side fooling with her phone.

"I'm not. I'm just trying to imagine how the hell I'm gonna clean this all up."

"Well first, you're not going to do it alone. We all can help." Sey tucked her phone away. "Second, you're not going to do it tonight. It's gonna take the cops a while to go through everything anyway, so you probably won't get back in there until tomorrow. That's how it was when some punks broke into my shop and trashed it last year."

Suzie remembered the mess and the time it had taken to get the store set to rights. Seychelles had said the building was cursed so she'd packed up and moved to another place downtown. Fortunately, a building had come up for sale and she bought it, the store space and the two story apartment upstairs. Suzie rubbed her face with her hands.

"I hope it doesn't take that long. I have real patients

who need help."

"I'm sure they'll be quick once they get their forensic team here." Sey glanced at Cathy. "What are you going to do about her?"

"At the moment, just let her rest. She'll sober up here and then her friends can take her home. I'll text Tom and he can find out who she came with."

Suzie turned toward the door when it opened and Tom poked his head in. "Hey Doc. You got a minute? The detective is here and he has some questions."

Suzie shared a look with Seychelles. "Detective? I thought the sheriff was coming."

They followed Tom out into the hall. They met Enrique standing beside another man in a suit with a salmon pink silk tie. He had dark eyes and a neatly trimmed beard that matched the short hair along the sides of his head. Despite his civilian attire, he gave the impression that he saw more than average people.

"Dr. Suzie Appleton, this is Detective Bastian Gutierrez from the Cheyenne PD." Tom waved at the bearded man.

"Welcome, Detective Gutierrez." She shook hands with him. "Is the sheriff coming as well?"

"Sheriff Taylor is an old friend and he's been laid up with a back injury. I happened to be between cases and said I'd help out." He gave her a friendly smile until his gaze switched over her shoulder. "Ms. Abernathy? What are you doing here?"

Seychelles frowned. "Do I know you?"

"Uh, probably not well. I was one of the detectives on your case under Detective Brinker." He gave her a deprecating smile as he held out his hand to shake. "I did help him catch the vandals, though, so there's that."

"Oh, well, thank you very much, Det. Gutierrez." Sey nodded and a small smile curled her lips.

Suzie had never seen her friend quite this taciturn and

she wondered if the young detective might have captured Seychelles' admiration after all.

"Seychelles was with me when we discovered the destruction of my office." Suzie gestured toward the office door. "It's through there."

"Thank you, ma'am." He turned on his heel but not without one last look at Seychelles.

Hmm, maybe the detective isn't only professionally interested in Sey.

Suzie shot a look at Enrique and he cracked a momentary grin before stepping beside her. He didn't touch her but his presence gave her a measure of composure as they strode through the waiting room and faced her decimated office.

"As you can see, someone destroyed everything in the room." Suzie bit her lip, holding her anger at bay.

"Where were you when this happened?" Det. Gutierrez lifted his phone and snapped a few pictures from the door then opened a notetaking app.

"We were all at the wedding. My dad, Trip Colton, got married today." Tom leaned against the wall outside of the office.

"Congratulations to him." Det. Gutierrez nodded. "Do you mind if I just talk to the people who found the room? I want to get your first impressions. Sometimes you don't know you've seen something until I ask."

"Sure. I'll be in the security office when you're ready to see the videos." Tom nodded and headed down the hall to the lobby.

"So who was the first person to enter the room?" Gutierrez turned his sharp gaze on them.

"I was." Suzie raised her hand a little.

"Actually, I was." Enrique placed a hand on her back. "When I saw the mess, I went looking to make sure the other rooms were clear."

The detective nodded. "Why were you all coming here

then? I thought you were at the wedding."

She nodded. "We were, but one of the guests had overindulged and fell during the reception. She was injured so we brought her here for some minor first aid."

"Did she enter the room at all?"

"Only to vomit all over the floor," Seychelles remarked, a grimace twisting her lips. She pointed at the orangish-brown stains on the papers near the door. "That's her stuff there."

"Have you touched anything in here since the break-in?"

"Just the scalpel that pinned the note to the carcass under her chair." Enrique shrugged. "You can have my prints to verify."

"And I straightened some of the papers on my way to my desk. I wanted to find the source of the smell." Suzie pointed to the piles. "They're there. I didn't touch anything else except the windows."

Gutierrez grimaced but nodded. "Did you see anything else while you were walking back to the lodge from the wedding?"

Suzie shook her head. "No. We weren't expecting anyone to be here other than Ethan, our security guy. Everyone should've been either off or at the wedding. And I keep this door locked when I'm not here. There are too many valuable things inside."

"Are you sure this wasn't an addict looking for a fix?"

Suzie frowned. "I can't be sure until y'all do some cleanup and we catalog what's missing, but most addicts wouldn't do this kind of damage. They'd go straight to the drug cabinets and break those. And none of them would bother leaving the carcass of a mutilated cat rotting under my chair."

Gutierrez snorted. "I've seen addicts do some pretty insane stuff when looking for a fix, but yeah, that seems like extra effort for no return." He made some notes. "Do you have any idea who would want to do something like this? Have you had any problems with patients or staff members?"

Suzie shook her head. "Not that I'm aware of. I haven't heard any complaints from anyone, including the administration of the ranch."

"I might have an idea who it is." Enrique spoke up and the detective's gaze swung to him.

"Why do you say that, Petty Officer?"

"Because the whole reason I'm here at the ranch is to recover from an injury caused by the collapse of my parachute during the rodeo." His jaw bunched as he gritted his teeth. "Your department should have the security videos from the rodeo that day. We think we've identified the shooter on them, but I want you to compare the videos to see if they match the person on the security videos here."

"You think the person who did this was the same person who shot your parachute?" Gutierrez's gaze sharpened. "Why do you believe that?"

"Because of this." He held up his phone with the picture of the note in the plastic baggie and handed it to the detective. "This was pinned to the dead cat in Dr. Appleton's office."

Gutierrez took the phone and studied the image. "How do you know it was meant for you?"

"The part about getting away from them – I survived and came here for therapy. And I've seen this cleaning lady everywhere on the ranch, like she's been following me. She'd have access to the offices through master keys. She could've easily done this." Enrique nodded to the image. "Check the security videos."

"All right, I'll have a look at those videos." Gutierrez fixed his gaze on Suzie as he handed Enrique's phone back. "I'll have the forensics team get your prints to eliminate them from those we find in your office."

Suzie nodded. "Mine should be everywhere, including

on the scalpel that was used to pin the note to the carcass."

"Do you have that?"

She shook her head. "No, I left it on the desk in the office when Petty Officer Sanchez removed the note."

Gutierrez grimaced. "Should've left it there, Petty Officer."

Enrique shrugged. "Seemed important to take it to Mr. Colton, but I put it in the baggie first thing."

"That's something at least. Okay, thank you for your time, Dr. Appleton. You and Ms. Abernathy are welcome to go back to the wedding." He gave Seychelles a warm smile. "If you can think of anything else, here's my card. I'll give you a call if I have any more questions."

Suzie took the card and nodded. "Not likely. I have to take care of that patient who vomited in my office. When you're done with Tom Colton, will you please send him to the clinic so I can find her ride?"

"Will do. Petty Officer, please come with me. I want to review the videos with what you know." Gutierrez retreated out of the waiting room but stopped at the door and waited for Enrique to follow him.

"Will you be okay?" Enrique laid a hand on her upper arm, squeezing gently.

"Yeah, I'll be fine, Petty Officer. I'll see you later."

"I still hope to have that dance you promised me, Doc." He flashed her a smile. "See you after." Then he was gone with the detective.

"Come on, let's go check on the Vominator." Seychelles turned to head back to the exam room, but Suzie caught her arm.

"You gonna fill me in on the cute detective givin' you the onceover?"

To her surprise, a blush colored Seychelles's cheeks. "What are you talking about?"

"Oh, come on. He was definitely checking you out. You didn't tell me he'd been looking into your case back in the day."

Sey shrugged. "I didn't pay attention then. There were several detectives on the case because of all the businesses the vandals had hit. Turns out it was an attempt to misdirect the cops away from the one being a front for meth distribution. They "vandalized" it to make it look another victim." She paused at the exam room door. "I didn't notice him then, but I sure as hell notice him now."

Suzie nodded. "He definitely notices you. Too bad he has to work during the reception. Maybe you could ask him for a dance." She winked and pushed open the exam door as Seychelles stood in the waiting room with a stunned look on her face.

CHAPTER FIFTEEN

Enrique shoved his cover on his head and ducked out into the summer evening. The clouds had rolled in and a cold wind blew out of the north. The discussion with the detective and Tom had lasted longer than he'd expected. *But what do you expect from a briefing?* They'd compared the security vids of the ranch and the rodeo, and Gutierrez agreed they could be the same person.

They'd watched the security videos for the better part of two hours, trying to find when this particular cleaning lady had shown up and where she'd gone on the ranch. She spent most of her time in the Bunkhouse cleaning rooms, but there were a few views of her in the lodge. It appeared she had a rental car parked near the barn, but they only had a blurry, partial plate. It would take time to track down.

About half way through, Seychelles had come in to ask Tom if he knew with whom Cathy had come to the wedding and he'd left with her to find Clair Knight, Ransom's sister. Gutierrez had tried to mask his interest in Seychelles, but Enrique caught the avid attention as the woman walked out. *Yeah, buddy, you got it bad.* Not that he was in any position to judge. He'd fallen hard for Suzie.

The forensics team Gutierrez called in went over the

office meticulously and piled the papers along the cabinets after dusting, photographing, and cataloguing each one. The place remained a mess, but at least the confidential information had been set aside. Suzie had come in to watch for a short time, but when they bagged the carcass and released her laptop, she checked that the files hadn't been accessed. No one appeared to have gotten to the data.

Enrique and Tom helped organize the stable hands to tidy the office while Suzie dealt with Clair Knight and Cathy. Clair apologized profusely about Cathy's actions and took her home, promising to make sure she drank plenty of water. Enrique hadn't been sorry to see them leave.

Suzie had gone home to her bungalow after saying goodnight to Seychelles. The other woman had walked Gutierrez out to his car before returning to the arena to help Mrs. Guthrie with the wedding cleanup. Enrique had finished up with Suzie's office and spent a few minutes talking to his team about what he learned. There wasn't much and they'd have to wait for the investigation, but Chin was already working his magic on the videos.

Taking a deep breath, Enrique released all the tension from his body. He wanted a beer, some quiet moments with his woman, and maybe some food. His stomach growled like he'd been on a ten day training op with a ninety pound pack rather than just at a wedding. *I'm getting soft.* He snorted. Bruiser would take care of that when he got back to the team.

Getting back to the team.

For the first time ever, he had mixed feelings about that. While he loved his job, he wanted to stay close to Suzie. That made him return to thoughts of what he'd do after he retired from the Navy. Anything he chose to do would have to be near Suzie.

He paused on the front step of her bungalow, letting the thought sink into him. Was he seriously considering making Suzie a priority? The future was always uncertain and he didn't have a way to see beyond the now, but his heart and his gut agreed. Suzie was everything he wanted in a woman and he'd do his damnedest to stay with her.

He knocked on the door and waited with a smile on his face, ready to spend the evening with the woman who held his heart. But the moment she opened the door with a look of exhaustion and a wan smile, he shifted his plans to take care of her.

"Hey, Enrique. Come on in." She stepped back to allow him inside and he pulled off his cover as he stepped under the lintel.

"Hey, what's going on, Suzie?" He set his cover down and reached for her, grasping her arms gently. "Are you all right?"

"I'm fine, just tired. Between Cathy and the break-in, I just hit a wall." She shook her head as her shoulders drooped.

"Let's sit down on the couch, crack open a couple of beers, and relax a little. Do you have any cheese and crackers here still?" He guided her into the kitchenette.

"Yeah, I think so. Some summer sausage as well, why?"

"I'm hungry enough to raid Mrs. Guthrie's fridge."

He winked and she laughed as she opened her own fridge. "We can't have that. Here's the beer and the cheese, and maybe I'll cut up some tomatoes and avocados."

"I'll help."

She raised her eyebrows. "You like to cook?"

"When I have the time. Mostly I would just help my *mamá* and *abuela* put together the meals when I was on leave." He took the cheese and worked on creating a small pile on the plate.

Suzie smiled as they worked in a companionable silence and he realized he wanted more times like this. They didn't have to talk, just share the space together. Of course, given his druthers, he'd rather be naked in bed with her, smelling her hair and licking her soft skin, but preparing meals was fun, too.

They brought the food to her little table and settled into the chairs, Suzie letting out a long sigh as she sat down. He popped the caps off the beer bottles and handed one to her before sitting in the chair opposite.

"Thanks." She nodded as she took a swig. "It's been a helluva day." She leaned forward on her elbows, resting the bottle on the table.

"Yeah, I bet. And it didn't help that Cathy puked on the mess already in the office." He snorted. "I'm kinda glad I wasn't there for that."

"It wasn't the first time for me and I'm sure it won't be the last." She shook her head. "Drunk people are a dime a dozen in a doctor's life."

"I'm sure, but let's focus on better things, like eating and possibly a dance."

"A dance?" She raised her eyebrows.

"Yeah, I promised I'd dance with you. Don't you remember?" He winked as she rolled her eyes.

"Yeah, I remember, but there's no music."

He pulled out his phone. "That's easily remedied. But eating is more important, then we'll dance."

She nodded, but made no move to make herself some food. So he put cheese and tomatoes on crackers and set them on her plate for her to prepare as she saw fit. He did the same for himself until the two plates sat full of little appetizer sandwiches.

"Suzie, you need to eat something. Come on." He held up a cracker with cheese, tomato, and avocado. "It'll be okay. Detective Gutierrez is capable. I watched him pretty closely while he went through everything. He's thorough and meticulous. He'll track down who did this."

"You think you know who did this. And she was here on the ranch." Suzie hugged herself and shivered. "It gives me chills that anyone would come here to do harm. It's a place of healing."

"Hey, come here." Enrique rose and took her hand. "Let's sit on your couch and eat there."

She didn't protest as he pulled her up and led her to the couch. She settled into one side of it as he went back for the food. He didn't like her reticence or her withdrawal. He made it his mission for the evening to make her smile again. *And a SEAL never gives up.*

He settled beside her and drew her against his side, gently running his hand along her arm.

"You know what I liked most about the wedding today?"

She tilted her head to look at him in surprise. "What?"

"The love shown by everyone who was there. Trip toward Henry, Henry toward Trip, the family and friends toward them both. You could see they cared a lot. Like a family that keeps getting bigger." Enrique smiled as he handed Suzie more food. "Family is important, but it's their support and love that make it all worthwhile. I see that here in the staff and owners of the ranch. You all care about each other. The world isn't like that, but that's the way it is here."

She shrugged. "We've all been through a lot. Trip hires not only professionals, but those who understand the struggles the clients have ahead of them. I'm just the medical doc, looking after their bodies, but their mental state often shows in the pathologies they suffer from, and understanding both helps them get better."

"You're a rare doctor to see that."

She scoffed. "There are a lot of doctors who see that."

"Not in my experience. Most of the ones in the military want to throw a pill at it to fix the problem. They don't have time to take a holistic approach." He shrugged. "Even at the VA they are more interested in moving us through than finding out what's really wrong. You're different and that makes you special. It make the whole ranch special."

She shot him a smile over her beer. "You're just saying that because you're sleeping with me."

Enrique laughed. "No, but that's a nice bonus." He ate a few crackers before growing more serious. "You are special, Suzie, and not just because I'm sleeping with you. Or maybe it's that I'm sleeping with you because you're so special. You make my days here easier to endure the pain and therapy. I have you to look forward to at the end of the day."

"What about your team? Don't they make your days full of excitement and that insane joy that makes you jump out of planes?" The snark in her voice showed in her smirk, but he took her question seriously.

"Yeah, they do and I like working with them. But we all need a place to land in the end, and you're my clear LZ." He took out his phone and selected the music app before laying on the table.

A soft mariachi ballad floated out of the little speaker, filling the room with gentle guitar chords. He loved this piece. It was the one his father used to sing to his mother. It always made Enrique think of silly things like soft summer nights, skies full of stars, and breezes ruffling palm fronds. He rose and held his hand out to Suzie.

"Come dance with me."

She took his hand and he pulled her against his chest, wrapping his free hand around the small of her back.

"You're beautiful, Suzie, and the person I most want to come back to when my tour is done." He met her gaze, putting all the sincerity he could find into his eyes.

"Back to Cheyenne, this little town that claims to be a city?" She raised her eyebrows. "It's not like the big cities of the world."

"I've lived in the big cities of the world. They have their features, but they don't have you. And you're what I want." He leaned down to kiss her lips in a soft promise.

"*Eres mi corazón.*"

"What does that mean?"

"You're my heart, *querida.*" He rested his forehead against hers and moved them to the music. He wanted her to know how much she meant to him but all he could do was show her. The silken words of the ballad echoed his feelings and he blended his voice with the song, singing the emotions he couldn't speak.

Suzie relaxed into his chest and moved with him, the tension and shock leaving her body. He wrapped his arms around her, giving her the strength he had for the moment. She was so strong and dealt with so much, but this was one thing he could do for her. He could take her woes and buffer her from the fear, if only for a short time.

At the end of the song, Suzie sighed and dropped her head against his chest. "I'm so tired."

"Let me put you to bed, *querida.*" He took her hand and led her to the bedroom, concerned with the exhaustion he saw in her face.

They didn't speak has he helped her undress, starting with her shoes. He caressed her feet before he stood and helped her out of her sexy sundress, enjoying her mostly naked form. He skimmed her arms and sides, unable to keep from touching her soft skin. He laid kisses on her shoulders, trying to give her pleasant relaxation rather than exhaustion.

He led her to the bed and lifted the covers for her to climb in. She raised her eyebrows as she settled, a smile crease between them showing her confusion.

"Aren't you coming to bed?"

"I'll be there in a moment. I'm gonna put the food away and turn off the lights."

"Okay." She closed her eyes and snuggled into the blankets with a soft sigh.

"*Te amo mucho,* Suzie." *I love you very much.*

She didn't react to his words, which eased his heartrate

a little. He half wanted her to hear them and swallowed against the fear of saying them aloud. What if she didn't feel truly the same? He shook his head at the unusual emotion and headed back out to the living room.

He took his time cleaning up the dinner bits and shutting down the bungalow. He checked all the doors and windows to make sure they were secure as his mind went over the intel he and the detective discussed. It was too early for answers, but he had a feeling there was much more going on than a trigger-happy malcontent.

Whoever she is, I'll protect this ranch and Suzie as much as I'm able.

Except he'd be leaving in two weeks. *We'll just have to find the shooter before then.* Not that he believed Tom and the detective couldn't handle themselves. But he didn't like the idea of leaving Suzie without his help.

He undressed and laid his uniform out carefully before crawling into bed with Suzie. She'd been sleeping soundly, but when he wrapped his arms around her, she sighed and more fully relaxed against them. He buried his nose in her hair and cupped one breast with his hand.

"You're safe, Suzie. I got you."

She snuggled closer, her ass pressed against his groin, and the world settled into pleasure and comfort for him. This was the woman he wanted to come home to. This was the woman he'd fight for.

CHAPTER SIXTEEN

Suzie sat down at her desk and ran her hands over her face. She didn't understand why she was so tired. Ever since the wedding and the break-in, things had been going well for her. She'd saved all the data on her laptop, her office had been deep cleaned, and she'd spent all her free time with Enrique. He'd been everything she wanted in a man: smart, funny, handsome, strong, fit, and attentive. They'd talked about their dreams and plans for the future, and she'd hinted at a family with him. Just the thought of him made her pussy cream and a smile curl her lips.

But the lack of progress on the mysterious cleaning woman who'd broken into her office weighed on her. Enrique told her Detective Gutierrez had contacted a colleague in the FBI to take a look at all the security footage from the rodeo and the ranch, and Agent Rick Sandoval had recognized a tattoo on the woman's neck above the uniform. It was the mark from the Casa de Catequil Cartel for their sex slave trade. They didn't have the identity of the woman and she hadn't been seen on the ranch since, but security had been increased and everyone had remained vigilant.

And yet I still feel like there's a threat out there.

Maybe it was because Enrique would be leaving in the next few days. Part of her knew it was time and he'd be able to email and call her when not performing or training, but another part felt his coming loss like a physical blow. She didn't want him to leave. She felt safer with him around even if he worked elsewhere on the ranch.

You're being silly.

Intellectually, she knew that. He'd only been here for therapy and recovery, then he'd return to his team and whatever other events awaiting him. She'd told Seychelles she thought he was the one to complete her dream of supportive lover and husband, father to her children, and the stupid white picket fence. Okay, she didn't need the fence, but she wanted Enrique for the rest, even if his job took him all over the U.S. and was scary dangerous.

It didn't help that Dr. Lyttle had been sending her frequent emails, inquiring about Enrique's progress and how she was doing. Why he'd suddenly gotten more electronically chatty she didn't know. She'd always been cordial with him, but never over email.

She checked her account again to find another email from him. She sighed, tempted to just throw it into the trash without looking at it, but something made her click it open. She skimmed the pleasantries and the fawning friendliness that made her skin crawl. He'd always been pushy when it came to their interactions, but she'd written it off as the way he was and reminded herself she didn't have to like everyone.

But when she got to the part where he asked if she'd seen the email he sent about Petty Officer Sanchez's medical history, she stopped and frowned. *What email about his history?* Why the hell would he be sharing that information? While she monitored Enrique's recovery on the periphery, that was private information between him and his primary care doctor.

She almost typed a response to Lyttle asking him what

he was talking about, but decided to check her deleted messages first. There were several she hadn't opened, but the first one came the night before the wedding and she'd completely forgotten to read it with all the problems with Cathy and the break-in.

Taking a deep breath, she opened the email and skimmed the smarmy greeting and pleasantries. *Damn, could this man every just get to the point?* But what she read after made her blood go cold and her gut cramp.

"Through analysis of Petty Officer Enrique Luis Sanchez's health records, I've found his sperm counts to be low and this sterility to be caused from actions in the field. Not to worry, though, as I ascertained the rest of his body is in perfect health and it's my opinion he should be able to return to his team at the end of this two week period."

The rest of the email went on to convey Lyttle's approval for medical release and more intrusive pleasantries. Suzie immediately closed the email program and sat back in her chair, fear, anger, and unease snaking through her with jagged spikes of pain.

She stared at the wall, her mind turning things over and over. Enrique was sterile? *When the hell was he going to tell me that?* How the hell would she be able to have a long term relationship with someone who couldn't tell her the most basic information about themselves? Her disappointment built until anger filled her gut and she couldn't sit still any longer. She rose to walk around her desk when the door to the office opened and Enrique stepped in.

"Good evening, *querida*. How are you?"

"Close the door please, Enrique." Her voice sounded cold and she tried to mellow it, but anger made it difficult.

He frowned as he did as she ask. "What's going on, Suzie?"

She gritted her teeth and took a deep breath to quell the anger. "When were you going to tell me?"

He raised his eyebrows. "Tell you what?"

"Tell me you're sterile. Don't you think that's something I should know?"

"Wait, slow down. Who told you I'm sterile?" He frowned deeper, putting his hands up palms down.

"Dr. Lyttle. He sent it in an email two weeks ago. When were you planning to tell me?" She glared at him, frustration pounding at her head.

"I don't know. It wasn't something I thought much about because it didn't change my service to the Navy. Why does it matter?"

"Why does it matter? It matters because now I can't be with you." She turned away, choking back tears.

"Whoa, wait. What do you mean you can't be with me?" He strode closer and grasped her shoulders gently. "What's going on, Suzie?"

She stepped out of his arms. "I can't be with a man who hides things from me."

"I'm a Navy SEAL, Suzie. I hide a lot of things from everyone. It's the nature of my profession." He gave her a dry look that only ignited her fury.

"Not the important things. Not about the possibility of family. Or lack thereof." She threw her hands out. "I need to be with someone who's honest with me."

"I've always been honest with you, Suzie. I've never hidden anything about me from you." He shook his head with a scowl. "And why the hell would Dr. Lyttle tell you about my sterility? That's my business."

"If you're going to be with me, it's my business too."

He held up a hand. "That's not what I meant. I meant it's my business to tell you. And I would've if you'd told me how important it was to you."

"Oh, you were waiting for the right time?" She snarled and crossed her arms over her chest in an effort to tone down her anger. "You know how important family is to me."

"Whoa, calm down. Of course I know how important it is to you." He held up both hands in a placating gesture. "I would've told you when our relationship had gotten deeper. But you never mentioned to me this overwhelming need for a baby. That's what this is, right?"

"No, it's not just a need for a baby. It's my need for a man to be honest with me and to tell me he's sterile first thing. So I can make the decision to waste time on him."

Enrique paused, his brows lowering. "To *waste* time on me? This has been a waste of time for you? All because I can't get you pregnant?" He raised his chin. "Sweetheart, it never messed up my ability to serve in the Navy, which was my goal until I met you, and it definitely never screwed up my ability to give my lovers pleasure. I certainly didn't hear you complaining."

The derision in his voice cut her, but she raised her own chin and stared at him with chilly disdain.

"Lovers, you say? I don't have time to be with someone who engages in such risky behavior." She straightened her back and clenched her fists at her sides. "That's a deal-breaker for me. I need someone who can be honest and true, who can put their loved ones ahead of themselves."

"That's all I do, Suzie!" He slammed his hands down on her desk. "That's all I ever do. I put my family, my friends, hell even my country first. That's my job. I'd have given you everything you wanted; love, friendship, back up. I was in this for the long haul."

"I need family, children, everything."

He stood up, his expression cold and remote. "I can't give you that."

"Then we're done."

The harshness of the words stabbed her own heart as anger crystallized in Enrique's eyes. He nodded sharply. "Roger that, Dr. Appleton. I'll pack my gear and I'll be out of here tonight. Please make sure to sign off on the release papers so my CO can reinstate my active status."

His cold formality shredded her heart like glass shards but she met his ice with her own.

"Of course, Petty Officer. Please drive safely."

He turned on his heel and left her office without a word or a look back, a stiffness in his back she'd never seen before. Tears threatened but she held them back as the door slammed. She had work to do and paperwork to finish.

But as she sat down at her desk and opened her computer, her anger overrode her need to work and she opened the email program. What the fuck was wrong with Dr. Lyttle that he'd betray Enrique's trust this way and share privileged information with someone else?

She immediately typed up a scathing reply to him, reminding him that his actions were highly inappropriate and she'd report him for it. She clicked send and tried to move on to the other things awaiting her, but with her anger spent, only sorrow remained. She rose to try to outrun the ache in her chest, but once it started, there was no stopping.

Tears cascaded down Suzie's cheeks as she realized Enrique had walked away and never once looked back. She looked out the window toward the parking area and saw him throw his things into the back of his rental car before climbing inside. He spun his wheels in reverse then shot away up the driveway. His taillights trailed into the darkness, disappearing quickly over the hill toward the freeway, and she was left with her distorted image in the window. The glass was old enough to have held her grandmother's reflection, and made her appear like a distraught ghost, her face contorted with black holes of misery.

Then it would be completely accurate.

She thought she'd made her peace with his profession, but she couldn't deal with hidden truths or lies. Not when it pertained to a dream she'd held close to her heart for ages. *And SEALs are full of them.* She thought she'd finally found a man to love with all her heart and they'd make a family. But Enrique's sterility crushed that hope and she'd been so angry at his lack of honesty. How could she be with a man who wouldn't be honest with her about something so important to her heart?

Suzie pressed her head against the glass, wishing it was cold enough to distract her from her heartache. If she could just go back to before she knew any of his medical history, maybe she could be happy with Enrique. But not even a Time Lord could unfold the origami of this mess to make it right. And now he was gone for good and she was alone.

****

Enrique slammed the door of his rental hard enough to rattle the windows and peeled out of the yard for the Triple Star Ranch. Fury and hurt radiated from his core, pouring out of him in the expletives of two languages and salty tears. He didn't cry often, but Suzie's accusation of dishonesty dug into his heart like a rusty knife. He might not be a Marine, but he lived by *Semper Fidelis*—always faithful to his team, his loved ones, and his country.

Especially his loved ones.

Aww glory, Suzie.

He'd never mentioned the condition that had afflicted him after he served in the Gulf. No one liked to talk about the shit they'd used over there, but anyone on the ground could've been affected. He'd become sterile, but it hadn't affected his active service in the SEALs. He hadn't mentioned it because it hadn't been relevant to his life in the Leap Frogs or with her. And hell, if it didn't matter to the U.S. Military, why should it matter to anyone else?

Today had been the moment he'd been planning to ask her to be his for all time. He'd talked to Bruiser and Seychelles and even found the perfect ring for his *querida*.

He'd been excited to see her right up to the moment she'd snarled at him and accused him of hiding things. *What the actual fuck?* He'd never deliberately hidden any non-classified information from her. But she'd told him it was a deal-breaker and that they were over.

The little ring box in his jeans pocket mocked him with its solidity as he headed back to Cheyenne to join the team at the hotel. He'd been all set to ask her to marry him, his sexy cowgirl doc, but then she brought up his medical history and accused him of risky behavior.

I'm a fuckin' SEAL. My whole damn life is risky behavior.

He scowled at the road through his damn tears. Why the hell did Lyttle tell her his medical history? She might be a doc, but she wasn't his doctor, and that was privileged information.

The smug expression on Dr. Lyttle's face when he left the VA filled Enrique's mind. What the fuck was his problem? They'd kept their relationship ethical. She wasn't his doc and he wasn't her direct patient. They were consenting adults and weren't cheating on anyone. Why would Lyttle feel the need to share that with Suzie? Just to sabotage their relationship?

"*Hijo de puta!*" He roared the words at the road in front of him, but the blacktop just continued into the darkness without break.

Dr. Lyttle had revealed patient details to Suzie without Enrique's permission. That was a breach in trust and doctor-patient confidentiality. *He'll probably say he was sharing between colleagues.* But the breach had ruined Enrique's chances with Suzie, all because of one little detail.

He hadn't thought it so important, but she'd looked at him with betrayal and distrust. All of his hopes and dreams, the life he'd wanted together, went up in smoke from that one omission. Everything gone, and he was on his way back to the team and an empty hotel bed, with a broken heart.

Call me crazy, but I'd rather be shot at. Oh, wait, he had been. That's how he'd met Suzie in the first place. And none of it mattered for shit. He slammed his hands on the steering wheel, but it didn't stop the pain spiraling out from the hole in his heart.

****

Consuela scowled at the retreating taillights. *Hijo de puta!* What was wrong with these people? Why couldn't they make things simple? She'd managed to get around the extra security and the cameras to get close to the bitch doctor and the *pendejo* she was fucking, but something must have happened because the weak military man ran to his room in the patient residence and cleared out his things.

She hadn't been able to shift gears fast enough and he'd been out to his car and down the road before she could even get to hers. She'd been hampered by that damn *policía* detective who'd been hanging around the ranch and all the new security guards they'd hired. In Peru, her husband had no problem taking out guards and police, but here in *Los Estados Unidos*, it was much harder remove such obstacles.

Swearing up a storm, Consuela walked to her new rental car like someone finishing a delivery. She'd been bringing flowers to hide the small handgun, but her plan was ruined and she'd have to find the fucking *pendejo* in Cheyenne or wherever he was going.

Sliding behind the wheel, her phone beeped with a message. She glanced at it, but didn't recognize the number at first. She ignored it and started her car, backing out of her spot slowly, and leisurely following the road back up to the highway. She hoped she'd be able to spot her target while driving, but it was dark and he was too far ahead.

She rattled the windows with all the swear words she'd

heard her husband use and tears of frustration slid down her cheeks. She'd hole up in the abandoned factory on the southwest side of Cheyenne and plan her next attack. The *cabrón estupido* would die. She'd see to it.

Her phone lit up with another text, but she didn't have time to look. She'd read them when she arrived at her little hideout and she'd find a way to take that U.S. Navy man down.

CHAPTER SEVENTEEN

Suzie sat on the front porch of her bungalow and watched the sunrise. She hadn't slept well despite going to bed early, and she'd finally given up on sleep at around five. The bank of low clouds predicted it would be a dark, cool, and rainy Wyoming autumn day, and it suited her mood completely. She held her favorite travel mug full of coffee between her hands, but it tasted like sawdust as thunder rolled in the distance.

Enrique was gone.

That's because you sent him away.

Her beautiful, sexy, attentive Latino SEAL lover had driven away after she confronted him about his medical history, a history he hadn't told her. She'd accused him of dishonesty, and he'd walked away.

Actually, stomped away would be more accurate.

All because of a rumor she'd heard from Dr. Lyttle about Enrique's risky health history and infertility. He hadn't denied it, just wanted to know who'd told her.

She shouldn't have been incensed at the question. Logically she knew that was private information and while she was a doctor, she wasn't his. But his demand had only confirmed her fears, and she'd told him they were over.

Correction: that you couldn't be with him.

Her heart had broken at the cold anger on his face, and her inner voice had screamed at her to take it back, to let his explanation stand.

And did you follow it? No, and now he's gone.

She gritted her teeth against the sorrow. She'd let her chance at love drive away all because he was shooting blanks. *And that's the dumbest reason to send someone away.*

Her phone rang, the cheery sound letting her know her best friend Seychelles was calling for an update on her hot date the night before. Suzie debated letting it go to voicemail but decided it wouldn't deter her best friend. Sighing, she picked up the phone and tapped "answer."

"Hello."

"Hey, Suzie. Can you walk this morning?"

She closed her eyes and fought tears. "Yes."

A short silence sounded on the other end of the phone. "Uh oh. What happened? Isn't Enrique there with you?"

"No. He drove back into Cheyenne last night." She cast her gaze south, wishing she'd gone with him.

Sey gasped. "Oh, honey. What the hell happened?"

"I was stupid and selfish and scared."

She snorted. "Those are all shitty S-words. Tell me how you could think you're all those things, 'cause that hasn't been my experience in the years I've known you."

"I accused Enrique of hiding the truth about his medical history from me."

"Whoa whoa whoa. What now? What are you talking about?"

Suzie relayed the story of the confrontation in her office the night before and how it had ended with her telling Enrique she couldn't be with him.

"Jeez, Suzie, all this over a little medical detail? Even I haven't told you my medical history. Why the hell would it matter?"

"Because he's sterile." The word came out in a wail, the tears finally bursting the dam of her resistance. "He can't give me babies."

"Oh, Suzie." Sympathy oozed over the phone line. "I'm so sorry. I know you want to have the husband, the kids, and fucking white picket fence, but doesn't that seem like small potatoes, darlin'? Certainly not big enough for you to toss away the heart of a good man like Enrique. There are other ways you can have kids."

"But they won't be his. Because his risky behavior caused his sterility, and he didn't tell me."

Seychelles laughed. "Honey, he's a Navy SEAL. His whole life and profession are risky behavior." She sighed. "Who told you about his sterility if you didn't hear it from him?"

Suzie brushed the tears away as she cleared her throat. "Edward Lyttle."

"Dr. Lyttle who works at the VA hospital?" Seychelles growled. "What the fuck are you listening to that pissant for? That guy's had the hots for you the moment you showed up there for the free clinics during CFD. He'd sabotage any man interested in going out with you. Hell, I know he has."

"What?" Suzie sniffed hard as surprise hit her between the eyes. "What are you talking about?"

"You don't know?" Seychelles growled and she could picture her shaking her head. "Oh my glory, Suzie. Edward Lyttle has been panting after you like a bitch in heat for years now. I've heard him talking smack about you to warn other guys off. He says you're driven. A ballbuster. A bitch. Married to your work. You know the drill. But Enrique's the first guy who ignored all that, didn't seem to care, and went after you anyway."

"Wait. How long has Lyttle been saying stuff like that?" Anger surged at the new betrayal.

Seychelles sighed. "Years. Every time a man showed

any interest in you. Hell, I once overheard some of the nurses say you were already his woman."

"The fuck?" Suzie damn near threw her travel mug into the grass beyond her little porch. Anger and remorse surged in her chest. "Oh my glory, I'm such a dumbass. I pushed Enrique away because of some obsessive asshole."

"Look, I know havin' kids is important to you, and you really wanted them to be Enrique's genetic code."

"I love it when you talk medical to me."

Seychelles laughed. "Shut up and listen. You're a healthy woman and have enough money to look into other ways of getting kids, whether you carry them yourself or adopt. But it's so much easier to deal with kids if you have a good partner. And honey, I've never seen a better partner for you than Petty Officer Enrique Sanchez. The man is sexy, smart, patient, driven, and strong in more ways than just his body. You can't let him walk away. You have to have faith in the man he is, not his past. And certainly not what Dr. Dickhead tells you."

Suzie barked a watery laugh then sniffed. "Sweet glory, Seychelles. Enrique was so angry last night. How will I fix this? I don't even know if he's still in Cheyenne."

"First of all, you gotta stop sniveling and call him. Even if he doesn't answer, you call and leave a message. Then you text him with a request to meet."

"Meet? After the shit I pulled?"

"Gotta start somewhere. See what he says and go from there. Slow and steady wins the race, darlin'."

"I look and feel like a waterfall raging out of control. I was such a bitch to him, Sey."

"Do you love him, Suzie?"

She let her eyes unfocus as she stared out at the sun gilding the fields around the ranch. The answer the Sey's question was easy. She'd loved Enrique pretty much from the moment they shared coffee in Cheyenne. He represented the very best of the men she'd ever met, despite his military and medical history. *And I want to be with him no matter what.*

"Yes, with all my heart."

"Well, then, you got your answer. Call him. Text him. Chase his ass to the ends of the earth if you have to. Slow and steady, relentless. He needs to know you won't ever give up on him."

Suzie coughed another laugh. "When did you get so wise, Sey?"

"Are you kidding? I can see problems in other people a hundred miles away. But in my own life?" She hissed a cuss word. "The problems I have with men are incomprehensible."

"I promise to help you should the need arise. Like with Detective Gutierrez."

Seychelles snorted. "I might hold you to that. But in the meantime, get off the damn phone and call your man. He needs to hear from you right now."

"All right, all right. I'm going. Bye, Sey. I love you."

"I know you do. Now call him." Seychelles hung up before Suzie could say more.

****

Enrique felt his phone buzzing against his ass and ignored it as he finished stowing his gear in his go-bag. The other guys had been surprised to see him last night, but they helped him get hammered on damn good whiskey. *Gotta say one thing for the Wyoming cowboys. They don't drink rot-gut.* He preferred Tequila, the gold label, but the stuff they drank worked well enough.

Except it didn't kill the heartache.

He closed his eyes and braced his arms on the counter where he'd set his bag, bowing his head. When the fuck would the pain go away? He hadn't known Suzie that long, just over two months, but she'd won his heart along with

SIOBHAN MUIR

his attraction pretty much from day one.

His phone buzzed again and he swore. Who the fuck was messaging him?

He yanked it out with a growl and swiped the front surface...and damn near dropped it. *What the hell?* Suzie had called twice and left a voicemail. *What, is she gonna tell me my genetic code isn't up to her standards?* He almost deleted it without listening, but he couldn't quite deny the siren's call of her voice. He ignored the shaking in his hand as he lifted the phone to his ear.

"Hey, Enrique, I know you're furious with me, but I wanted to say I'm sorry and I was so wrong. I listened to the wrong people and got hung up on my own bullshit. I'm not asking for forgiveness, I'm asking you to wait for me so we can talk. I'm driving to Cheyenne right now and I should be there in about ten minutes. Please give me a chance to apologize in person. Will you meet me at our coffee shop downtown? I don't know when you're planning to leave. Tonight, tomorrow, whenever, but I need to see you before you go. Give me the chance?"

Her message cut off at the end of a prescribed recording time and he stared at the phone. It buzzed with an incoming text from her and he pushed it away. Could he give her a chance? Did he want to see her again after the hurtful things she'd said?

Do you want to lose out on the best person in your life over your ego?

The question burned in the back of his mind as the phone chirped again. *Damn, the woman just doesn't give up.*

"What the hell's wrong with you, Sanchez?" Bruiser scowled at him as he shoved his duffle into the luggage cart. "What's up with the sourpuss face?"

"Nothin'." Enrique shook his head and turned his back on his friend. "I have a hangover thanks to you assholes. I'll get my gear."

"Fuck that. The only time you've worn that expression was when some of the rigging was wrong on one of the chutes, not when you're hungover. What the fuck's going on?" Bruiser crossed his beefy arms over his massive chest and scowled deeper.

"It's nothin'."

"Don't give me that horseshit. I've smelled enough of it while here in Wyoming for the rodeo." Bruiser shook his head. "Does this have to do with the doc?"

Enrique tightened his fist around his duffle's handles to keep from throwing a punch. Anything to move the hurt from his heart to somewhere else. A broken hand was easier to deal with than a broken heart.

He shook his head. "She told me we were done last night. You remember getting me drunk, right?"

"Yeah, but since she's blowin' up your phone apologizin', I thought you'd be smart enough to snatch your second chance with her." Bruiser held up the little electronic traitor and raised an eyebrow.

Enrique snatched at it, but Bruiser held it out of reach. "Give me that. I'll respond when I'm ready."

"And when will that be? When hell freezes over?" Bruiser shook his head, still holding the phone. "Don't fuck this up if you don't have to, Sanchez. She messed up and from what I can see, she wants to apologize for it. I shouldn't have to remind you how hard it is for SEALs to find women who put up with their "don't ask don't tell" shit. My wife left me long before the Leap Frogs. You got a chance with the doc. Grab it with both hands and don't let go."

He extended the phone back to Enrique with a solemn look.

Enrique curled his hand around the little plastic rectangle and it vibrated in his palm with another incoming text. Could he take a chance that everything would work out like the happily-ever-afters in the books his sisters talked about?

Oh sure, sparkling swirls will erupt around us like a geyser of magic. He snorted. *This is not an anime with talking animals who sing catchy ditties.*

No, it was real, fuckin' life and a real woman was trying to make a real apology and he'd be a real asshole if he didn't at least hear her out. Besides, the only easy day was yesterday. Facing an emotional and apologetic woman should be easier than facing insurgents with automatic weapons bent on killing him.

"Yeah, roger that. I guess I'll go meet with her."

"About time you pulled your head out of your ass. Leave the gear. I'll make sure it gets stowed." Bruiser waved at him to leave. "Go talk to the doc. Maybe she has some medicine to fix that bad attitude you got goin' on."

"Shut up." Enrique growled.

Bruiser snorted. "Not gonna happen. Besides, I don't need this attitude infecting the others. Go get inoculated before it spreads."

Enrique scowled but turned on his heel and headed out into the rainy morning, feeling suspiciously lighter than he had in hours.

CHAPTER EIGHTEEN

Suzie opened her eyes and wondered why it was raining up. And why did her hair keep swinging into her face? She tried to reach up to sweep it aside but her shoulder and chest spasmed with deep pain. An involuntary whimper escaped her lips and she settled back into her seat. Or tried to.

What the ever-loving hell?

Turning her head, she caught sight of the grass against the roof of the car, but it set her rocking as she hung from the seatbelt. *Holy shit, I'm upside down.* She grabbed the steering wheel to stop the motion but all her muscles protested. *Damn, I feel like I was hit with a truck. Wait...*

The thought brought back memories to the forefront of her mind. She *had* been hit by a truck. She'd been driving through the rain to Cheyenne to get to Enrique before he left Wyoming. She'd called him several times on the drive, but during the last call, she'd looked in the rear view mirror at the last moment to see the headlights and grill of an old Ford pickup closing in on her. She'd screamed and dropped the phone as she jerked the wheel to avoid the looming truck, but it had hit her anyway.

Suzie frowned as she tried to remember what came

next. All she could recall was the world flipping. Glancing out the front window again she suspected she'd been the one flipping. Or at least her car.

Fuck.

She had to get out, if for no other reason than to figure out what damage there was. She bit her lip and slid her hand along the shoulder strap toward the center console. The seatbelt buckle had to be close. She wanted to turn her head but it would set her rocking again and she was already dizzy. *Must've hit my head when I rolled.*

Her fingers found the buckle and she pushed the button. Release came with a drop to the ceiling and another groan as her shoulders hit. She allowed her body to relax so she could determine if anything had been broken. She ran through her personal checklist, focusing on each part of her body to assess pain and functionality.

Her head and shoulders ached, as if she's slammed her face against something hard. Her chest felt bruised from the seatbelt and her knees hurt as if they'd been shoved into the steering column. Nothing felt broken, a definite plus, but everything felt twisted and bruised.

She moaned as she tried to right herself, getting her knees under her on the ceiling of the car. She didn't have to look to know it was totaled, and tears started in her eyes. Her poor car.

What is wrong with you? It's a damn car. Yeah, it was, and she could always buy a new one, but with her relationship with Enrique damaged, possibly beyond repair, the loss of her car proved too much to bear. A sob broke through and she folded into the fetal position, letting her grief roll out like a tidal wave.

Tears and minutes passed as she allowed her losses to overwhelm her. Enrique's departure was her own fault and she'd been trying to get back to him. She had to find a way back to him. So why the hell was she upside down on the side of the road? Who'd hit her? Was it just a freak accident?

She tried to think back to what she'd seen. She remembered the pickup's grill coming straight for her and she'd swerved to avoid it. The sound of the impact still echoed in her head but she'd managed to get ahead of it enough that the other vehicle hit her back door and rear fender, spinning her car. The wheels must have grabbed purchase on the grass beside the road because the car had tilted on its side and rolled over and over until it stopped on its roof below the berm of the freeway.

Shit. If it rolled hard enough, the doors might be crunched too tight to open. She'd be trapped.

Panic rose in her chest and she grasped the door handle, yanking on it to open the door. It wouldn't move. She shoved as hard as her bruised body would allow, but other than a groaning complaint, the door didn't budge. Fear and frustration built up as she pushed and pulled, hoping to loosen something enough to give.

But nothing moved.

She slumped back against the seats. *How am I gonna get out of here?* She looked around for another way to escape. Her gaze rested on the windows, only two of which remained whole from where she knelt. *Windows.* Too bad her car didn't have the old fashioned crank shafts.

She scrambled to look at the back ones, but the seats got in the way. She almost banged her head on the gearshift and frowned. Would the electrical system be dead if the car rolled? She scrunched down and looked for her keys. They hung in the ignition and waved as if taunting her to try them.

Come on, baby. Turn on enough for momma.

She tried listening for engine sounds, but she couldn't hear over the pounding in her head. She grasped the gearshift and shoved it into Park then listened for the engine. It was still running. Relief shot through her as she reached for the window controls. *Just down far enough for me to slip out the window.*

She pressed the button and the window started to move, but it stopped, humming in protest as it refused to retract into the crushed door. *No, no, no.* She leaned the other way and tried the passenger's door with the same result. The window dropped half way and quit.

"No, no, no! Come on." She gritted her teeth and grasped the edge of the window, hoping to pull it down farther. It moved a few inches and stopped. "Dammit!"

She crouched down and looked between the front seats. One of the back windows had shattered into tiny pieces, and glass spread in a path away from the car. But a significant amount remained in place and the struts of the cabin had compressed during the roll. She frowned. She might be able to kick out the rest of the glass…if she could get into the back of the car. But she didn't know if she could fit through the remaining opening.

She tried to work her body along the ceiling to the back, but the seats sat too close. Backing up, she fought tears as she pulled down on the seat recliner lever. The seat lurched toward the dashboard, almost taking out her knees and her arm.

"Shit." The tears spilled as she remembered she had to push the lever up for the seat to go back. But now the seat was in the way. "Fuck a large duck with a flamethrower."

She pulled the seat back to its usual position and grabbed the lever.

"Push down and push the seat back." She had to pause to make sure she understood which direction things had to go. Taking a deep breath, she pressed the lever and shoved the seat upward.

It groaned but moved and she damn near fell into the back of the car. She braced herself with her hands and managed to land on her discarded phone. Remarkably, the screen wasn't cracked and the phone illuminated her face and the space around her, making her realize just how dark it was. The clock said it was only ten in the morning but the light made her think it was closer to twilight.

Maybe that's because the car is on its roof.

And she had to get out of it to assess the damage, both to her car and herself. *No use whimpering in here. Get after it, sister.* She sat down on her butt and put her feet against the damaged window, praying that she'd be able to break it.

Taking a deep breath, she slammed her feet against the glass. It felt like hitting stone, but the damaged window cracked some more. *Come on.* She thumped her feet against the window again, harder, and the fractured glass bowed a little more. *That's it.* Two more impacts and the glass broke away, allowing the smell of water and the hiss of rain to flood the cabin.

Suzie whimpered and rested a moment, relief cascading through her. She could get out. Tears returned to her eyes, but she swept them away as her logical mind kicked back in. *Need my keys, my purse, and my phone.* She reached back to the steering column and twisted the keys, trying to free them. *Idiot, you have to do it the opposite way because you're upside down.*

She turned them the other direction and the car released them. She didn't waste time, just gathered her purse, and phone, and scrambled for the open window. It was a tight fit with the frame warped and crushed, but she wriggled and contorted until her shoulders and hips made it through.

Rain soaked her immediately as she crawled away from the wreck but she settled into the wet grass, grateful she was free. She swung her gaze over her car and swallowed hard. It was amazing she'd survived with all the damage to the frame and doors. Hell, she still felt like death-warmed-over just looking at the car.

"Sweet glory." The sound of her own voice brought her a little comfort. "Gotta call the ranch." She grabbed her phone and searched for Tom Colton's number, wishing she had a hat to keep the rain off the screen.

The phone rang in her ear and she tried to find a comfortable position as she waited for Tom to pick up.

"Hey, what's up, Doc?"

A tired smile curled her lips at the old tagline. "Tom, I'm sitting on the side of I-25 heading southbound, just north of the Vandehei exit."

"Are you all right?" His voice lost all the humor.

"I think so. My car rolled and I'm pretty banged up, but nothing's broken."

"Holy shit. What happened?"

She shook her head. "Some truck came barreling across the road and slammed into me. I tried avoiding it, but my car went into the berm and flipped."

"Sweet glory, Suzie. Okay, I'm coming to get you. Can you see anything nearby? Mile marker? House, anything?" Sounds of him grabbing his keys came through the phone.

She swung her gaze toward the freeway but the rain shrouded it from clear sight. "No, the rain's coming down too hard." She gave thanks there wasn't any hail. "I've reached the section where there's a frontage road, but I can't see if there are buildings beyond it."

"Shit. All right, hang tight. Have you called the cops?"

"No, I just got out of the car and called you." She bit her lip as tears joined the rain. "Could you please call Petty Officer Sanchez and tell him what happened? I was on my way to try to meet him before I rolled."

Tom paused. "Why don't you call him, Suzie?"

Tears fell harder. "He won't answer my calls and I've already left several messages. Could you please call him for me?"

"Tell you what, I'll call Sanchez and you call the cops."

"And what do I tell them? I don't even know where I am and I can't see anything that'll help." She looked around again, hoping that a building or sign had come into view, but the unrelenting rain turned the world into a field of gray.

"Don't turn your phone off. They can use the GPS on it to find you. I'm comin' and I'll call Sanchez."

Suzie bit her lip to keep from whining. "Okay. Thanks, Tom."

"Just hang in there—"

The call cut off mid-sentence and she looked at her phone in time to see it power down.

"No, no no no. Dammit!"

Something must have gotten damaged in the crash to make her phone just quit. Her gut sank as the thing up and died in her hand. How the hell would the cops know where to find her now? She hadn't managed to call them.

She glanced back at the highway looking for the truck that hit her, but the rain made everything just shadows and water. Where the hell was the other driver? Were they unconscious or hurt? The rain plastered her hair to her scalp and soaked through her coat as she tried to move around the car. The wet grass made her footing precarious and she went down a couple times, soaking the knees of her jeans.

By the time she got around the back of the vehicle, she realized she'd taken the long way and stood farther from the road. She could hear cars passing but the rain shrouded them. Would anyone see her car off to the side of the road? She moaned in frustration and gathered her strength to push toward the blacktop up the wet berm.

But a dark figure appeared in front of her out of the rain, making her cry out and lurch backward to fall on her butt in the grass.

"Dr. Appleton? Oh my god, Suzie? Are you all right?" The figure cleared up to be Dr. Edward Lyttle dressed in jeans and a flannel shirt without a coat.

"Dr. Lyttle? What are you doing here?" She tried to focus her thoughts, but nothing made sense. "Are you doing a ride-along in the ambulance today?"

"No, I was coming back to Cheyenne from visiting the Triple Star Ranch. I was looking for you but I'd just missed you." He offered her a hand up and she took it, still trying to figure out why what he said didn't make sense. "It's a good thing I happened along."

"Yeah…Why were you looking for me?"

"I thought I'd stop by to see how you were doing since you haven't been in town much." He gave her a smile that made her skin crawl. "You know, catch up after that last email you sent. You sounded upset."

Last email? She thought back to the email she'd written to Lyttle and a warning light flashed in the back of her head. She hadn't been polite or understanding. She'd told him straight up he'd violated doctor-patient privilege and she'd be reporting him to the medical board.

Did he drive all the way out here to confront me?

While the idea seemed farfetched, he wasn't acting normal for a doctor. Shouldn't he be checking her over for injuries? Something about his demeanor made her cautious. She straightened as the ground flattened out.

"Guess that was lucky you were here." She tried to pull her hand back but he tightened his grip. "Please let go of my hand."

"I have to make sure you're all right. My vehicle is just down the road a bit."

He started to drag her along the freeway. Other vehicles could be heard and seen in the gloom, but they were nothing but vague shadows speeding along in the rain. She pulled back on her hand again, trying to get free. She didn't want to follow him, no matter how "well-meaning" he appeared.

"Now, now, you're all shaken up, Dr. Appleton. Let me get you to my car and I'll take you to the hospital. It was a nasty tumble you took in your vehicle."

How the hell does he know that?

The answer became clear when she saw his ride. Older

model Ford pickup, with the grill smashed in and one of the headlights broken. Her memory served up the last thing just before her car rolled. She'd been hit by an old Ford pickup.

She dug her heels in and yanked them to a stop.

"Wait, is this your truck?" She pulled back against his grip, trying to dislodge his hand. "Were you following me?"

"Don't be ridiculous, Suzie. I saw you go off the road. I'm here to help."

The front fender under the broken headlight lay caved in and the truck sat askew to the road as if it had collided with something. *Yeah, like my car.* The red side panels looked like dried blood in the dim light. She jerked her hand free and backed up a few steps.

"Oh my glory, you hit me! I saw you in the mirror. You hit my car and pushed me off the road." She wiped her hand on her thigh though it was as wet as everything else in the downpour. "Is this because of my email? Because I was going to report you to the medical board?" She hadn't yet, but now it would be her first priority. She wanted to scream at him, demanding what the hell was wrong with him, but given his actions, antagonizing him more didn't seem wise.

"You shouldn't have said that, Suzie. I was doing you a favor. Protecting you from heartbreak." He gave her a smile of entreaty. "Come here now. Let's get out of the rain."

"Protecting me? How were you protecting me?" She shook her head, wiping her face with one had to clear the water from her eyes.

"Suzie, we need to get you inside. You're in shock." He used his careful, doctor's voice, the one to placate hysterical patients, and the one she realized only infuriated them. *Note to self: Don't use that voice.* "Come on now, we'll get in the truck and everything will be better."

"No, answer the question, Edward. How is revealing personal information protecting me? How is shoving my car off the freeway protecting me?" She moved farther out of reach, not trusting him.

"I didn't shove your car off the freeway, Suzie. You're just remembering wrong. You lost control and I stopped to help." He sounded patient and conciliatory, but he kept moving toward her. "And I know how much you want to have children. That's why you want to find the right man, marry him, and have a family. The Petty Officer is sterile, infertile, and he'd never give you the family you want. He's defective. I made sure you didn't make a mistake with him."

"Defective? And how do you know that's what I want? I've never told you any of that." Suzie groaned as her chest tightened with stress and movement, but she couldn't let him touch her.

"Sure you did, at one of our shared coffee breaks. Come back to the truck now, Suzie." Lyttle gestured at her, moving slowly so as not to spook her, but she didn't like his focus. He looked like someone getting ready to pounce.

"I never told you anything like that and we haven't had shared coffee breaks. We're always on different schedules when I come for the clinic." Anger surged in her chest at his narrative. He'd made up his own story to fit what he wanted. "Get away from me, Dr. Lyttle. I've called the police. They should be here soon."

For the first time, his expression cracked and angry derision sneered back at her. But then it smoothed out into solicitous concern. "That's good, Suzie. They'll bring an ambulance I'm sure. But let's get out of the rain and into some place warm and dry."

As much as she wanted to avoid the rain, she wouldn't get into a vehicle with him. "That's okay. I'll just wait with my car. Why don't you get into your truck? That way you'll stay dry."

"No, you need to come with me, Suzie. I can't leave you out here in the wet." He moved toward her again. "You aren't well. You need help."

Oh yeah, I definitely need help.

She kept backing up, not wanting to take her eyes off him. He'd run her off the road. Who knew what he was capable of? She wished she was more sure of her footing, but when she shot a look behind, he lunged for her.

"No!"

"I'm here to help you, Suzie. I was always here to help." His snarled words didn't convince her.

He tried to secure her arms, but the rain and her wet clothes made her slippery, and she twisted out of his grip, shoving him away. He lost his balance enough for her to gain distance and she staggered a few steps before launching into a run. She'd be damned if she sat there and let him catch her. The question was, could she stay ahead of him long enough for Tom and Enrique to get to her?

CHAPTER NINETEEN

Enrique threw himself into the rental car and peeled out of his parking space. After Tom Colton's phone call, his gut had solidified into a panic he hadn't felt since the first time he'd been shot at.

Suzie's been in a car accident. Her car rolled off the freeway just north of the Vandehei exit on I-25.

He swore someone had scooped out his heart with a rusty spoon. He'd been idly waiting at the coffee shop for Suzie, wondering why she hadn't answered his texts, when Tom's name lit up his caller ID. He'd thought maybe he'd forgotten something at the ranch when he left and quickly picked up. But his hopeful morning had turned into dark panic with Tom's message.

A rollover accident. Holy fuck.

He fishtailed around a corner onto Lincoln Way, hoping the cops wouldn't notice his erratic driving. Or maybe that would've been a good thing. He'd give them a good chase straight to Suzie. He kept his speed to ten miles over the limit while in town, but the minute he hit the northbound onramp, he floored it. The rental didn't have much power, but it was the only wheels he had. It would have to do.

He went over the last few messages Suzie had sent in his mind. Had she been crying while driving? Had she swerved to miss an animal on the highway? The low ceiling and the rain would've made visibility problematic. Even now with his lights on and his attention sharp, it was hard to see the oncoming traffic on the other side of the guardrails.

He made the Vandehei exit in less than six minutes, but he kept driving north under the overpass, scanning the road side for her vehicle. The guardrails disappeared into nothing on the grassy median and the southbound lanes became visible.

There!

An old Ford pickup with a dark red side panel sat parked at an odd angle on the side of the road, the tailgate down. Enrique frowned. Suzie drove a pale green Subaru hatchback, not a truck. He scanned the median looking for a way across when he spotted someone walking on the side of the road.

It looked like a man, but the mist and rain made it difficult to tell. He found an emergency vehicle turn around and jerked the rental into it, skidding to a halt as he scanned the southbound lanes for traffic. *Would be stupid to collide with someone while trying to provide a rescue.*

He managed to find a break in the traffic and shot across to the shoulder, suddenly seeing the skid marks and the roadside damage from another vehicle.

Holy fuck.

Had she been run off the road by someone? He threw the rental into park with his flashers on and got out, trying to take in the scene despite the driving rain. He almost called out for Suzie, but he held back. His gut told him there was more going on here than just a simple rollover accident.

Enrique pocketed his keys and pulled out his phone while scanning the misty world around him. "Tom? Yeah,

I'm here on the freeway, but there's no sign of Suzie or her car."

"What? She's there. She called." Tom's voice echoed like he sat in the cab of a vehicle.

"Yeah, I can see where a vehicle went over the side, but the mist and rain is hiding things. Call the cops. I'm gonna go look for her."

"I did. Her phone cut off in the middle of our conversation so I wasn't sure she could. They should be there soon. Call me when you find her."

"Roger that."

Enrique thumbed his phone to silent and shoved it in his pocket as he moved forward to the pickup truck. The person he'd seen walking was gone but the truck steamed in the wet weather and his gut grew colder as he approached. Where was the driver?

He moved quietly around the front of the old pickup and anger blazed through his chest. The front end showed impact damage with the grill smashed in and a broken headlight. Had the asshole actually hit Suzie? He swung his gaze back to the tailgate, wondering why it was down. Had the driver been hauling something? The only things in the back were a wet tarp and an old climbing rope. Innocuous items on their own, but their combination made his neck prickle with unease.

He left the truck behind and made his way down the berm, looking for Suzie's car. It took a few moments with the mist and rain obscuring it, but he found her car upside down in the ditch between the freeway and the frontage road. His breath stalled in his chest as he scrambled down to it, terrified he'd find her bleeding out or crushed to death.

No, Tom said she'd called after *the crash. She was alive then.*

So where the hell was she now?

He glanced at the ground, looking for foot prints in the

wet grass, but everything had been matted down from the crash. He stood up and searched the rainy world around him, listening for things that didn't belong.

"Suzie, you know this isn't the best thing for you. Come back to the truck where it's safe and warm. I promise I'll take care of you."

A man's voice carried just over the hiss of the tires on the asphalt and the white noise of the rain. *I know that voice. What the fuck is Dr. Lyttle doing here? Was he the fucking pickup driver?* Enrique headed into the misty gloom across the frontage road. A barbed wire fence stretched between metal posts on the far side, but the land dipped into a gully choked with reeds and cottonwood saplings.

Enrique ducked through the barbed wire and made his way closer to the gully. The silhouette of a man poking through the brush became visible the closer he got to the gully and Enrique had to hold back a growl of fury.

Dr. Lyttle lunged into a thicket of reeds, but pulled back with a sneer of disgust when he came up empty.

"Look, I know you're confused and I saw you limping. You're hurt. Let me take you to the hospital where I can take care of you." The mild voice didn't go with the furious grimace on his face as he searched more of the gully.

Enrique half expected Suzie to answer with a sarcastic comment, but when only wind and rain greeted Lyttle's remark, Enrique wondered if Suzie couldn't rather than refused to answer. He moved closer, trying to decide between searching for Suzie and taking Lyttle down.

"You ran me off the road, Lyttle. Stay the fuck away from me." Suzie's voice carried from farther up the gully and Lyttle turned toward it with a malicious smile.

"Now, that's not true. I came to help, remember? Your car rolled and I'm here to save you."

Fury ignited in Enrique's chest and he made his decision. Using the poor visibility and the cover of the wind and rain, he shifted closer, taking care to watch his feet. The wet grass and the slant to the ground made the footing precarious.

And I don't want to give him any advantages.

Enrique remembered the doc saying he'd been a Navy Corpsman with the Marines. The man might be rusty, but he'd had training. *But I haven't been sitting on my ass for years.*

Enrique crept closer before he launched himself across the wet ground at Lyttle. The man turned at the last minute, his eyes wide, but Enrique slammed into him, taking him down with a cry.

"What the fuck!"

Lyttle struggled and rolled, trying to get on top of Enrique, but Enrique kept the motion going until he straddled the man's squirming body and landed a punch against the side of Lyttle's head. The doctor slumped, stunned. He yanked Lyttle up by his collar, and wrapped him in a headlock, cutting off his air, a snarl pulling his lips back from his teeth. The other man yanked at Enrique's arms, but his strength failed him and he quickly went limp in the headlock.

Enrique waited long enough to be sure the man was completely out before letting him go and rising to his feet. He took a moment to catch his breath and make sure Lyttle stayed down. Then he searched the gully with his gaze. Suzie had hidden herself pretty well and he'd have to comb through the reeds to find her.

"Suzie, it's Enrique. You can come out now." He pitched his voice to carry over the wind and rain, praying she'd hear him. He scanned the gully, hoping she'd stand up, but he didn't see any movement beyond the wind in the reeds. "Suzie?"

"Where did we go on our first date together?" He voice floated out of the brush but he still couldn't pinpoint her.

"We went to the Tilted Tea Cup and you asked me not

to open your door for you while I was injured." He searched the reeds, hoping to see her move. "Come on out. Dr. Lyttle is down."

Sirens started in the distance, the cops and EMS vehicles closing in on their location. *About damn time.* He moved along the stream edge, listening and looking for any sign of movement.

The reeds shivered and Suzie's face appeared between them. "Enrique?"

"*Sí, querida.* I'm here." He waved as he made his way down the bank and into the reeds. "Come out."

"I can't. I twisted my ankle getting in here and I can't put any weight on it." Her voice shook and he gritted his teeth.

"All right, I'm coming. Show me where you are and I'll help get you out." He shot a glance back at Lyttle to be sure he remained out before he turned back to the gully. "Can you see me?"

"Yeah. I'm about thirty feet to your right." A hand shot up out of the reeds and waved, and relief crashed over him like a balm.

"I see you. Hold tight, I'm coming."

****

Suzie sighed as she settled back on the downed log left to rot in the creek. When she'd found her hiding spot, she'd intended to keep moving upstream until she encountered a residence or other building to hide in. But her foot had slipped on the wet wood and she'd landed hard, her ankle twisting painfully in the wrong direction.

The pain had made her breathless and it had taken precious seconds to regain enough equilibrium to get moving again. By then, Lyttle had been too close and her ankle refused to support her weight. She'd hunkered down and kept silent while he thrashed around in the reeds, praying he wouldn't find her before help came.

"I'm almost there." Enrique's voice brought tears to her eyes.

When he'd first called out to her, she wasn't sure she'd heard correctly, and worried that somehow Lyttle had masked his voice to find out where she was. But she'd rolled her eyes and called herself all kinds of fool. Lyttle didn't have that talent and she'd been wishing for help to come. But she also didn't trust that it wasn't a trap so she'd asked the question about their first date.

"So, are you comfortable there in the rain, or would you like to come sit in a warm ambulance?" Enrique appeared in front of her with a warm smile and even warmer hands.

"Oh, sweet glory, thank goodness you're here." All her fear and adrenaline drained out of her in the form of tears as he pulled her into his arms. "I was so scared and my phone died and he ran me off the road and I didn't know what to do." The words poured out of her in one long rush, interrupted only by a sob as she wrapped her arms around him.

"I've got you and you're safe. *Te protegeré para siempre, mi amor.*" He kept whispering more words in Spanish, but she closed her eyes and melted into his embrace. He made her feel safe.

Eventually he pulled back as other voices called out to them. "Come on, I better get you to the paramedics so they can check you out."

She grimaced but nodded. "I'm going to need your help. I'm pretty sure my ankle's sprained beyond all use."

"Do you want me to carry you or just help you balance?" He eyed her face as the rain sheeted down over them.

"I think it would be easier for you to help me balance. There's no use in twisting your ankle too." She rolled her eyes. "That would ruin your chances of jumping out of airplanes any time soon."

"All right, wrap your arm around my waist and hold tight."

The next five minutes were an act of will and determination on her part. Her ankle throbbed, she'd started to shiver with the cold and wet, and her stomach reminded her she hadn't eaten anything that morning despite her early wake up. By the time he helped her to the barbed wire fence, the frontage road swarmed with cops, EMTs and firefighters. Tom supplied the wire cutters and Enrique helped her into the hands of the EMTs.

"Stay here while I take the police to Dr. Lyttle."

"Is he dead?" She hadn't meant to ask so bluntly and all the cops around them shot Enrique sharp looks.

"No, ma'am, just unconscious." He gave her a cocky grin before he turned away and disappeared into the rain.

The EMTs gave her a warm blanket and wrapped her ankle while the cops rounded up Dr. Lyttle and hauled him to the back of a squad car. They took her statement of the events and another statement from Enrique and a third from Tom before they asked her if she wanted to press charges.

"Yes."

The EMTs wanted to take her to the hospital to get checked out, but she declined treatment and had them wrap her ankle so she could go home. She promised the cops she would come into town the next day and file formal charges, but at the moment she just wanted to go home.

"I'll take you home, Dr. Appleton." Enrique held his hand up for her to step out of the ambulance.

"Thank you, Petty Officer Sanchez. But if you don't have time, I can get a ride home with Tom." Suzie tried to smile, but he needed to go back to Cheyenne. "I know you have to leave soon with your team. I don't want to take you out of your way."

"It's not out of my way. I realized I'd left something at the ranch and need to pick it up anyway, so it's not a problem."

"Oh, well in that case, I'd appreciate the ride, thanks."

She grasped his hand tighter and hobbled along beside him to his rental car. The big black SUV looked like something out of a secret agent movie and she had to laugh. *Boys and their badass toys.* He helped her into the vehicle and hurried around the front to climb into the driver's seat. He turned over the engine and cranked the heat to warm her after sitting in the rain.

"That should warm you up and we'll get you home quick. Just let me call my CO so he knows what's going on."

She nodded as he eased the vehicle into motion onto the freeway. He put on his hazard flashers and got them up to speed enough to take the exit. The conversation was intense and full of military jargon that she couldn't quite follow so she closed her eyes and let the warm air from the heater settle into her bones.

"Suzie, wake up. We're here."

"What?" She opened her eyes and found them parked outside of her bungalow. "Oh, I must've fallen asleep." She inhaled deeply and rubbed her eyes, but grimaced when her face came away wet. "Ugh, I need dry clothes."

"Hand me your keys. I'll get the door open so you don't get as wet." Enrique held out his hand for her keys and she frowned.

Had she remembered to take them out of the ignition? She searched her pockets and pulled them out, grateful for old habits. He took them and squeezed her hand briefly before he ducked out into the rain. She watched him run to the bungalow and unlock the door before returning to the vehicle to open her door.

"Come on, *querida.* I'll carry you inside so you stay off that ankle." He reached in and moved his arms under her knees.

"Why do you call me that?"

"What, *querida*?" He raised his eyebrows.

"Yeah."

"It means 'lover' or 'beloved'. It's an endearment." He pulled her against his chest and she wrapped an arm around his shoulders. "Why wouldn't I call you that?"

"Because I treated you so badly and accused you of things that weren't true." Tears started in her eyes from the cold, the wet, and the stress of being run off the road by a psychopath. "I'm so sorry, Enrique."

"Shh, let's get you into dry clothes and then we can talk, okay? Don't cry. We'll work it out." He carried her through the door and into her bedroom, setting her down gently on the bed. "Do you need help getting out of your clothes?" Despite the suggestive words, his smile was gentle and concerned.

"No, I'll be fine."

"Okay. I'm gonna make some tea for you. Call me when you're ready to come out to the living room." He cupped her cheek a moment before he turned and left the room without a kiss.

Glory, I'm dumber than a bag of hammers.

She sniffed, but managed to get out of her wet clothes. They fell into a sodden heap at the foot of her bed as she limped to the closet for sweats and a long-sleeved t-shirt. She didn't bother with underwear, but she threw her robe over everything and wrapped it tightly around her. The dry clothes warmed her body, but they couldn't chase away the chill of what she had to face in the other room.

Best to get it over with.

She took a deep breath and limped into the living room. Enrique had hung up his jacket on the coatrack and filled two mugs with hot tea. He sat on the couch, his expression withdrawn and his arms crossed over his broad chest. She took a moment to admire the breadth of his shoulders and the thickness of his thighs, suspecting this would be the last time she'd get to enjoy his physique.

He looked up and rolled to his feet with predatory grace. "Hey, I told you to call me. I would've helped you out here."

She shook her head, but gratefully took his arm when he came to her side. "I can do it. It's a little painful, but not that bad. Besides, you've already done so much for me today I figured I should do a little on my own."

"Suzie, I will always help you when I can."

"Stop, give me a moment to catch my breath and get my thoughts in order."

She settled into the couch and closed her eyes, trying to settle her mind and her heart rate so she could do right by him. He sat down beside her and remained silent. She couldn't even hear him breathe, but given his profession, she supposed that was an asset.

"Okay." She opened her eyes and turned her body to face him. "I'm so sorry, Enrique. I was stupid, and scared, and unreasonable, and thoughtless. I had this idea in my head of how my life would go. I'd become a doctor, and a championship barrel-racer, and then I'd meet the man who'd light me on fire and we'd marry and have kids, and life would be perfect. Then you came along and you were more than I could wish for in a man. You're handsome, sexy, strong, patient, intelligent, funny, generous, and loveable. You're everything I wanted."

"Except for the part where I can't get you pregnant." His voice was quiet. She couldn't hear condemnation but she didn't hear forgiveness either.

She nodded. "Right, and I got hung up on that. I was so sure I knew how things would go and when you didn't fit the idea in my head, I panicked and blamed you." She grimaced and tightened her hands in her robe. "But it's not your fault and you didn't deserve all the horrible things I said. I'm the one who was stuck on the idea of how we'd have kids. I'm the one who was stupid. And I'm the one who's really sorry for being that way. I made a mistake and

I hurt you, and I'm sorry for all of it. I know you have to leave with your team today but I needed you to know that I love you and I want to be with you, no matter what."

He looked at her for a long time, considering her words. She held her breath, hoping she hadn't lost him forever. *But if you have, you deserve it for being so rigid.* She'd been manipulated by Lyttle into losing the best person in her life, and now she was paying for her inattention and lack of faith in their relationship.

At last, Enrique took a deep breath and Suzie braced herself for his response.

"It's been a helluva morning. I started with pissed off and hungover because of last night, then your texts and messages gave me hope. I was doing pretty good until Tom called me and told me you'd been in an accident. That scared the living shit outta me, especially when I found Lyttle hunting you." He reached out and tucked a strand of wet hair behind her ear. "But the moment I held you in my arms again, I realized that I'd been stupid to think I could just walk away from you. I wasn't much of a badass if I didn't stick around to talk you down and argue my side of whatever we disagree on." He grimaced and rubbed the back of his neck. "I'm sorry I didn't stay and fight for us. You're too important to me to just walk away without trying to work it out. *Te amo mucho, Suzie, y te protegeré para siempre.* I love you very much and I'll always protect you in whatever way I can."

He paused and picked up his tea mug, rubbing the glazed sides with his thumbs. "I'm sorry I didn't mention my sterility. It never mattered before because I hadn't met a woman I wanted to have children with. I would've told you if we discussed kids, but we hadn't gotten there yet."

"I know. I jumped the gun with my stupid attachment to my dream future." She rolled her eyes and sipped her tea.

He nodded. "Are you sure you're ready to give up on

that dream?"

She raised her chin and met his gaze squarely. "It's not much of a dream if you're not in it."

"Are you sure, Suzie?"

"Yes, completely sure. I don't want anyone else. I want you to be part of my family, and I really want to be part of your team." She bit her bottom lip as tears started in her eyes. "I need you, Enrique. We'll figure the kids thing out, but I want you and I love you, and I don't want to spend my life without you in it."

Warmth filled his eyes and a smile curled his lips. "That's exactly how I feel, *querida*. Now I have something I need to ask you. I was gonna do it last night but we got a little sidetracked."

She frowned. "What?"

He slid off the couch onto his knees and dug something out of his pocket. A little black velvet box sat in his palm.

"*¿Suzie Marie Appleton, quieres casarte conmigo?*" He pulled back the lid of the box and held it up. "Will you marry me, Suzie?"

A slender gold ring with seven diamonds of varying size embedded in the band winked at her from the white satin interior. She gasped and raised her gaze to his. When had he learned her middle name? How had he figured out she didn't want a ring with upright stones?

The answer to her questions were the same: Seychelles must have told him. No wonder she'd been so excited to hear how Suzie's evening had gone. She must've known Enrique was planning to propose.

"Oh, Enrique. Are you sure? After that stunt I pulled?" She grasped his hand holding the ring box with both of her own.

He laughed. "I admit you threw me for a loop last night. But I told you I was in this for the long haul and I'm not gonna give up. I've never been so sure about something as I am about this. I love you, Suzie, and I want to be your husband, no matter what life throws at us."

He pulled the ring out and grasped her left hand. "Please marry me."

"Yes." She grinned as the ring slid into place. "Glory, yes, I'll definitely marry you."

He whooped and lifted her off the couch into his arms, kissing her with all his enthusiasm. She laughed and kissed him back until his phone chirped with an incoming text. He sighed and set her down again before dragging the phone out to check.

"Damn." He grimaced but his eyes danced. "I gotta go wheels-up. The team's heading out in an hour and I gotta get back to Cheyenne." But he crouched in front of her and took her hands with a wide smile. "But I'm gonna be back here at Thanksgiving and I'll text and email and call you when I can. I love you, Suzie, and I'm gonna marry you."

"That's good, Enrique, because I'll be looking forward to it. I love you."

He kissed her hard, tangling his tongue with hers before pulling back and standing up.

"I gotta go, but I'll see you in two months, and we can make more plans then." He strode to the door where he paused long enough to look back. "*Te amo*, Suzie."

"*Te amo,* Enrique. *Buena suerte.*"

His eyes flashed with love and joy. "Roger that."

THE END

AUTHOR'S NOTE

I hope you enjoyed Suzie and Enrique's tale. I didn't know it when I started writing, but this became a crossover tale that connects a lot of different series. Though this story is part of the Triple Star Ranch series, it has connections to the Bad Boys of Beta Squad series in DELI'S TAKE OUT, the Ultimate Recon series in DARWIN'S EVOLUTION, and to J.M. Madden's Lost and Found series. Happy reading!

Siobhan

ROPE A FALLING STAR
TRIPLE STAR RANCH, BOOK 1
SNEEK PEEK

Only the best stars fall...

Three time bronc-riding champion Tom Colton's dream of a fourth title ends when he draws Wooden Nickel, a mean little bronc with more twists than a maze. With his heart no longer in rodeo, he figures it's time to go home to the Triple Star Ranch, the PTSD therapy ranch he and his dad founded to help others with trauma in their pasts. Tom just wants a little time to nurse his hurts and consider his next move.

Amber Hillcrest started out as a Triple Star client and stayed on as a massage therapist. Her dog Nimbus keeps her PTSD in check, but her heart remains bruised. She knows she's too old and too broken for love, especially with the son of her boss, but he's hot enough to fill her fantasies for years to come.

Amber tries to keep it professional between them, but Tom proves too irresistible with his big heart and charm. But someone is sabotaging the Triple Star and the neighboring Fantasy Ranch, and an ex-girlfriend keeps coming around, trying to reconnect with Tom. Tom's hands are full of problems instead of the luscious massage therapist. But when Amber gets kidnapped, Tom will move heaven and earth to get her back and tell her how he truly feels.

STAR LIGHT, STAR BRIGHT
TRIPLE STAR RANCH, BOOK 2
SNEEK PEEK

Sometimes the brightest stars need to come home…

Henry Bright has a picture-perfect life as a rising star in the country rock scene—fortune, fame, and more lovers than he can shake a stick at. But something is missing. The glitz of Nashville is nothing more than glitter and tinfoil. Searching for authenticity in his life, he completes his DVM in veterinary medicine and returns to Wyoming. He takes a job as a vet at the Triple Star Ranch, hoping to find meaning and connection. He just didn't expect to find love.

Trip Colton's wife died over thirty years ago and he figured that was it for love. But the moment he meets Henry, he can't get the younger man off his mind. The problem is, he's never been attracted to a man before and the realization throws him for a loop. Dating is hard at any age, but Trip's out of practice and wooing a man is completely different than wooing a woman.

When Henry's former manager, Jordie, tracks him to Wyoming and begs the star to come back to the music biz, tensions damage the fragile connection between Henry and Trip. Jordie will do anything to convince Henry to return, even playing on his prejudices and hinting at Trip's infidelity. But when the bank keeps calling with alerts on Henry's accounts, he suspects there's more going on with Jordie than a simple comeback music tour. Ultimately, Henry must choose where his heart lies, and who to trust, before he loses more than his chance at love.

OTHER BOOKS BY SIOBHAN MUIR

Her Devoted Vampire
Queen Bitch of the Callowwood Pack
Second Chance Succubus
Darwin's Evolution
Wildfire's Heart

Bad Boys of Beta Squad Series
Bronco's Rough Ride
The Navy's Ghost
Rimshot's Hard Target
Bam-Bam's Inked Hart
Deli's Take Out

Cloudburst Colorado Series
A Hell Hound's Fire
The Beltane Witch
Christmas I.C.E. Magic
Cloudburst Ice Magic
Cloudburst Coffee & Spa

Concrete Angels MC Series
My Forever Cocky Biker Encounter
Dude With a Cool Car

Rifts Series
Take the Reins
A Centaur's Solstice Wish
In Death's Shadow

Triple Star Ranch Series
Rope a Falling Star
Star Light, Star Bright

The Ivory Road
A Walk in the Sand
Outback Dreams

Warbler Peninsula Series
Order of the Dragon
The Valkyrie's Sword
Burning Yuletide

Coming Soon
Angel Ink (Concrete Angels MC #3)
Second Chance Whiskey (Capitol of Second Chances #2)

ABOUT THE AUTHOR

Siobhan Muir lives in Cheyenne, Wyoming, with her husband, two daughters, and a vegetarian cat she swears is a shape-shifter, though he's never shifted when she can see him. When not writing, she can be found looking down a microscope at fossil fox teeth, pursuing her other love, paleontology. An avid reader of science fiction/fantasy, her husband gave her a paranormal romance for Christmas one year, and she was hooked for good.

In previous lives, Siobhan has been an actor at the Colorado Renaissance Festival, a field geologist in the Aleutian Islands, and restored inter-planetary imagery at the USGS. She's hiked to the top of Mount St. Helens and to the bottom of Meteor Crater.

Siobhan writes kick-ass adventure with hot sex for men and women to enjoy. She believes in happily ever after, redemption, and communication, all of which you will find in her paranormal romance stories.

Connect with Siobhan online at:
https://siobhanmuir.com
https://www.facebook.com/siobhan.muir.35
https://twitter.com/SiobhanMuir
https://siobhanmuir.com/blog
https://pinterest.com/siobhanmuir.35

www.ingramcontent.com/pod-product-compliance
Lightning Source LLC
Chambersburg PA
CBHW031953240626
47153CB00003B/975